NORTHWEST
OF NORMAL

Also by John Larison

The Complete Steelheader

NORTHWEST
OF NORMAL

A NOVEL

JOHN LARISON

BARCLAY CREEK PRESS
Bolton, Massachusetts

Northwest of Normal: A Novel
Copyright © 2009 by John Larison

ISBN-13: 978-1-936008-01-8
ISBN-10: 1-936008-01-7

Barclay Creek Press, LLC
PO Box 249
Bolton, MA 01740-0249 USA

www.barclaycreek.com

Publisher: James D. Anker
Page design: Dutton & Sherman Design
Jacket design: Dutton & Sherman Design
Jacket and chapter art: Ellie Rose
Author photo: James R. Larison

For Grandpa Smith,
who shared the magic of dawn
and the mystery of place.

What is that feeling when you're driving away from people and they recede on the plain till you see their specks dispersing?—it's the too huge world vaulting us, and it's good-by. But we lean forward to the next crazy venture beneath the skies.

Jack Kerouac
On the Road

There were the letters, there was the word: plain as water, in a flowing, utterly uncrabbed hand, current, erosion, gravity and chance had written WHY upon the valley floor!

David James Duncan
The River Why

ACKNOWLEDGMENTS

Some say it takes a village to raise a novel, but in the case of *Northwest of Normal*, it took a small city.

This book exists only because four generous, brilliant people devoted hours of their time to teach me about words, about emotions, and about how the two can become one. Thank you: Tracy Daugherty for, most specifically, the deftly taught craft lessons and the always inspiring example; Marjorie Sandor for the sometimes painful but always spot-on marginalia, notes that eventually revealed how writers read; Ted Leeson for, among other things, the glimpse at the ropes and pulleys behind those magical sentences; and Ellie Rose for the secret readings and candid appraisals, but most of all for the sublime friendship, partnership, and loveship (your passion is the loam from which all this grows). There's a monument to each of you in downtown Ipsyniho.

Also thank you to Oregon State University's English Department, and more specifically the MFA Program there, for the financial and intellectual support during the years it took to complete the manuscript. I'm especially indebted to Keith Scribner, who will be receiving a life-time supply of All-Nighter passes to the Cascadia Carnival.

Many splendid writers took time away from their art and families to read early drafts: Joe Aguilar, Claire Carpenter, Reuben Casas, Quinn Dmitriv, Chris Drew, Lauren Fath, Isabelle Haskins, Melissa Hough-ton, Adam Kroll, Jason Ludden, Amanda Richter, Stephanie Wisniewski, and Joshua Weber. Thank you for shooting out my high beams and handing me a headlamp.

Also thank you Michelle Barnes, Benjamin Barnett, Julia Betjemann, Peter Betjemann, Isaac Bloom, Morris Bloom, Betty Campbell, Tom Christensen, Marcia Diamond, Paul Dresman, Rebecca Egbert, Ellie Graeden, Ryan Graeden, Nate Koenigknecht, Jim Larison, Sarah Larison, Ted Larison, Jay Larkins, Marcus Looze, Steve Perakis, Scott Powell, Alison Ruch, Sara Rushing, Chris Seifert, Sarah Sheldrick, Sky Silga, Amanda Sever, Rachel Teadora, Nathan Warren, and a very special thanks to Jim Anker.

And finally (but only in terms of reverse chronology!) a profound thanks to my mother, Elaine Larison, for sparking it all by never saying no to a book.

CHAPTER 1

What hadn't changed was the smell: first the purple sweetness of ripe blackberries, then deeper, the green spice of Doug fir needles. Deeper yet was the chocolaty musk of the river at dawn, its fog ghosting over the riffle. This was the Ipsyniho he remembered, and Christ had he missed it.

Every river smelled unique, its own body odor. He could name a few by whiff alone. The Rio Blanco in Chile: milky blue water fed by a receding glacier; it smelled as chalky as a blackboard eraser. Fall Creek back in his hometown of Ithaca: yellow stones wearing a brown skin of fertile growth; after wading its flows in sandals, the smell of compost clung to your legs. But no river pheromones were as sublime as the Ipsyniho's. The chocolate notes would fade as day revealed its diamond-clear water and jade and turquoise stones—there would be a clean smell like icy snow over a lavender garden.

He took a deep breath and shut his eyes. The Ipsyniho: not paradise, but closer than he deserved.

Andy Trib's nose was still sunburned from the Micronesian sun. He had only been back three days, just long enough to retrieve his belongings from storage and pay the deposit on his old place. He needed work— three or four trips plus this one would give him the cash to reestablish himself in the valley, buy a new set of oars, a fridge full of food, a few

1

bottles of good wine for his friends. All he needed to do was call the Ipsyniho Fly Shop, tell Gordon, the owner, he was back in town and ready for work. Fall always provided a surplus of paying clients—the steelhead were willing and the weather was nice. But Danny Goodman might answer. Any given day, it might be Danny at the counter.

So he had called Northwest Stream Born, a fly shop an hour away, in Eugene. He had bailed them out a few summers before, a week's worth of work when Starbucks held a corporate play date on the upper river. They owed him a favor, and they delivered, three trips—although not without giving him a little shit.

"But you've been gone a year," Alan, the owner, had said. "Take a few weeks. Get to know the river again. The Ipsyniho had a big flood while you were gone."

"It's my homewater," Andy replied, using a toothpick to pry a popcorn shard from his teeth. "Flood or not, I know the water."

But now, as he struggled just to recognize the old runs, he realized how severe the flood must have been.

His client said, "You've fished this river before, right?"

The Honey Bucket, formerly a fish-laden tailout, was buried under a landslide. The river had carved a new course.

Prefontaine, an impossibly fast and long riffle, was streaked with hundred foot Doug firs and their waterlogged root balls—totally unfishable.

This hadn't been just any flood. A boomer deluge, the dreaded hundred-year flood maybe, had scraped the river valley clean. It had probably come in March when the snowmelt met an errant tropical monsoon. Back in March, Andy had been pointing out brown trout to rich Americans in Tierra Del Fuego.

He backed the drift boat to shore and dropped anchor. Even if the river had changed, the steelhead hadn't.

"This is the Hippie Hole," he said. Or it used to be. The two Volkswagen-sized boulders near the tailout were gone, buried under tons of displaced gravel. "Most of the fish hold in that trough." He pointed to no place in particular.

"Where?" The sport was waiting for Andy to help him out of the boat.

Andy offered the man a hand, helped him find his footing in the current, and gave him a 7-weight. "You're best off casting quartering downstream."

Once the man was busy casting, Andy climbed the bank and stepped into the blackberries, careful not to touch the skin of his waders to the thorns. Just two minutes, he promised himself, then he would get back to work.

He plucked a couple berries, popping one into his mouth and eyeing the other. The chunky globs held to the center like the moon held to the earth and the earth to the sun. Glistening sunlight formed constellations in its moist surface. He turned the berry in his fingers, staining his skin with the purple juice.

It was a shame his grandfather hadn't come west. These berries were sweeter and juicier than the little black orbs they had picked together on the Upstate farm. He would have appreciated the complexity of their flavor, how they made the rocky shoreline their own.

He plucked a baseball-cap worth and watched the sport throw wide loops toward the center of the current. The man chronically overpow-ered his forward stroke, which is probably how he lived his life too. Before the line could complete its swing, before the fly had even entered the best water, he was already lifting it back into the air.

Andy hadn't just missed the river and its blackberries. His drift boat glowed against the dark water, a marvel of old-school simplicity. With a hull as flat as a pizza pan, it sat a scant three inches in the water when fully loaded. Curved like the leg of a rocking chair, it would swagger through the heaviest Northwest whitewater. The boat's physical dimen-sions coupled with its feather weight—only three hundred and fifty-two pounds—allowed an experienced oarsman to hold it dead still in the fastest current and actually guide it upstream in slower water. Rowing one was as close as a human could come to defying the physical proper-ties of flowing water, to moving upstream with the supple grace of an anadromous fish, to taking tender treads on open water.

A backcast hit the brush nearby—and the fly was stuck.

"I got it," Andy said.

But the sport tugged anyway, and the leader broke.

Andy made his way back to the shore. "Any strikes?" he asked, already knowing there had been none.

"One or two."

"Good start," he said, reaching for the line. "What do you say we try a new pattern?"

A pair of twenty dollar bills make a disproportionate bulge in an empty pocket. Andy passed his fingers over the lump as he pulled out of the boat ramp parking lot and onto River Road. It was a good tip, considering he hadn't found the man a fish.

He needed to do some fishing on his own, learn the river's new contours, where the steelhead stacked up. He needed to talk to somebody who still knew the water.

He couldn't avoid Danny forever. The valley was too small, the river too intimate. Before long, they would surely see each other on the water. And then what would Andy say? He had been in town for how many weeks and still not called?

The town of Ipsyniho, twenty thousand people clustered between the mountains and the banks of the river, spanned highway mile marker sixty-nine. The valley there widened slightly, the steep ridges spreading and making way for thin strips of farmland. Organic blueberry farms, hazelnut orchards, and endless rows of tear-shaped Christmas trees lined the road. Between the Co-op and Nearly Normal's Diner sat the fly shop. If he kept heading downstream, the valley would meet the Coast Range at mile thirty-two, the ridges pinching the highway and the river through a narrow canyon before spilling into tidewater. For a moment, he imagined driving all the way, selling his truck and boat at the port, and stowing away on a ship back across the Pacific.

In the fly shop's parking lot, he chose the slot furthest from the shop door. Danny's truck sat in front of the shop, backed into the same slot he had been using forever. The same gray scars lined the body, old dents where paint had peeled free. But on the bumper he saw something new, a yellow and blue bumper sticker: *BIODIESEL*.

Andy pushed through the shop door, the familiar bells announcing his entrance.

There he was, near the rod rack, wiggling a two-hander for a customer. The same Danny he had known for a dozen years: strikingly tall, permanently sunburned, red hair curling out the bottom of his baseball cap. He looked even stronger than Andy remembered, with the wide and thickset shoulders of a career oarsman. His T-shirt read: Got Steelhead?

"So you're sure I want to use a Skagit line?" the customer asked.

"If you're new to Spey casting, definitely," Danny said. No one could earn the confidence of a client faster than Danny—his sports always came back. "Trees crowd the famous runs on the Ipsyniho. The Skagit will let you keep a smaller D-loop but still send a long line. And this is the rod for it."

The customer glanced over at Andy, and Danny did the same. He looked again and said, "No shit!"

"What?" Andy said, "You act surprised to see me."

From the glazy redness of his eyes, Andy could tell instantly that Danny was stoned. He offered his hand, but Danny pushed it aside and embraced him.

A few sun wrinkles had emerged on Danny's forehead, the only sign time had passed. Except for the ring on his finger. "I'm sorry, you know, about that," Andy said.

"What, the wedding? Nah. Just some talking and a well-funded bender." Danny checked his feet. "Tell me where? The Bahamas?"

Andy hit the highlights, Chile during their summer, Micronesia during their winter.

Danny punched him in the shoulder. "Fuck you, that's great. Working the lodge scene?"

"I wasn't teaching English. They're desperate for Americans who can give casting tips down there. In the islands too. One lodge sent a car two days through the mountains to pick me up. Easy money."

Danny's forearms were stronger than before, each wider than the fist below it, rowing veins bulging over the muscles. "I bet Bridge you were on some Jamaican cove living off dope and shellfish and that we'd never see you again."

"You knew I'd come back. I can't leave this place."

Danny scoffed.

5

Andy stuffed his hands in his pockets and glanced around the store. He had known Danny Goodman a long time and he had never felt short on words before.

"Well, goddamn," Danny said. "You got to get your skinny ass over to our new place. Have some dinner. What do you got tonight? Shosh will scream when she sees you."

Shoshana.

"Excuse me," the customer said, still holding the rod.

"Sorry, bud," Danny said. "We're closed."

"But I'd like to buy this. You've convinced me to buy it."

"Ring it up," Andy said. "I've got time."

The man also wanted a reel and line to match the rod. Danny ran his credit card, bagged his new tackle, and guided him to the door. "Good luck out there," he called, already flipping the *open* sign to *closed*.

"Let's go," Danny said. "Follow me up River Road."

This wasn't the time to face Shoshana, not yet. "Yeah, I probably shouldn't. Got a trip tomorrow, and today didn't go so well."

"Fuck off," Danny said. "You're coming over." He leaned over the counter and turned the key on the cash register. "Today? You hit the river already?"

Andy examined some flies in the "Traditionals" bin. "Stream Born sent me a trip before I'd even gotten settled. Hadn't even fished once yet."

"Stream Born?" Danny said. "Why didn't you call here? I could have switched the bookings and given you a few trips."

"And stick you in an awkward spot with Gordon?" Gordon, the owner, kept a suspicious eye on everything, including the guiding schedule. "Not a chance."

"It wouldn't have been any big deal," Danny jammed some papers into a drawer.

Andy checked his watch. "What will Gordon say about you closing this early?"

"Gordon can lick my balls. He's drinking bourbon with those White Oak bastards. Won't be driving past the shop anytime soon."

"White Oak?" Andy asked.

Danny pointed toward the door, flipping off the lights. "A lot has changed around here my friend."

Andy followed Danny upstream along River Road as the evening shade climbed the mountains. Soon they left the flat agricultural section of the valley, and the ridges rose to ten and two overhead. Huge Doug firs held their mossy arms over the road, their fingers bowing to speeding log trucks.

The road swerved in and out from the river's edge, and would keep it up for the next forty miles or so. But as the foothills gave way to the Cascades, the river views would become increasingly sparse. Eventually, River Road would leave the river altogether—becoming Highway 128 East on a map—before summiting the pass and dropping into the high desert of central Oregon.

Houses were few and far between along the upper river, the land rarely providing a flat place to build. There were the mega-mansions along Missouri Bend, a dozen or so three-story vacation homes built within casting distance of the river. And there were the old hippie cottages scattered through the hills. And of course, the tiny Calapooia Community up Deer Creek. But most Ipsynihians lived within a mile of the town center. He wondered now, as he followed Danny upriver, where he and Shoshana had scored a place this high. A lucky find for sure.

Danny still drove the same, too fast around the corners. He drove like a crab walked, each limb shifting and turning and clutching and gassing, always in motion.

Years ago, they had piled into Danny's truck and raced upstream in the morning darkness, trying to beat the dawn crowd to the Hatchery Hole. Just as they came around a blind corner near the Millican Boat Ramp, a deer appeared in their headlights. A white deer, perfectly albino, its eyes laser red. Danny had braked just when he needed to accelerate if the truck was to hold traction around the corner, and they had spun wildly through a stand of short trees and into a meadow. For a moment, neither of them said anything: staring at their limbs, wiggling their toes. Then Danny broke out laughing and Andy did too, twenty-year-olds, still alive, as always.

Just past mile marker eighty, Andy followed Danny's truck up a thin gravel road that threaded Buckskin Valley. Buckskin Creek, a small trout stream, paralleled the road. Andy had often fished the confluence of Buckskin and the Ipsyniho, the smaller creek drawing fish to its cool flows in the heat of summer. But he had never known there were houses up the slender valley. Of course, he didn't get away from the river much.

At the top, just past a mailbox painted the color of a sunset, they turned down a driveway, and there, tucked along the ridge, sat a yurt—or actually, two yurts connected by what looked like a hallway. The cedar siding glowed orange in the dusk, and a deck protruded off into the woods. A domed skylight blasted a beam of warm light onto the surrounding fir trees.

The soil around the home was still bare, probably cleared only a few months prior. A high elk-proof fence guarded a garden—Shoshana's work no doubt. On a wooden sign above the fence's gate, in wobbly aquatic letters, read the words: *Arousal From Below*. She surely appreciated the double meaning.

Danny's aluminum drift boat sat tipped up in the driveway. Beside it was another, a new fiberglass boat, "Osprey Guide Service" written on the side, the name of Danny's company. A fiberglass boat cut silently through the current, bounced off rocks without chattering the occupants' teeth, and flexed its hull to help clear shallow riffles. Danny had the most expensive version, low sides for easier mobility in strong winds, and a second casting platform on the back. Probably cost twice what a new aluminum boat did, enough that few other guides in the valley owned one.

The yurt's door opened. She appeared, peering over reading glasses, a book in her hand. Shoshana. She wore flip-flops and paint-smeared jeans and an old T-shirt. Her brown hair, back in a loose bun, looked red in the evening sun. It would smell like rosemary if he got closer.

Andy took off his baseball cap, wiped the sweat from his forehead, and stepped out of the truck. This was it.

She stayed on the porch, a finger keeping her page in the book. She was biting her lip, and he knew she wanted a cigarette.

"Look what I found floating downriver," Danny said, slamming his truck door.

Their eyes met—the first time in fourteen months. "Some flotsam," she said.

They needed to hug. This is what old friends did. But she wasn't coming his way.

He followed the railing up the steps, and she laid her arms around him. Hardly a hug. A balloon's distance stayed between their bodies. Her hair blew across his face, and he held his breath.

"You look like a tomato," she said, stepping back. Her finger slipped from the book.

"You should see my bikini line," he said.

"I'd rather not."

He searched for words. "You lost your place."

She was staring at him.

"In the book."

"Right," she said. It was a worn copy of *Sometimes a Great Notion*, Kesey's Oregon epic, the sprawling tale of the Stamper family and the world set against them. She had told him about it nearly a decade before, insisted he read it. They had always had books in common.

Danny put his hand on her arm, and she turned and kissed him instantly. "Come in," she said. "For god's sake, come in."

The yurt smelled of cedar and flowers. It wasn't rustic like he had expected. Tile. Stone. Stainless. Some old-time string band played quietly from speakers in the ceiling.

"What do you think of *Sometimes a Great Notion* this time through," he asked.

She tossed the book on a chair. "It never gets easier."

"He wants a tour, not a college study group." Danny laughed, like he always did when people talked about books or college.

As Shoshana guided him around the house, he did his best not to look at her.

Her charm hadn't changed since she was twenty. It grew from a casual, almost messy sophistication, that when coupled with her unerring confidence became entirely intoxicating. Somehow she was elegant without being uppity, regal without being snotty. She could make the most slapdash attire appear utterly graceful. But most of all, she knew who she was and what she wanted—and that made her impossibly attractive.

She was looking at him, awaiting an answer. He pointed at something. "What about these?"

"Those?"

They were a pair of large copper plates, each engraved by a precise hand. "Yeah."

"From Turkey," she said. "I've had those a long time. You've definitely seen them before."

In the years between college and meeting Danny, years he had spent learning the Ipsyniho, she had traveled.

Danny signaled Andy to follow him down the hallway, and they stopped at a wide doorway. "You've got to see this." Danny stepped inside, and signaled for Andy to do the same.

The bed. Red and orange and big. The imprints of their bodies discernable in the disheveled sheets. Andy leaned against the doorframe.

"Get in here," Danny said. "You've got to feel the ambiance."

Andy took off his hat, and took a half step.

"What's this?" Andy pointed at something that wasn't the bed, a framed document on the wall. The large writing on top appeared to be Hebrew, and the flowing cursive on the bottom looked to be an English translation. The English section was longer, the modern language filled with superfluous turns on the path to the same meaning. Shoshana could have read the Hebrew if he asked—he still remembered the glottal sounds, her voice like sandaled feet on cobbled ground.

"The ketubah," Danny said.

Shoshana's voice from the doorway: "He won't know what that is."

"The Jewish marriage contract," Andy said quickly—wishing now that he hadn't asked about the thing in the first place. He remembered when he saw the word "consecrated."

"We all signed it," Danny said, pointing to the signatures along the bottom, four of them. "When you couldn't make it, I got Ethan."

"Right."

Silence.

Shoshana cleared her throat.

"Want a beer?" Danny offered.

In the kitchen, Danny filled a bowl with nuts and sliced a few slivers of sharp cheddar cheese. There was already a bowl of blackberries, probably gathered that morning, based on their matte appearance. Andy picked at the food, drinking river-cold IPA between bites. Shoshana disappeared into a bathroom.

"Ethan left, you know. Had an accident, in Coffin Rapid. He was guiding when it happened. A radiologist and his daughter." Danny ate a blackberry. "The guy died."

"No shit."

"Ethan lost an oar on the cliff, went broadside through those first waves, filled the boat. By the time he got the extra oar ready, he couldn't pull free from Steel Rock, sucked the boat into the hole. They think the gunwale hit the radiologist's head. Took almost two days for Search and Rescue to recover his body."

Ethan had started guiding about the same time as Andy. Wasn't much of a fisherman, but he could sure handle a pair of oars. "How'd he lose the oar?"

"Didn't ship it fast enough. You know how the cliff sneaks up on you. He left town as soon as he could. Florida or Georgia or some shit. No more rivers."

The Ipsyniho flowed through Ethan's veins. He loved the river every bit as much as Danny or Andy. What would Ethan do without the valley? He would probably come back, after he realized how demented the outside world had become since those planes.

Last time he remembered seeing Ethan was that trip on the upper river last year, six golfing buddies and their six bottles of scotch. The three of them had worked the trip, Ethan, Andy, and Danny, and afterward, they had gone up to Cougar Hot Springs for a soak.

"Energy efficient gas-powered heating. Bamboo floors." Danny had moved on to the house. "Salvaged lumber, most of it. The rest was sustainably harvested. We went all out to do it right."

He couldn't remember Danny ever saying words like "energy efficient" and "sustainably harvested." Shoshana had been a good influence. Andy nodded toward the driveway. "I see you're running biodiesel."

"Only way to go. I looked into electric, but nothing that runs on volts has the horsepower to pull the boat. Shosh and some other neo-hippies convinced the Co-op to put in a biodiesel pump behind the shop."

Maybe one of these neo-hippies owned the house. "Who you renting from?"

"Rent? Oh, no brother. We bought the land from Bridge and he and I built the place."

"This is yours?" Andy reexamined the ceiling, the tile floors. Not cheap.

"Bridge was sweet to sell the land," Danny said.

Bridge was a native of the valley, a contractor who lived up Steamboat Creek with his longtime ladyfriend, Rita, Ipsyniho's midwife. Good people.

Shoshana walked back into the room, drying her hands on her shirt.

"Wow," Andy said. "You guys won the lottery while I was gone, eh?"

Shoshana opened the refrigerator and grabbed more beers. "We got some cash from the wedding. Figured we might as well put it to good use."

Danny's parents didn't have money to give, Andy knew that. They both worked blue-collar jobs in Eugene and rented their own house. "Your mom?" Andy asked, avoiding Shoshana's eyes. She lived in Boston, old money.

Shoshana began popping the caps off with a lighter. "You know how she is."

Danny said, "Shosh's mom thought she'd never find a nice Jewish boy way out here on the fringes of the Diaspora."

"I don't know if you count as 'nice.'" Shoshana smiled at Danny—that coy glancing smile.

Andy chewed a fistful of nuts.

Shoshana handed him another beer, and took a swig of her own—hers was a ginger ale.

"To life," Danny said, holding up a fresh bottle.

The first beer had helped, but the third really did the trick. He was able to look Shoshana in the eye.

She told him of her new studio in town, how she had been making good money selling her mosaics. She had never been so productive.

Danny tossed a hazelnut into the air, threw back his head to catch it in his mouth, and blinked as the nut hit him in the forehead.

"Let's make some dinner," Shoshana said. "I need to eat."

"Will you make it?" Danny asked.

"It's your turn."

"I'll rub your feet later," Danny begged.

"Feet and shoulders, or no deal."

"Deal."

She squinted at him. "You better not fall asleep on me."

Andy asked about Carnival, if the executive committee had granted her booth space again this year.

"They did," she said. "But not a spot with camping space. If it wasn't for the Community Booth, I'd have to sleep under my display table."

"Community Booth?"

Shoshana frowned. "Danny hasn't told you about Trey?"

"I told you lots has changed around here since you left."

"Trey is Danny's new best friend," Shoshana said into her ginger ale.

"Come on," Danny said. "Trey is starting a new community in the valley. Homes like these."

"This guy is a developer?" Andy said.

"He's not a developer, exactly."

"Bullshit," Shoshana said. "He's a realtor from down south who's drooling to develop the river. Ask where he wants to build the community."

Danny walked over to the woodstove and opened its door.

"Where?" Andy asked.

Danny crammed a quarter-round into the heat. "You know how land is out here." The fire crackled as the new wood disappeared in a yellow wall of flame. "Near the confluence of Steamboat and the Ipsyniho."

About ninety percent of the Ipsyniho's remaining steelhead spawned in Steamboat Creek and its tributaries.

"Can you believe that?" Shoshana said. "Danny Goodman helping to develop the Ipsyniho."

"Fuck that," Danny said. He walked back to the counter. "The confluence is getting developed. The zoning commission decided that for us. Now it's just a matter of how it gets developed." His temper hadn't abated in the last year.

She smiled at him. "All I'm saying is you weren't interested in any of this until Trey came around."

Danny pushed the bowl of blackberries across the counter. It slipped off the edge and exploded over the floor, surprising everyone.

Shoshana handed him a broom. "Damn it, Danny. My Bubbie gave me that bowl."

Andy pushed away from the counter and found the hallway bathroom.

Danny was known in the valley for his lava temper. Once, years before, when Andy was desperate for clients and Danny was already guiding full-time, he had nearly drowned a client. The story had raced through the guiding grapevine. Supposedly, the client had chuckled under his breath at Danny while casting from the bow of the boat—over what, no one knew. When Danny realized he had become the butt-end of the sport's joke, he punched one oar and pulled the other, dumping the guy into the cold river. Danny left him there to freeze—luckily another boat came by and picked the guy up. Later, when asked about the incident, Danny shook his head and said, "Douche bag got what he had coming." He would say no more. But for weeks, other guides were buying Danny beers.

Andy had always traced Danny's temper to his origins in the valley. He had grown up in Ipsyniho, a first-generation local. His parents, both from southern Oregon, had been children during the short but terrifying resurgence of the KKK there in the late fifties. While Jewish by lineage, they had gone to great lengths to assimilate; after marrying and moving to Ipsyniho, they even changed their last name from Goodman to McDonald. Jon and Nancy McDonald spent almost twenty-five years working as a millwright and a waitress in Ipsyniho, each year cutting the biggest Christmas tree and cooking the fattest Easter ham. They had even attended the Methodist Church in town, dragging Danny and

Joel—their first son—with them, a fact Danny resented deeply. "It was like waterboarding," he had once said. "Everybody knew we were Jews except them." Upon turning eighteen, he had changed his name back to Goodman and had the Star of David tattooed on his shoulder.

Maybe Joel had felt the same way; there was no way to be sure. He had died not long after Danny's fourteenth birthday, during the Methodist Church's annual Back Road Derby, an event to raise funds for charity. Joel's four-wheeler had slid off a logging road and tumbled a hundred feet down a clearcut. According to local accounts, Danny had been riding behind Joel at the time of the accident, and had been the first person to his brother's mangled body. The details of that day were not something Danny discussed. In fact, at no time in the twelve years they had known each other had Danny once mentioned his brother.

What was clear was that after his brother's death, Danny took to the river. He fished every day the river was in shape, walking from his parent's home to the riffles and pools just upstream from Ipsyniho. Lots of people fly fished—it required a level of single-mindedness that blinded a person to the shoreside irritations of life. But Danny didn't fish to hide from irritations. When they first boated the river together, Danny had said, "I like the way you fish, Andy. It's like there's a monster on your ass, and if you slow down, you'll end up somebody else's bait."

Danny's adolescence arrived at the end of an era, just as the trees ran out. And as the mills closed and the last of the money was trucked down River Road, a flood of cheap land hit the market. In less than a decade, every available acre had been bought—mostly by out-of-staters looking for a slice of paradise. As Danny's parents followed the work downriver, their house was bought and demolished and a grand new summer cottage built. That was another thing Danny wouldn't talk about.

If Andy knew anything about Danny Goodman, it was that he would sooner trample a person than back down. When the muscles in his jaw flexed into ridges, he might as well have hardened into a dam, unable to relent no matter the weight against him. At such moments, Andy would turn and leave. Give the guy a few days to recover. But now, as he flushed the toilet, he wondered how Shoshana dealt with it.

He cracked the bathroom door and peered into the kitchen. At first he could only see Shoshana, her thin frame leaning against the counter.

Her shirt hugged the soft edge of her breast, and he knew he needed out of this yurt.

Danny took her in his arms, and they stood there holding each other, their foreheads pressed together.

He stepped into the kitchen. "I better go."

"We haven't even had dinner yet," Danny said, looking up. "You can't go."

Shoshana slapped Danny affectionately with a dish towel and walked toward the refrigerator.

"Hey," he said. "I'm sorry about . . . about that little outburst. I'm working on things."

"Don't worry about it," Andy said. "I really should go though. Flies to whip up. That trip tomorrow."

Danny shook his head. "I've got all the flies you need. Stay for dinner. Then a soak. Hell, just spend the night here. Might as well."

"Let him go home," Shoshana said. "He wants to go."

"Who doesn't want a soak?" Danny said. "We've got a new hot tub. It's screaming your name. Besides, you'll be closer to the ramp if you sleep here."

It was true, he would be.

Shoshana turned to him. "Don't let him pressure you. Do what you want."

It would look suspicious if he turned down Danny's offer. Two years ago, this wouldn't have been an issue. "Okay," he said. "But I better tank out early. Dawn trip."

"Excellent," Danny said. Then, suddenly, he walked out the front door and left Andy and Shoshana alone.

She was washing a plate. Andy looked at the window and saw their reflection in the glass. He wondered if Danny was standing out there in the dark, watching to see what Shoshana and Andy would do when left alone.

He needed to act normal. He opened the refrigerator. On the bottom shelf, a pile of zucchinis and tomatoes and onions, most still covered in garden dust. He shut the refrigerator, organized the magnets on the door.

Only ten feet away, Shoshana lathered a large salad bowl. "What can I do? Need some help?" Andy asked.

"I got it."

He cleaned some crumbs off the counter. There was her ginger ale. "This is the first time I've seen you turn down a microbrew."

"In the freezer, could you grab the Ziploc bag with the steelhead burgers in it? It's marked." She didn't look up from the sink.

He set the frosty package on the counter. "Shoshana," he was whispering now, "I want to clear the air, set things right again. That's why I came back. I couldn't keep living—"

"Shut up about that," she snapped, still lathering.

He whispered, "You obviously haven't told him anything."

She shut the water off, her eyes squarely meeting his. "Don't you dare, Andy. Don't you even—"

The door opened, and suddenly, Danny was back inside, grinning at Andy. "You know my favorite part of this house?" He waited for Andy to ask 'what?' Then, finally, continued anyway. "It isn't the energy bill or the sound system. It's being able to arc my fluids from the deck. Aren't I blessed, Andy?"

The hot tub scalded Andy's toes. He watched as Danny slipped his legs in, then cupped his hands over his balls, and submerged the rest of his body. "What? Try it. Keeps them from melting off." Danny shrugged. "I've become quite the hot tub pro since we got this thing."

Shoshana had gone to bed inside, waving goodnight to Andy from across the room. She claimed the meal had made her too drowsy for a soak.

The blue hot tub lights glowed through the steam: an artificial aurora borealis. Danny lit a joint, puffed twice, and passed it. Andy shook his hand dry and pinched the paper. "So, Shoshana isn't drinking beer, eh?"

"I love this thing. Soak in it after every trip. Loosen the muscles and drown the memories. One thing hasn't changed since you left: Guiding still ties your back in knots."

There weren't many reasons why she would pass up a beer.

"You going to hit that?" Danny said.

He brought the joint to his lips. The wind rustled the trees, and as the smoke filled his lungs, the limbs began to sway in a hypnotic rhythm, a rhythm that then appeared in the swirling mist, and a moment later, in the bubbling water. The pulse of the Ipsyniho.

A coyote howled on the ridge behind the house, chatty and broken, not long and sustained. Another one yelped nearby. Their voices in perfect rhythm.

He passed the joint, overpowered by a profound appreciation for this singular moment. What a beautiful house. What a striking sky. How stellar to be back with Danny again.

Danny flipped the joint over the deck, even though it was only half gone. "You still haven't told me."

"Told you what?" Andy said.

"Why you're such a dirt bag?" He wasn't laughing.

Andy wiped his brow, dizzy again. Might Danny know? He lifted himself from the water, putting a little distance between them.

"Skip town a week before our wedding? You committed to being part of it, for fuck's sake."

Andy climbed out of the tub. He had practiced his confession a hundred times. A thousand times. Perfecting his elocution, his intonation. But now he had nothing. Shoshana hadn't told him, hadn't paved the way. He hadn't expected this. "I snapped, I guess," he heard himself say. "Didn't have anything to do with you or Shoshana."

"Snapped?" Danny wasn't smiling. "You owe me something better than that."

"I had a little freak out. Like when you dumped that client in the river."

Danny was watching him.

"I had personal things going on. Family things. We were coming up on the fall rush. I just couldn't do it. I had to get away."

"Why not tell me what was going on?" Danny asked. "At least me. One day you're here, the next you're gone."

"Like I said, I snapped. Booked a flight and that was it."

Danny squinted as if they were on opposite sides of the river. "And you don't call for fourteen months?"

"It was crazy, I know. And ridiculously selfish. I thought I needed a fresh start."

Danny turned and dried his hand on a towel and plucked a second joint from the edge of the hot tub. He struck a wooden match and held it to the end of the paper. A ball of smoke left his mouth and disappeared up his nose.

He came across the tub, his eyes cold and stoned, and handed the joint to Andy. "Well, you're back now anyway."

CHAPTER 2

Andy told the clients to fish their way up a side channel Danny had suggested, to cast toward the seams between fast water and slow, that he would be right behind them. A mossy rock, flat as a table, offered a place to sit and organize his thoughts. He just needed a couple minutes.

The skin along the backs of his hands had changed in the last year, darkening and cracking. They looked foreign to him now, older than his memories of them. The last year had also delivered his first gray hairs, silver threads above his ears, maybe a dozen on each side; in the mirror, they stood out against his dark hair. He tucked his hands in his wader pocket and looked toward the water.

Behind the rock, a small eddy twisted, bringing the same submerged leaves around and around. A drowned mayfly, a *baetis* it looked like, did circles there, floating on a billion water molecules. Two hydrogens and an oxygen, whatever that meant. Once an individual molecule spun into the riffle, how long did it take to drift downriver, past Ipsyniho, past the Coast Range, and into the tidal flats?

Things with Shoshana hadn't always been so twisted. It was simple love in the beginning. They were university sophomores—a full two years before he met Danny. It was her hips, how narrow they were. So petty and childish it seemed now. But then, they were everything. The hips of a runner, not a mother.

Under an umbrella, the winter rains dragged the clouds to the ground, and she told him of her father. "He and my mom were never married. They didn't even fake being in love. Just two academics devoted to the concept of a child. Of course, his devotion proved a bit fickle."

"When was the last time you saw him?"

She shrugged. "Not important." A moment later, her lips were pressed against his.

Later, she told him he kissed funny. Too much tongue and not enough lip. "The lips are the most persuasive organ, you know. Here, let me show you."

It was his smile, she would say later, that first attracted her, a smile that seemed to transform his otherwise "steely" face. He generally looked pensive, she said, even intimidating, but each smile, no matter how small, cracked that wall. "Like you were showing me—and only me—the real you. It was your smile, well, and also your calloused hands. I've always had a thing for guys who actually do things."

They sat on her dorm room bed, wrapped in a quilt, and watched the first major storm of winter, the wind shaking the building, the rain glazing the window. "It's like we're deep in the river, staring up at the surface."

She leaned forward, a match in her fingers, and lit the first candle of Chanukah. "It's fire for fire's sake," she said. And as she sang the Hebrew words, he watched the flame flickering against the river's surface.

Then, she asked about his family.

"My grandparents came from Portugal," he said, hoping she wouldn't ask any more.

"What about your other side?"

"We're not real sure. What about you?" Maybe his response had come a little too quickly.

She narrowed her eyes, on the verge, it seemed, of asking again. Then she looked away and said, "They came over in '46."

But later, as they cuddled under the covers, the lights dimmed, she asked again. "So where's the other half of your family from?"

"I don't really know. I've never really been close to any of them. Probably one of those boring Everywhere-Europe lineages."

"Are you lying?"

"Me?" He ran his fingertip down her spine, over the bulge of her hip, and along her thigh. "Of course not." He kissed the flesh of her abdomen.

She lifted herself from the bed, wrapped her body in a robe, and sat in the chair at the foot of the bed. She was waiting for the truth.

If he'd lied just one more time, everything might have gone differently. But he didn't. "They might be, at least partially, from Germany."

The menorah still sat on the desk.

In a low, nearly inaudible voice, she probed, "They were sympathizers."

"It's not like you think," he said.

She squeezed shut the top of her robe, as if she were suddenly afraid to reveal anything to him. She was imagining the worst, creating a story far more atrocious than reality.

So he told her, starting with how his grandfather had been conscripted, forced to march to Poland. He hadn't wanted to, but there was a war on, and a tyrant in power. Luckily, just outside of Warsaw, shrapnel broke his knee and he spent the war's remaining years back in Germany. He'd been a college student before the war, studying film and cameras. So they gave him an Arriflex and assigned him to an engineering corp. "He hid behind straw bails, the camera running just over his head, and filmed the test detonations of bombs and stuff. He was pretty much deaf because of it."

She didn't say anything.

"He hated the Nazi Party, hated their ideas. He disagreed with the regime." Andy heard his own voice, the begging tenor of it. "Shoshana, he was a good man, a good man stuck in a country doing bad things. Just imagine if one day, for no good reason, we invaded some other country."

"Your grandfather," she said in that same low, disbelieving voice, "was a Nazi."

"No, he wasn't. Only technically. After my parents split, I spent summers with him on his farm. The only part of the year I looked forward to. He taught me to fish. Made me my first rod." He didn't tell her about the man's nightmares, about how he sometimes shouted German words in his sleep, the throaty sounds echoing through the dark farm house.

He didn't say more, and she didn't ask anything else. Eventually, she came back to bed—although she slept with the robe on.

Her mom and grandmother came from Boston just before spring break and took a suite at the Best Western across the street from campus. In front of the mirror, Shoshana changed her clothes five times, asking his opinion while examining her profile.

"Great," he said, looking at his own clothes. "Do I need to change?" He wore the same things he always did, the work pants, the sandals—his college uniform.

She glanced at him and took off her shirt. She was wearing a bra. She never wore a bra. "Maybe you shouldn't come," she said.

"I'll change."

They walked along the millrace, the water mud brown and burping over its banks. He knew the Ipsyniho, a short drive to the south, must be flowing near 8,000 cubic feet per second—blown out by the same spring rains. "Just don't say anything about us," she said. "Don't say anything about my bedroom." And then she'd pulled her hand from his as they neared the hotel.

He met Ms. Weissman in her room, the low hotel ceiling squeezing his breaths. She did all the talking, her sentences complete and precise, as if lifted from the page. A pair of reading glasses hung at her navel, suspended by a long piece of green yarn. Shoshana had told him earlier that her mother was an English professor, "Does feminist lit crit," she had said. Now, as the woman spoke, he struggled to overcome the sensation he was in office hours.

"And this is Shoshana's Bubbie," Ms. Weissman shouted for the benefit of the old woman beside her. The grandmother took his hand and waited for him to kiss her cheek. As he leaned forward, he saw a faded tattoo where a sailor would put an anchor—a number maybe.

"Where did you grow up, Andy?" Ms. Weissman asked.

"I moved around a lot. But I'd say Ithaca if I had to pick one place."

She beamed. "Oh, we have great friends in Ithaca! Did you go to Temple Beth-El, then?"

He looked to Shoshana, but she didn't interject. "Actually, I'm not Jewish."

"Oh," Mrs. Weissman said. "Of course, of course. Excuse me for assuming."

Shoshana launched into an animated explanation of how great Oregon was, the rivers, the trees, the mountains, the liberal culture. How they were going to love it. And before she was done, they were safely on their way to dinner.

Later, once back in his dorm room, her mom and Bubbie sleeping in the hotel room, Shoshana apologized. "I'm sorry if you felt awkward earlier. I should have told them before that you aren't Jewish."

"I didn't realize it would be an issue," he said. "You acted embarrassed or something."

"It's not that," she said. "That's not it at all."

He found a gum wrapper in his pocket and balled it between his fingers. "Because that's what it kind of felt like."

She touched his arm. "I'm sorry. I'm not embarrassed."

"It was something."

She walked to the window, the trees bare and quivering in the wind. "Let's talk about this some other time." She turned and headed for the door. "I should get some sleep. I've got that Spanish final tomorrow."

"You're leaving?"

She pulled on the door's handle, but a basket of laundry pinned against the bed stopped it from fully opening. She yanked and when the door wouldn't budge, she tried to squeeze herself through the narrow gap.

"Shoshana?" He saw the terrible urgency in her eyes—it was panic really. She had become wedged in the gap. He kicked free the laundry basket and the door opened.

But instead of leaving, she spilled into him.

Later, in the darkness of the winter night, she told him of her grandmother's tattoo. She delivered the words quickly and without emotion: Bubbie had survived the camp, bearing witness to the murders of her parents, sisters, brother—her whole family. Shoshana herself was named after one of those sisters, one who on the way to her death had spit on a Nazi guard. One day, Shoshana would name her own daughter Miriam after the youngest sister, the only sister yet to be honored. "And now I'm in love with the grandson of a Nazi."

He slept at his own place for rest of the week. And her family left without seeing him again, although according to Shoshana, they passed along their goodbyes. "My mother liked you," she said.

For the next year, he and Shoshana lived as if they had never come, as if she'd never told him about the tattoo. They studied at a campus coffee shop during the day, shared her single dorm bed at night, and escaped to the river on warm afternoons. One day, on a sunlit beach, the emerald water gliding by, she wandered through the gallery of driftwood, collecting pieces that caught her eye. The wind pressed her skirt tight against her thighs. "Art everywhere," she said.

He sat on the bank, looking out over the river, at the way the currents fractured the emerald stones along the bottom. "This river is magic."

She walked over, pulled up her skirt, and straddled him. She wasn't wearing panties. "Think anyone can see us?"

They started going to the river more often. Sometimes he would coax her into a rock-skipping contest. She'd grin that coy smile and hop a stone a dozen times over the surface before it planed high and dove under in a spray of white. She always won—he never figured out how to get more than four or five skips. But no matter. Winning put her in a kissing mood, and they'd end up with whole-body sunburns.

That summer, she took him to see The Grateful Dead—Autzen Stadium stuffed with more people than came to the Oregon Ducks football games. He didn't like the music then, thought it was too twangy, too hippie. But he liked how happy it made Shoshana. She'd wear her torn jeans with the teddy bear patch on the hip and spin as if she were the only person in the stadium. Afterwards she asked, "We should go to more shows. After we graduate, we should spend a year on tour, don't you think?" "Definitely," he said. But Jerry died that August.

And a few months later, she couldn't raise herself from bed. He brought her a cup of soup, instant ramen he'd nuked in the dorm microwave. She sat up against the wall, her hair matted and tangled. The soup's steam misted the space between them. She looked at him, her lips quivering—then vomited over the side of the bed. On the test, two blue lines appeared. Three more tests confirmed it.

She stared out the window, watching the rain slide down the glass, her knees pulled up to her chest. She didn't say anything, and he didn't dare ask. What did people do in this situation? Was it assumed that they'd keep the pregnancy, or end it? How could a guy even broach the subject? He struck a match and touched it to a candle, but the flame flattened when she let out a breath.

He imagined a baby between them, smaller than a fish. Imagined holding it to her breast, keeping it warm with both their bodies. He'd have to get a square job. Nine to five. He might make it to the river two Saturdays a month. And he'd have to call his father and ask for money.

When around her family, would she be made as anxious by their child as she was by him?

Later, they walked the sidewalks, talking about everything except what mattered. Conversations about the weather or politics took on a feverish urgency. Anything to fill the space between them. She ate crackers to keep the stomach acid down, and he snuck a few for himself. Once, while she used a public restroom, he vomited in a trash can.

That night, in the blackness of her dorm room, he said it. The words slipped out in the truthful-consciousness before sleep. "Maybe a baby isn't the best idea?" He almost went on, but she rolled and faced the other direction, and he figured she was lost in a dream.

But the next morning, she asked him to leave. "You should go," she said.

"Okay," he said. "Will you call me?"

An entire day passed, and then another. Finally, he knocked on her door, and her friend Becky answered. "Shoshana is on the phone," she said through an eye-sized crack.

"Can I come in?"

The door didn't move. Becky just watched him. "You're getting what you want."

Back home, hours later, his phone rang. Shoshana's voice: "I made an appointment. Tomorrow, three o'clock. Can you take me?"

At Planned Parenthood, Shoshana left him in the waiting room and followed a woman with a clipboard down a hallway. A boy and a girl sat nearby, laughing. Around him, fetuses lived on the walls. At three months, at six, at nine. He shook his head against it all, and from his book bag, extracted the new issue of *Fly Fisherman* magazine. Had his words brought them here? He held the magazine before his face and didn't see anything.

He didn't see anything until Shoshana was beside him, watching him read about fish.

As they taxied back to her dorm, she kept her hand on her abdomen, her teeth clenched. He helped her upstairs to her bed, and she rolled her back to him. That night, he couldn't tell if she was asleep or awake. He waited up until dawn, running his fingers through her hair. Starting on her cheek and swirling over her ear and dropping down her neck. On the pillow, his salty tears mixed with her rosemary hair, and he wondered what amniotic fluid smelled like.

He had loved her more in that moment than in any before; this was their pain and they would survive it together. But part of him—a loud part of him—resented her too, resented her for letting him think that his words had caused them to go, that his words had cast away this child. As if her fear of her mother's reaction hadn't influenced the decision, hadn't scared her into scheduling the appointment. She owned this too. But the longer he laid there beside her, the longer he watched her, the more he hated himself.

Afterwards, she took up smoking. She took up smoking in her pajamas in the middle of the night. He would wake up to find himself alone, the sheets beside him cold. She would be on the roof, the night breeze rippling through her clothes, her feet dangling over the edge. The first time he found her there, he thought he was looking at her ghost. "Leave me alone," she said. "I need to be alone."

A couple nights later, he found her there again. This time, rain soaked her shirt, and she shivered against the cold. He laid a blanket on her shoulders. "Tell me everything is okay," she muttered.

"Everything is okay."

And eventually, things seemed okay again. Or at least they did the same things they used to when things were okay. Except now, when they'd walk along the Millrace or have beers with friends, Shoshana kept a pack of cigarettes nearby. And now, there were subjects she avoided. The future, for instance.

In late May, they went to the river to spend the day in the sun. While on a quilt spread over the ground, they ate an entire bag of cherries from a farmer's roadside stand. Andy stood and hopped a stone. It skipped once, twice, then maybe a half-dozen times before diving. "Holy shit. Did you see that?"

She spit out a seed and looked downriver. "Would you ever convert?"

"Convert?" He wasn't the religious type. She knew that. He was pretty sure God had been invented by people, a perennial super-parent there to order the chaos. Occam's razor—it just seemed like the simpler explanation. "Why would I convert? I'm already circumcised."

She didn't laugh. Instead, she said: "Forget it." She would never ask again.

In June, over a jug of four-dollar merlot, she ended it. "I need to move on," she said. "I need something else. I'm thinking of spending the year in Chile."

He should have sensed it coming. But he hadn't. And the pain swelled with each passing day, sprawling through him, squeezing him shut. He saw the story of their relationship, the bitter finality of it, the permanence of his shortcomings. There would never be another child to annul his failing. And he saw into the future, how he would always be left wondering if that abortion had cost him the one woman he was built to love.

After failing his exams, he fled to an apartment along the Ipsyniho and spent six months living on his meager savings and fishing the river. One July dawn, a tall guy with red hair appeared along the bank, holding a hatchery steelhead by its gill. "Hey, cowboy," the guy said. "Try swinging your fly by that rock." As soon as Andy made the cast, a fish took.

Within a couple months, Danny had found him a boat and he was guiding a couple days a week. The Ipsyniho was becoming home.

He thought of her often, wondering what she was doing in Chile, if she had met someone. Fall became winter, winter spring, and the pain slipped further into the background.

Eventually, he found himself desiring new people, usually as the nights grew colder and longer. Nothing serious, just friendly romances, a dinner, a bed shared, maybe a midnight trip to the hot springs. Once, years later, a woman even moved in with him, Meredith, an elementary school teacher. They laughed at the same things, and she was simple, no trap doors. Plus, she was crazy in bed. She wouldn't so much as swear in public—even when a dog peed on her grocery bag outside the Co-op one time—but she would moan the dirtiest obscenities in the dark of night.

They had been living together for three months when, a few days after his twenty-ninth birthday, something strange happened.

After another dull day of guiding, he stopped at the Co-op for some dinner ingredients. Meredith had begged him, for the fourth time that month, to make a pepperoni pizza, the most boring entree in the history of cuisine. In the Italian aisle, a man with a ponytail and a beard kneeled, talking to his little daughter. She might have been five or six years old. A pair of pink, oversized sunglasses barely stayed on her nose. She giggled and said, "Don't be silly, Daddy." The man smiled, and with his pinkie finger, tucked a lock of her hair behind her ear. "It's always something new with you, isn't it?" And suddenly he realized how much he missed the child.

That night, and many nights after, he woke with a start, the smell of rosemary still in the air. "What's the matter?" Meredith asked, her hand on his bare shoulder.

He needed to explain, to tell her about the dream, to tell her about the child, but something stopped him. He turned to find Meredith, her blond hair illuminated by the moonlight, dabbing the sleep from the corner of her eye with a precise fingertip. Everything in this woman's life was calculated, calibrated, no missteps or mistakes. She'd been the vale-dictorian at her high school and gone straight from college to her first teaching job. She cleaned her car every Saturday morning. The moment she caught a whiff of her own body odor, she took a shower. This woman possessed little sympathy for people who—for even a moment—lost control of their lives. She insisted on using condoms *and* birth control pills, for christsake. "Would you ever want babies?" he asked.

"Right!" she laughed. "I've got enough of them at work." She yawned. "Get back under the covers. You're letting the heat out."

A few days later, as if he'd conjured her, Shoshana appeared—in Danny's truck. They'd met a couple days before, when Danny went to Eugene to pick up a new boat trailer. He'd stopped at the Saturday Market for a burrito and she'd stepped into line behind him, grabbing some lunch while someone watched her booth and the mosaics for sale there.

Danny stepped out of his truck and saw the look on Andy's face. "Do you two know each other?"

She stood frozen in the dusty afternoon light, a braid hanging down each shoulder. Small wrinkles fanned from the corners of her eyes, only noticeable because they weren't in his memories.

Neither said anything and the moment sprawled into awkwardness. Finally, Danny saved them with some semi-witty remark and they all laughed a little harder than it warranted.

A couple weeks later, while fishing Prefontaine during sunset, Danny admitted he had fallen for her. "I think this could work. But knowing what I know," he said knotting on a Lady Caroline, "out of respect for our friendship, I'm asking your permission."

Danny had been lonely for years, living in a basement apartment, rarely doing anything but fishing or guiding. And in that moment, he looked up and the sunlight caught his eye.

"Of course," Andy said, turning back to the river. "What happened between us was a lifetime ago."

And less than a year later, Danny showed up at his door, gushing about Shoshana, a wedding band in his palm. "Do you think it's too soon?"

The trip went poorly. The sports, whatever their names were, turned out to be *avaros* as the Chilean guides would say—too stingy to tip. They had complained most of the float about one thing or another. It was little wonder they'd gone fishless. He swung the truck around the house and backed the boat up under the carport. He had completed the maneuver so many times over the years that even now he barely needed his mirrors.

His house sat in the middle of a hazelnut orchard. The river lay a quarter mile down a razor-straight orchard row, the blackberry bushes purple and green in the distance.

His wrists ached from rowing all day, gritty cement hardening along the tendons. It happened to older guides, their fingers forever bent as if around an oar. But he was still young, and tomorrow he knew he'd wake up with his wrists as strong and flexible as ever. A privilege that wouldn't last forever.

He grabbed a bucket and headed through the hazelnuts, toward the river.

River blackberries were the crème of the crème. They were different than inland blackberries. The water kept their roots moist all summer, swelling the ripening fruit with black syrup. Inland berries might be as big around as a bottle cap, but river berries looked more like black golf balls dragging their parent limbs to the soil. The trick was to find a patch on high ground near the river, a patch that could be watched and guarded, allowed to grow to its fullest potential.

Just past the orchard, Andy found his familiar patch. Clumps of juicing purple glistened in the last rays of the day. He held a clump in his hands, two pounds worth maybe, careful not to bruise the delicate bunch. Three-quarters of the berries were still green and inedible. The peak would come late this year, in another two weeks maybe. He plucked three ripe berries, biting each down the center and letting the violet juice run between his fingers. He inhaled on the bite, like he had seen the owner of Harris Bridge Vineyard do after swirling a glass of pinot.

The first berries of the year always delivered a sweet forebite—the promise of what was to come in the later fruit—and a metallic finish. The metal flavor, he figured, was the vine flushing its limbs of the soil's metals. He savored these early nuggets. With each bite, he swallowed land, microscopic flecks of the Ipsyniho Valley. He'd heard that metals never flushed from the human body; they became an intrinsic part of the flesh. He licked the escaping juice from between his fingers, then picked a few for the bucket.

The rows he had cut two Junes ago were overgrown now—the patch would give fewer berries. But the floods had been good for the soil, helping hydrate the crop through the summer. What this crop lacked in number, it'd make up for in flavor. Two more weeks.

His grandfather could always predict when the berries on his Upstate farm would peak. They weren't blackberries, but they were close, tasting more like a tart raspberry; the neighbors called them "blackcaps." They ripened at highly variable times—the exact date determined by the last snowfall. His grandfather took pride in deciphering this latter detail, and each spring as they talked on the phone, the old man declared with absolute certainty which day the berries would be at their prime. After summer recess began and Andy arrived on the farm, he'd track the days on the calendar—and each time his grandfather had been right, give or take a day or two. When Andy was fourteen, he deciphered his own detail: the arrival of the year's biggest hatch event, the green drakes—an aerial orgy that brought even the most reclusive trout to the surface—occurred simultaneously with the ripening of the berries. He could still remember the exact moment now—it had been his first intimate discovery about a particular place. They sat on the porch drinking Folgers coffee, as they always did at midday. His grandfather wore overalls and a flannel shirt, both clean of course. He may have lived on a farm, but he was no farmer. The dairy cows had been sold off before he bought the place, and he rented the corn field to the neighbor rather than tend it himself.

"Opa? Don't we always fish the green drakes when the berries are ripe?"

The old man cupped his hand to his ear, fighting the deafness. He'd heard too many explosions. Andy repeated the question, and his grandfather pulled a rag from his pocket and wiped the fluid from his upper lip—his nose ran ceaselessly, day or night, hot or cold. He pondered the question, then walked inside. A moment later, he returned with a leather bound notebook and began flipping through the pages. He was never overly congratulatory. "I think you're right."

In that moment, a wave of pride had rushed through Andy as he looked out over the farm, the beech trees, the corn, the stream in the distance. He owned this place, every square yard of it, and not in some frivolous monetary sense. Not like his father owned a house in Atlanta one year and another in Arlington the next. He owned this place in a deeper, more profound way, as if he had been born here, as if his grandfather had been born here too, as if his entire genealogy had originated from this point. He owned it as if this place owned him too.

Now, walking back through the hazelnuts—the smell of blackberries in the air—he wished he had a child of his own, someone he could teach about the Ipsyniho.

For several years, Andy had rented the one-room house from the Keping-ers. It'd been built in the forties, in a time when farmers still housed their hired help. He took care of it, fixing the gutters when the orchard leaves clogged them, building a shed for firewood, a carport to cover the boat. No one had lived in it while he was gone; the same wood was still stacked next to the stove. And although Mr. Kepinger said he'd tried to find a renter, Andy figured he hadn't tried hard. "I knew you'd come back," Kepinger had said when Andy showed up at his door the week before.

Now if only he could find enough work to pay the rent through the winter.

A guide made more than half his money from repeat business, cli-ents who called every year or every season or every month wanting to book a trip. He'd been gone for a whole cycle, and his established cli-entele had surely found someone else—Danny probably. Hell, maybe his old clients had paid for that new boat. He'd need to get the word out that he was back, and wrangle as many trips from the fly shops as possible. The profit from three trips would pay his rent. Another trip for food. A trip for gas. And a trip for insurance and odds and ends. Six trips a month weren't hard to find in early fall when the river was always in shape and sports took their vacation time. But winter was a different story—the river often flowed unfishably high for three weeks or more. And if the numbers of winter steelhead were down—which they were more often than not these days—an article would run in *The Oregonian* and the few sports interested in fishing in the rain would go to another watershed where their prospects weren't as grim.

He knew he could call his father, tap into the man's guilt, and money would be wired instantly. After the divorce, his father had all but cast him away, choosing instead to devote himself to a blooming legal career. Andy could count the months they'd spent together on one hand. But then, right about the time Andy went to college, his father suddenly appeared wanting to make up for lost time, to be the dad Andy had needed ten years before. He offered to take Andy and a friend of his choice on a snorkeling tour of the Caymans. But Andy turned him down, and chose instead to leave for Oregon early.

A simple phone call would deliver any needed money, but then he would have to talk to the man, feign interest in his new family, a prospect at least as depressing as sleeping in his truck.

It was time to get his shit together. He was too old to lean on his father anyway. He needed to learn the river's new holding water. Stop thinking about Shoshana when he should to be pointing out fish. He called Danny.

"What do you got tomorrow?" he said.

"Nothing," Danny said. He was chewing something. "Had a trip reschedule and Gordon is working the shop. Chromers?"

"It'd be nice to get a tour."

"Done," Danny said. "Let's meet at Millican at five a.m. I'll show you the new water."

Meeting at Millican Boat Ramp meant they'd leave the runner car there and put the boat in at the dam. The thought of that cement wall, the roar of the water coming down its face—the image of Shoshana shaking with tears . . . He couldn't go to the dam with Danny, not yet. Not before he cleared things up. "What if we meet at Missouri Bend?"

"Yeah, right." Danny laughed.

"No, seriously," Andy said.

Silence.

"For real? There's no good water in that drift. Wasn't then, isn't now. What did that tropical sun do to you?" Danny took another bite of whatever he was eating—probably a donut—and his voice became muffled. "I'll meet you at Millican. Five a.m. My boat."

Andy hung up and popped a berry in his mouth. It would be okay. He would just not think about her. He paced the room, eating two berries at once.

Just days after Danny and Shoshana had first pulled up in Danny's truck, she appeared at his front door, a smile on her face. Behind her, the sky was smeared dirt red—the Willamette Valley's grass seed farmers had set fire to their fields again.

He must have looked like a hermit, wearing no shirt and red long-john bottoms. His sport had cancelled. Meredith was at work, although she was supposed to be home any time.

Strands of her hair rode the wind. On the thigh of her jeans, there was a patch, a dancing bear.

"You look good," he finally said. "Come in. Let me get you something." He pointed inside the house. "I have frozen blackberries." The bed wasn't made. He remembered a condom on the nightstand, rolled up in a tissue, waiting to be thrown away.

She wasn't coming in. "It's been a while, Andy. It's been a long time since we knew each other."

He leaned his weight against the doorframe. "Sure, it's been a while."

She extended a finger and chipped a piece of paint from the door jamb. "You and Danny are good friends?"

"Yeah."

"You guys guide together." A lock of hair fell out from behind her ear.

He nearly reached for the lock, to tuck it back in place—an ancient habit.

"Because," she said, "I don't want to cause a rift."

"Is that why you're here?"

She stepped back, out of the door jamb, and surveyed the landscape. "Nice place you have, by the way. I've always loved this valley. The orchards, the blackberries. The art scene. Is that the river just over there?" She pointed into the distance. "I always imagined you'd end up near a river."

"Yeah, that's the river." He answered without looking.

She bit her lip. "What I wouldn't do for a cigarette."

Her car sat in the driveway, kicking out small bursts of exhaust—she'd left it on. And the farmer's smoke drifted over the sun, casting red over the land. "I don't smoke," he said.

"Me either. Not anymore. Old habits, you know?"

He wanted to tell her of the child he had seen in the Co-op, to ask if she felt like he did, that they had made a mistake. But he couldn't ask that, not now. "Why are you here, Shoshana?"

"Danny," she said. Again, she chipped at the paint. "I want to make sure our seeing each other won't cause any trouble between you two. I don't want to cause a rift. You're important to him."

Anger flamed within him—he could feel its heat in his face. She had come to him to talk about Danny. "You probably shouldn't do that," he said. "That is weather-proofing paint."

"Sorry. I like Danny," she said. "Danny is a good guy, and—"

"He's Jewish, if that's what you mean."

And right then, Meredith pulled up in her car.

He quit pacing—he had finished the fresh berries—and went to the heap of boxes in the corner. Since he had returned, he had yet to unpack his novels.

A slice of the knife opened the box, and he fished around until he found exactly what he was looking for: *The River Why*, the story of Gus and his fishing cabin along Oregon's Tamawanis River. He had read it as a kid, a gift from his Opa, and the moment he finished it, he decided he would someday move to Oregon. He rarely reread novels, but now he needed the familiar story, the familiar setting. He sat near the window and opened the book.

Shoshana would love the story. He'd recommended it years ago. Maybe she'd read it by now.

He read, then reread the first line: *Having harbored two sons in the waters of her womb . . .*

He snatched up his fishing journal and a pen and started an entry. But he couldn't finish the first sentence. He moved to the kitchen. Maybe he was hungry. Maybe that was the problem.

In *The Moosewood Cookbook*, he found instructions for "Zucca-noes." He had picked up a half-dozen zucchinis at the Co-op on the way back from the river, and now he ran the knife down each, lengthwise.

Good cooking depended on good music, so he switched on KIND, the college station. There was some spacey reggae, and he left it.

Just as he flipped on the burner and began sautéing the mushrooms and onions and garlic and sunflower seeds, the phone rang.

"Trib?" said a voice.

"Yes?"

"I just got a call from Mr. Anderson." It was Alan, owner of Northwest Stream Born.

"Mr. Anderson?" Andy asked.

"Your client from today?"

"Right."

"Listen." Alan's voice was stern, almost paternal. "I never thought I'd have to have a conversation like this with you, but you leave me little choice."

He wouldn't cancel any future trips just because of one bunk day. Andy was sure of that.

"I'm pulling your trip day after tomorrow. You're not ready. You've been in goddamn Timbuktu for a year and our clients deserve better."

"You can't cancel a trip inside of forty-eight hours," Andy said.

"Take it up with the Marine Board. I've got a business to run, and I can't have guides sitting on their asses while their sports go fishless."

"You're right," Andy said. "You can't. But today was a fluke. I promise." He walked outside, away from the hiss of the sizzling vegetables. "I know this river and I know its fish. Today . . . it was a personal issue, Alan, it involved a woman."

"Like I said, my clients deserve better."

"But I worked it out with her. It's fine. I'm a hundred percent healed and healthy."

The receiver was quiet. Surely, he was convinced. "Andy, you bailed us out on that Starbucks fiasco a few years back. I haven't forgotten that. So, here's what I'll do. I'm pulling your trip day after tomorrow. But I'll put you down for another next week. Give you time to screw your head on straight."

"Next week is Carnival."

"This is what I'm willing to do," Alan said.

"You'll give me a trip then because you can't find any guides working those days."

"Take it or leave it."

Andy paced from the house to the boat, turned and came back. He could always leave Carnival and work one day. He needed the money. But more than the profit from one trip, he needed to be back in Stream Born's good graces by winter. "All right, Alan. But tell me, who'd you give my trip to?"

"Danny Goodman. Should have called him in the first place."

The fire alarm sounded inside, and he caught a whiff of burning zucchini.

A few months after Shoshana showed up at his door, Meredith met Andy in the driveway. He had just returned from the river, his forearms still hot with the exhaustion of rowing. Her blond hair was in a bun, and she held a Co-op bag in her arms as if she were carrying groceries from the house to her car. "What are you up to?" he asked.

As always, her mascara was fresh. "I'm leaving you, Andy."

"Where are you going?" He tried to hang his keys on the rack by the door—but the rack was missing. Across the room, the couch's quilt was missing too. So was the little television Meredith kept on the counter.

She pushed past him, out the door, stumbling over the weather seal.

Leaving. He heard the word again and rushed to the car, beating her to the door. "Seriously?"

She yelled, "Why would I stay?" Then caught herself and restated her words calmly.

He tried to think of some reason. Any reason. They were in the middle of the cozy, cuddly rainy season. But he couldn't exactly cite that.

His hesitation angered her, and she pushed at him. The Co-op bag fell to the ground and kitchen utensils spilled into the mud.

"Come on, Meredith. We have something . . . " The sky reflected off the utensils. "That's my spatula, by the way."

She lifted the spatula and threw it into the orchard. "Why don't you call your beloved Shoshana?" She pushed him again, and this time he stumbled backwards. "Don't think I don't know about you two."

"Meredith—"

"What, Andy? What?"

"Beloved Shoshana? What are you talking about?"

"I know where you were last night."

He had been with Ethan and got a little too drunk to drive. He had called and told her.

"I just feel bad for Danny," she said.

"I have no idea what you're talking about. You're acting a little crazy, M."

"The hell with you." She laughed. "What? Did you think I'd stay with you in this dung hole forever? Little FYI: Kids want to grow up and be fishing guides—you're supposed to grow out of it."

She started the car and reversed all the way down the long driveway, onto River Road. He was still standing there as she accelerated toward town.

He went back inside, cracked a beer, and found all the ingredients he needed to make a jerk chicken pizza. Nice of her to at least leave the pizza pan.

Sure, maybe he had been thinking about Shoshana a lot lately, but he hadn't acted on any of those thoughts. Meredith had always been a bit cuckoo.

Andy called Danny, just to be sure. He thought of an excuse as the phone rang. The four of them were supposed to go to Wildfire Grill together the next night, but in light of the break-up, Andy would offer to stay home.

"I wouldn't want to be a third wheel," he said.

"No, no, of course you're still coming." Danny was acting normally. "You need to meet somebody new. She wasn't right for you anyway. A little too prissy, if you ask me."

So he went. Before the food would be served, a bouquet of dry flowers on a nearby table would fall into a candle and catch fire, and they would be forced to flee into the parking lot as the restaurant's sprinkler system kicked on. But in the forty-five minutes before the fire, they sat together at an intimate table, drinking cocktails and laughing.

"So what happened?" Shoshana asked. "If you don't mind me asking."

Since Shoshana had started staying with Danny, they'd seen each other on several occasions. And each time the awkwardness had subsided a little more. So far tonight, it seemed their progression had reached a new level: they were socializing without any clumsy, self-conscious stumblings.

She looked more gorgeous than ever.

Andy sniffed his tequila, his third. "She has issues. I have issues. And as it turns out, our issues don't exactly dovetail. Plus, she listens to soft rock."

Shoshana cringed.

"And she didn't fish," Danny said. "That's a major issue."

Shoshana slapped Danny's shoulder. "I don't fish."

Danny smiled. "You will."

"Not likely."

Danny stood. "Got to use the head. Order me the ginger glazed salmon." He nodded toward Andy. "We'll see if they have anything on your fish."

Alone with Shoshana, Andy quickly finished his drink. "What's the point of serving tequila in a receptacle the size of a petri dish?" he joked.

"You don't seem too broken up by the whole Meredith thing," Shoshana said.

"It's getting to be spring anyway." He laughed. "No time for a lady friend when the river is in shape."

She rolled her eyes. "You guides have some wacky priorities. That river is like a mistress."

Andy signaled the server for another round. "Danny is probably the worst cheater in the valley."

"At least when he's not home, I know where he is," Shoshana said. With both hands, she pulled back her hair, and while her speech was cluttered by a hair pin, said "And anyway, everybody has got to have their thing."

"Right." Was she sending him a subtle missive? Of course he was slightly drunk and so was she, but . . .

And suddenly he remembered, as if he were smelling it right now, the peachy musk of her inner thighs.

"Downed your drinks already?" Danny's voice.

Andy jerked and slammed into the empty table behind him.

"Whoa there, cowboy," Danny said.

And then a server yelled, and Shoshana leapt from her seat. Andy turned to see a ball of fire on the table behind him. He'd knocked over the vase when he had jerked back.

Outside, standing in the pouring rain, a siren screaming in the distance, Shoshana started laughing and couldn't stop.

"What?" Danny said.

Andy saw the neon Wildfire sign, and started laughing too. "Irony is a bitch," he said.

Danny laughed, but it was obvious he didn't get the joke.

CHAPTER 3

He heard Danny's truck coming through the darkness, first the gurgle of the biodiesel and then the familiar rattling of a drift boat trailer at speed. Danny's headlights crossed the parking lot, blinding Andy for a moment.

"Brought you some coffee," Andy said, passing a cup through the window.

"Let's move," Danny said. "I saw Roy Haggard's boat sitting at the gas station, probably waiting for clients."

Andy heaved his dry bag into the bed of the truck and snapped his rods into the rod rack. Roy lived in the Rogue Valley, two hours to the south. He was a different kind of guide, one who would travel to any river within five hundred miles for a paying client. He spent time every fall on the Ipsyniho, swiping clients from locals. Roy fished fast, in the Rogue style, covering lots of water in a single day. If he got to the river first, he would pluck out the eager fish.

Danny's tires squealed, gaining traction on River Road.

"I tied these up last night." Danny unhooked a big black fly from the visor and handed it over, never taking his eyes from the road.

"You trying to put me in the poor house?" Andy joked. "Raymond called last night."

"Raymond? He called me too." Danny shifted into fourth gear and pointed at the fly. "Check out how I wrapped in those ostrich plumes."

"He gave my trip to you."

"Oh, that was your trip? Shit man, sorry about that."

Andy pinned the fly to the visor without looking at it. "No way you could know. I just need that money, that's all."

Danny pointed at the fly. "Should get better action in those slow tailouts."

Andy only glanced at the fly. "It's just I don't have another trip lined up for a week."

"Oh."

"I got totally shafted on this."

Danny downshifted and gassed through a corner. Now the truck was roaring, and Danny wasn't saying anything.

Andy unpinned the fly. "Those plumes will dance underwater. Smart design."

Finally Danny said, "If you're low on money, why don't you call your daddy?"

They rode the rest of the way in silence.

In the darkness, the dam's orange lights gave the place a strange urban feeling, more like the Santiago Airport than the place he had met Shoshana on that day before the wedding.

Danny pulled up into the neck of the boat ramp and reversed into the throat. He stopped with a jolt and jumped out. "Damn it." Roy's truck and boat pulled into the lot. "He's going to hop us first thing."

Andy ran to the trailer, loosening the crimp strap. Danny tossed the gear bags into the boat and laid the pile of rods along the gunwale. Together, they gave the boat a push and dropped it onto the river's surface.

"Look who's trying to steal our fish!" The voice of Roy, always too loud, always as if you had just tried to sneak one past him. His clients swung their feet out of the truck's cab, testing their footing as if the pavement might be icy. "Thought we'd beat the recreational dudes, getting here twenty minutes before fishing light. What, did you boys bring your spotlights?"

Danny dropped the anchor from the boat, while Andy walked up the ramp for the requisite handshake. Roy always tried to crumple your knuckles when he shook. This time Andy was ready.

"Roy," Andy said.

"Trib." The man's eyes were dark under the brim of his cowboy hat.

Andy squeezed as hard as he could, but his wrist was still sore from the day before. Roy had him beat, and continued to tighten even as Andy went limp, the knuckles grinding under the pressure. Finally Roy let go, but not without a parting throb of pressure.

"Goodman," he called over Andy's shoulder. "New boat? Didn't think you boys found enough work to buy yourselves anything nice."

Danny pushed past Andy and shook Roy's hand. At the sound of the snap, the clients stopped whispering and turned to see their guide drop to one knee, trying futilely to extract his hand from Danny's vise-grip.

Danny didn't release. Instead, with a deceptively calm voice, he said, "It's always a pleasure to see you, Roy."

They had the river all to themselves. The only other boat on the water decided to spend the morning on the first pool.

"Nice work back at the ramp, by the way." Andy laughed. "I've never seen Roy so tightlipped."

Danny said, "The big ones always go down easy."

The new boat moved through the river as silently as a leaf. And it was stable too—more like a mobile dock than a traditional drift boat. Danny oared while standing, his osprey eyes always calculating their position in relation to the features of the bottom. He slowed the boat with a pair of powerful backstrokes and dropped the anchor by tapping the rope release. They stood on their seats and Danny pointed to a dark patch of water in the middle of a long riffle. "The slot's only ten feet long, right there where the current moves at walking speed."

"A trough?"

"Only six or eight inches deeper than the rest, but it works. Producing hook-ups about sixty percent of the time this summer."

It had been years since Danny gave Andy a tour of the river, pointing out the hidden holding lies, spots he had learned through countless hours of trial and error. For the first year after Andy moved to the valley, they spent every free moment in Danny's boat, drifting each section from the uppermost ramp to the ocean. "If you're going to guide on a river, you've got to learn every pool and riffle," Danny had said.

During those trips, Danny had also taught Andy to oar the boat. He had given him control of the oars for the first time above the Cheese Steak Hole. "Okay, a few things you got to remember: Every rapid is run one move at a time. When in doubt, straighten her out. And always—always—go slow to go fast. Slow is steady and steady is fast."

Now, as Andy watched the water, he remembered how much he'd loved that time, how exciting it'd been when the river and his new friend possessed more mysterious features than understood ones. What did it mean when the broken surface of a riffle suddenly glided flat, or the curved corner of Danny's lip suddenly fell straight? What was coming when the steady northwest wind swung around to the south, or an older fisherman chuckled under his breath? In those moments when most details remained shrouded in insignificance, there existed only the promise of exploration, of discovery, of deepened connection. He'd taken it all for granted, the lack of complications.

His fishing log detailed each of those trips, providing an account of the drift. More than once, he'd gone back and reread those entries, less for their precise drawings of the pools and runs and more for their optimistic tenor.

Just as the morning sun reddened the ridge tops, Danny anchored the boat above a short run. "We've been calling this spot 'Mojo.'"

They broke the run in half, Andy taking the tailout, Danny the head. Andy waded out to his waist and delivered his first cast and the current brought the line into swing.

Swinging like this was a systematic way of covering a run, of presenting a fly to every possible lie. The trick, Danny had taught him long ago, was to maintain the lightest possible tension on the line while still guiding the fly's shoreward progress. The task seemed simple enough, but to do it well, to do it as effectively as Danny, required precise and preemptive mends of the line; the angler had to anticipate the currents and prepare the line for their effect. The first time down a run, even an experienced steelheader would inevitably botch most swings—the fly racing when it should be gliding. But over time, over years of swinging the same water, the right way to fish it would eventually emerge. In this way, swinging—more than any other manner of fishing—bonded the angler to the river; eventually, the presentation revealed each pool's unique hydrodynamics, each riffle's fingerprint.

Danny's reel squealed out line and Andy looked upstream to see a slab of chrome thrashing at the surface. The fish turned and torpedoed past Andy, through the tailout, and out of the run. "I'll get the boat!" he called.

Danny was straining against the fish. "I think I can hold him."

And he did. By adjusting the rod pressure at the precise moments, Danny confused the fish and stopped him behind a boulder in the rapid. He fed some slack into the current, which bellied below the fish and applied downstream pressure—soon the fish was moving back into the run, toward them.

"Pro move."

"I think we can land him there."

Andy got into position, and Danny bent the rod into its cork. Soon the steelhead, a thick-shouldered buck that would probably go ten pounds, was in Andy's hands—the first steelhead he had touched in fourteen months. He cradled it in the current, one hand on the tail joint the other under the pectoral fins, and Danny unpinned the fly.

Its adipose fin, the small fatty deposit behind the dorsal fin, was whole—uncut by a hatchery employee's scissors. Its parents had probably spawned somewhere up Steamboat. The young fish, then, had lived a trout's life for a couple years in the shadowy holes of that watershed before descending to the ocean. Once at sea, it had probably chased schools of baitfish to the end of the Aleutians and maybe as far as the Japanese coastline before submitting to the magnetic pull of its home river and the work to be done there. These fish were precious, rare, vulnerable. They needed pure water, unmolested forests, and free-flowing rivers. Holding this one as it regained its strength, Andy felt connected to the Ipsyniho, to the Pacific, to a disappearing world.

The fish gave a massive tail stroke—splashing them in a wall of river—and was gone.

A short time later, they drifted past Steamboat Creek. The clear water sloshed over a staircase of stones and collided with the Ipsyniho at one of the river's deepest holes. The turquoise currents spun wildly here, their upwellings pulling mounds of water onto the surface.

"I never thought you the type to help develop the river," Andy said.

"It's not that simple," Danny said, pushing hard downstream. "It's either us—people who care about the river and fish—or it'll be those White Oak assholes. Sports looking for another vacation rental. Whoever can make Mr. Willis the best offer come December."

"Just doesn't seem like something you'd get your claws into, that's all."

On a shaded pebble beach where the Patriot Hole used to be, they sat cross-legged, leisurely chewing roast beef sandwiches Andy had made the night before.

The sun dappled through the trees, laying emerald patches on the shaded water. Fingers of spring water extended from the mossy bank, tickling the pool. It must have been ninety degrees.

"I might take a swim," Andy said.

Danny didn't respond. He was staring at his sandwich, not eating.

"Nice fish today," Andy said.

Danny wrapped up his sandwich and said, "There's something I got to tell you. Shosh asked me not to, but I'm going to anyway. It's not right to keep it from you."

"Did you win the lottery?" Andy joked. "I knew you were lying about buying that house with wedding money."

"Yeah, right." Danny laughed unnaturally. "Wedding money."

And Andy knew instantly wedding money hadn't bought that house. "What were you going to tell me?"

Danny stood and tucked his free hand in his pocket. "Shosh is pregnant."

Pregnant. He could have guessed, but still. There it was: the empty look in Shoshana's eye after the abortion, after what happened at the dam. "Oh, that's terrific. Great news." He offered Danny his hand. "Congratulations to you and Shoshana."

"Because of your guys' history," Danny said, "I wanted to tell you myself."

"How many weeks?"

"Twelve. We've been trying for a while." Danny checked his feet. "That's why I couldn't say anything in the hot tub. Shoshana wanted to wait, to make it all the way to twelve weeks before we went public." He looked up, his eyes drooping. "We've had some trouble. We miscarried over a year ago and nothing has taken since. If you make it to twelve weeks, odds are good you'll make it all the way."

"Wow. I didn't know."

Danny nodded, pinched his lips. "After that there was nothing for over a year. We were starting to think a baby wasn't in the cards for us."

"You'll make a great father. And Shoshana," he reached for words. "I can't think of a more compassionate and—"

"It was just days before you left, actually."

"It?"

Danny picked up a stone. "The miscarriage. It happened just before the wedding, just before you left." He skipped the stone over the water. "It was—it was hard. Caught us off guard."

She must have miscarried in the days before meeting him at the dam. Or right after.

"We're throwing a little party tonight to announce the good news. Can you make it?"

"God, of course I'll be there. Danny Goodman, a father. How stoked are you!"

"Infinitely," Danny said.

"Must be scary. Totally intimidating. You'll be responsible for a helpless little being."

Danny removed his hat and, with the same hand, scratched his sweaty red hair. "Should be okay. I mean, I think we'll do okay."

"You'll do fine."

"I just don't want to raise him poor," Danny said. "And it's hard to make a family wage guiding."

"But you two got plenty of love, and kids don't know if they're poor or not."

"Yeah, they do. Especially in a place like this. Besides," Danny swatted at a horse fly on his shoulder, "Shoshana was raised rich, so she's got expectations."

Andy looked to the river. "Her mom must be elated."

"This has got to be weird for you," Danny said. "Shosh and me having a baby, I mean. After what you two went—"

"No, don't think about that. Ancient history. Don't clutter your mind. You're going to be a father!"

Danny watched him like he watched a fish under a heavy current. "Be honest with me."

"Be honest with what? Come on." Andy swatted at the issue. "You know, you're going to have to get in your fishing while you still can."

Danny looked to the river and nodded. "Trust me. This is something I've considered."

A cool breeze wafted upriver, and they turned to face it.

An osprey soared high over the water, riding the thermal winds. Then, the bird tucked its wings, tipped head first, and fell toward earth— a blur of white crashing into the green pool. A long moment later, the osprey lifted back into the air, a silver fish writhing in its talons.

Andy heard a rustling and turned to see Danny building a joint, his third of the day. With practiced precision, he tapped a sideways film canister and sprinkled green flecks into a carefully cradled rolling paper. Even from a couple feet away, Andy could smell it: blueberries, pineapple, and skunk. "You're smoking a lot these days, eh?"

"Not really."

"You going to keep burning when you're a daddy?"

"You sound like Shoshana. Better pot than whiskey." Danny rolled the joint, licked the paper, and passed it to Andy. A second later, he tossed over a wooden match.

"To the Goodmans," Andy said, striking the match with his thumb nail.

This was right, the way things were meant to be. Danny and Shoshana would be attentive and passionate parents. This would be a lucky baby.

The osprey shrieked—it was a male—and flew circles around a tree-top nest, the fish still in his talons. A small white head emerged from the sticks and debris. But the second bird ignored the first. It appeared to be looking down, at them.

Andy exhaled, put on his polarized glasses, and focused on the river.

Later, as they climbed into the boat, Danny said, "Listen, if I'd known that was your trip tomorrow, I wouldn't have taken it."

"I shouldn't have mentioned it," Andy said. "Besides, you're going to need the money more than me."

Danny stepped in front of Andy, less than an arm's length away. So close, Andy could see the black dot the size of a pepper grain in the olive sea-grass of Danny's eye. "And I'm sorry about what I said, you know, about your pops."

"No worries."

But Danny didn't look away. He continued to hold his stare, as if awaiting something—as if awaiting Andy's own confession.

But he couldn't come clean now. Not with a baby on the way. Nevertheless, he heard himself saying, "There's something I've got to tell you."

Danny frowned. "Oh yeah? What's that?"

A new chapter had begun. Danny would have a child soon. A real nuclear family. Shoshana was right: what had happened at the dam was old news. Confessing the details would only hurt Danny unnecessarily. In truth, confessing would be a selfish act, one to clean Andy's own conscience at the expense of his best friend's marriage, his happiness. Andy would have to swallow this, take it to his grave.

He stuck out his hand and said, "I'm glad for you."

"I'm glad for you too." Danny scanned the river. "Well, enough of this sappy shit. We won't catch fish standing here."

They finished loading the boat and climbed in. Danny lifted the anchor, oared forward, and the current caught their bow. As the boat neared the tailout, the river coming together in a rush of white, Andy searched for something to say. Anything grounded in this moment, in the current chapter of Danny's life. "We should get a hatchery fish for the party tonight. Barbeque it up right. I could make a blackberry sauce."

"We were going to do pizzas," Danny said.

"No, no. We should do something special."

Danny shrugged. "Shoshana would like that. She wants fish protein. Rita told her it's good for the baby's brain." He oared downstream. "I'll anchor us up in the Hatchery Hole. See if we can't convince a keeper or two."

When the sun dipped below the horizon, they still hadn't caught a fish for the party. Soon the remaining rapids before the take-out would be unrunnable, darkness hiding the rocks and holes. They'd spent hours wading the riffles and pockets around the hatchery facility's outflow, the hatchery that raised young steelhead before setting them free to roam the ocean. Like the wild steelhead, the hatchery-reared fish returned to the precise location of their birth. A metal grate was the only thing stopping them from refilling the cement tanks in which they had spent their youth.

A few were visible in the clear fast water, gray torpedoes tucked behind current-blocking rocks. But other anglers had spent hours putting flies and lures and bait past their noses over the summer months. Most anglers avoided other sections of the river, not wanting to catch wild fish that they would just have to let go, and concentrated their efforts right here. Some days, fisherman stood shoulder to shoulder, two hundred people visible along a short stretch of water. Only those hatchery fish immune to an angler's offerings remained this late in the season.

"You'd think between the two of us, we could convince a dumb hatchery clone," Danny said while walking down the beach, his fly line kept aloft by short strokes with his single-hander. No one could cast like Danny. He leapt onto a rock, the movement of his torso and arms already gaining speed, and released the forward stroke: the rod arching into a C then snapping straight, a tight curl of line unfolding toward the distant horizon—the whole fly line, at precisely the same moment, leveled and settled to the river. Danny's casts wrote cursive across the sky.

Andy D-looped another cast and felt the current bring the line into its swing. He looked to Danny, and the rod nearly jerked out of his hand. A fish. He raised the rod and instantly felt the telltale thump, thump, thump of a steelhead on the other end. Danny shouted, "About time!"

The line razored open the water, a thread of river climbing the monofilament. And then it was beside them, airborne, its silver body contorting wildly—a heavy bird taking flight. The fish dove under the rushing rapid, the neon line giving chase off its tail, and strained against both rod and current. When it finally tired and came near shore, Danny swiped it with the net.

He trotted up the bank, beaming at the weight in his hands. "Good fish," he said.

Andy reached in, took the hen by its gill, and pressed it to the stones. He lifted a rock and smashed its head. The body throbbed under his grip, trying to find water and escape. He came down two more times, fast and hard, and finally the body quivered—its spinal cord cracked and its misery ended. *Thank you.*

"Andy."

He lifted the fish by its gill. A stream of blood ran down its lateral line.

"Andy," Danny said, pointing at the tail.

There, fat and obvious even in the low light, was a healthy and natural adipose fin. The dead fish, still quivering in his hand, wasn't a hatchery clone at all, but a native steelhead.

Danny ran to the boat and grabbed a towel. "Give it to me."

Andy just stood there as Danny grabbed the fish and wrapped it. How could this have happened? How could he have killed a wild fish? Nausea was flooding him.

Danny tucked the roll in his dry bag, under his rain coat. No game officer would search Danny's boat—how many times had Danny or Andy reported a fish poacher?

"Let's move," Danny said, his eyes scanning the banks.

They made it to the take-out and loaded the boat without seeing another soul.

Andy followed Danny up River Road, past the dam, sweating a fever's chill. He rolled down his window and mist from the cascading water dewed his face—as it had her sunburned cheeks that day.

Andy had begged Shoshana to meet him, and finally she said she would between errands for the wedding. He had picked the dam; it was neutral, public space. She didn't smile when he pulled up.

Why couldn't they just talk on the phone? she asked.

A breeze carried a wave of mist from the dam, and miniature rainbows flashed between them.

He needed to see her in person, talk to her in person.

She was nervous about being seen, she said. So they sat in her car, which she had parked in the shade near the trees, hidden from anyone passing by. She asked why they were doing this. She had worn a thin summer dress, just like she used to in college, and sweat glazed her neck. She seemed out of breath and desperate for air.

He had to ask her a question, he said.

Oh, she said. And then she was reaching for his arm. She stopped herself halfway, but then she was reaching again. And then she was kissing him and he was trying not to kiss back and trying to ask her what was happening but then she was unzipping his pants and climbing onto him and he was kissing her now and looking up into her hair and breathing her in. This was so wrong, so not what he had wanted, and yet he wasn't stopping it and neither was she. They were silent, voiceless, moanless, as if someone was in the same room and they didn't want him to hear.

Whether it was five minutes or fifteen hardly mattered. What did matter was that somewhere along the way she had begun crying, though he didn't see the tears until it was over, until she pushed herself away and straightened her dress.

I didn't come here for this, he said.

That hardly matters now.

Why?

Please get out. Please. Please leave. She was staring at him and her tears had run dry. They had been replaced by fear. This should never have happened.

Why did it happen?

Please.

He opened the door and climbed out and she pulled the door shut behind him. He knocked on the window, hoping she would roll it down, but she just looked at him through the glass. She looked at him like he would have looked at himself. Her cheeks had gone ashen, and she stared at him, through him, as if he wasn't even there. He would carry that look with him to the rivers of Chile, to the flats of Micronesia. He would see it in the ceiling when he tried to sleep. He would see it in the mirror after a shower. It would be looking back at him from every pool of water. That look would become the face of every wrong he had ever committed.

And then she drove away, onto River Road, and disappeared behind a veil of trees, and he was left standing there, wondering what had happened, and what he was to do now.

Cars and trucks lined the driveway leading to the yurt. A few had California plates. By the house, one spot remained, for Danny's diesel and boat. Andy turned around and finally found room back on the gravel road.

Danny waited for him on the driveway. He had the fish on the ground, a knife in his hand. He had cut the adipose fin free. "Won't fool Johnny Law, but it'll get us to the barbeque." He handed the quickly blackening fish to Andy—the fresh cut an obvious white line.

Andy kicked the severed fin into the ditch.

"There's a dude here I want you to meet," Danny said. "He's a little different, a little California maybe, but you'll like him."

"Trey?"

"Exactly. The wife and daughter are still down south. You'll meet them at Carnival."

People peppered the porch, drinks in their hands. A few he recognized from the valley: Isabelle, a rafting guide in summer and ski patroller in winter; Sky, the owner of a café downtown and a fine bait fisherman; Joshua, who taught English at the high school and snuck the students copies of *Howl*; Arielle, someone he had dated when he first moved to the valley. Dozens of people Andy recognized but couldn't attach a name to, The Wildfire Grill's owner, the counter jockey at Ipsyniho Mountaineering, the town's librarian. But most of the faces were new, clean cut, nice clothes, swirling wide wine glasses. Andy followed Danny through the crowd, his fingers through the steelhead's gills, a bag of blackberries in his pocket.

Voices came at him: "Of course Andy Trib wouldn't return from the Sahara without a fish to fry. Where'd you go, anyway?"

"I heard you died in some Nicaraguan mud bank."

"Skip your best friends' wedding?"

Andy laughed and gave the requisite pleasantries, then held the fish up between them and said, "Better get this to the coals, eh?"

"Of course, of course."

Along the quiet side of the house, Danny flipped on a light, revealing a table made from an aluminum frame and a long plastic cutting surface: a fish-cleaning table. Two knives sat ready. Plastic containers for the fillets. A hose for washing away the mess. A drain tube directed the waste off the deck and down the steep hillside.

Andy slipped the blade into the fish's belly, and pink and brown organs bulged through the slice. Two long strips of pea-sized red eggs ran the length of the body cavity. Eggs that should have ended up in Steamboat's gravel. With a quick finger, Andy removed each strip, laying it on the table. The rest of the organs he tore free and dropped into the wide drain tube.

"Yum, Northwest caviar," Danny said.

Andy ran the knife down the fish's back, working as quickly as he could, and sliced free a fillet of meat, fat marbling the grain. He flipped the fish and did the same on the other side. With the smaller knife, he sliced out the steelhead's cheeks, two more nuggets of fatty meat. He wouldn't let any go to waste.

"Do you have a pot?" Andy asked holding up the boney remains. "I'll boil this and make stock."

"Don't bother," Danny said. "Toss it over the rail. A bobcat—Shosh calls him Leo—comes around every few days to check for scraps."

"I'd rather boil it."

Danny grabbed the remains and flipped them into the woods. They crashed through the leaves and landed with a thump. "You didn't know," he said. "Be done with it."

Inside, Andy poured the blackberries into a bowl and mashed them into a purple pulp. A handful of crushed hazelnuts, a little honey, a dollop of sour cream, a pinch of salt. The sauce blanketed the fillets. He added a sprinkling of thyme—he could at least make it beautiful.

Danny handed him a teapot of nearly boiling water. After stirring in a palm's worth of salt, Andy poured the water over the roe and began separating the eggs from the gray tissue holding them together. Danny placed a half-dozen of the bright orbs on a cracker and popped it in his mouth. "Perf," he said, still chewing. "I'm going to check on Shosh."

Andy carried the fillets to the grill. A pair of huge flannel shoulders hunched over it: Bridge. "You live!" Bridge said. His voice had a way of being deep and soft at once. He lifted Andy in a hug. "You've been missed, brother." A little stick protruded from his waist-length, graying beard. He was looking at the fish. "Blackberry hazelnut sauce? You knew I'd be here!"

"Your handiwork," Andy said, waving at the yurt. "Stunning. You've got a way with wood."

"Sweet of you to say. But it's simple, really. Put the beam where the plan tells you to."

"How's Rita?"

"A bit lonely since Neil moved out. She'll want to see you."

Neil and his brother Cameron, Rita and Bridge's children, were a half generation behind Danny and Andy. "How are the boys?"

Bridge chuckled, looking off into the trees. "Neil is down in Eugene now, started at the university, says he's going to do Peace Corps like his mom. And Cameron got a great paramedic job up in Seattle, big check and only works one day out of three. They were just here for archery season. Cammy got himself a little bull." Bridge pointed to the grill, at a thick roast splattering fat drops into the heat below. "Passed on a few pounds to the old man."

"That time of year already?"

"Elk season ends in a week, son. A bit out of touch, are we?" Bridge cleared grill space for the fillets—sliding over the roast, and a dozen or so black bean burgers. "For those with Disney-marinated imaginations," he muttered.

Rita appeared beside Bridge, her silver hair pulled tight into two braids. A more regal version of her younger hippie-self Andy had seen in pictures over their mantel.

Rita and Bridge had met at Berkeley in the mid-sixties. Bridge was the son of the son of the son of some of the Ipsyniho's first white settlers, and Rita had been born and raised in California. Andy had pieced together traces of their early lives from Bridge's stories. He knew they had gone their separate ways after college, Rita heading to Mexico— where she had studied midwifery—and Bridge dropping off the draft's radar just in time. He had holed up with some of his La Honda friends, including Ken Kesey who he had met in Eugene years before. He claimed that Kesey wrote *Sometimes a Great Notion* in an apartment in Florence, Oregon, over the course of one winter, a winter spent in a steady Benzedrine frenzy. "That's why Keys didn't write much after—he charred himself that winter." Bridge had been invited to Kesey's funeral when he had died a few years back.

Rita was the valley's midwife, a celebrity of sorts. She knew most of the valley's babies from their first breaths, and guided their parents through some of their most intimate moments. At Carnival, she could hardly make it from one booth to the next without families she knew showing off their toddlers, and in some cases, their teenagers. Boxes of garden-fresh produce and homemade bread and jams appeared at her door regularly—Bridge would occasionally trade what they couldn't finish for fresh fish. Andy imagined Rita's skirts sweeping through the night, appearing beside the worried sides of mothers-to-be, her hands wiping the sweat from their brows. Each dawn birth had worn a wrinkle into her skin, and she wore them with pride. She plucked the stick from Bridge's beard and flicked it over the rail. Then did a double take at Andy.

"Hey, Rita," Andy said, feeling his face flush—which made him flush more. He had maintained a slight crush on her for years.

"Andrew!" She smiled, wrapping her arms around him. Her hugs were long and meaningful, never trivialized by social etiquette. "You're so tan, I didn't recognize you. A bit too thin though, if you ask me."

"You know me. I'm on a strict regimen at the gym, twenty-three sessions a week."

"Yeah, right." She slapped Bridge's chest. "Andy here needs a good meal. What do you say we cook him up something nice tomorrow night?" She looked to Andy. "Are you free?"

"As a bird."

"Hell, yes," Bridge said. "Come over. Have some wine and catch up."

"Wouldn't miss it," Andy said. Over Bridge's shoulder, he saw Shoshana coming through the crowd. "Would you mind dropping those fillets on the heat for me?"

Inside, the party pulsed. An impromptu band played in the corner. Takken, wearing the same dirty overalls he'd worn a year ago, tickled a mandolin. Stephanie fingered a banjo, her baby sleeping in it's sling. And a man wearing business pants, a clean white shirt, and sunglasses kept a simple rhythm on a soup pot.

Two women laughed and clanked their wine glasses.

Rachel and Benji, organic blueberry farmers, were pressed into a single form, swaying a half beat behind the music. Andy had gone to their wedding a couple years back, a small affair in the midst of a flowering blueberry patch.

Then Shoshana was beside him.

"Jesus. You scared me."

Her hair was back, held aloft by two chopsticks. A pair of silver earrings swayed as she surveyed the crowd. "You fished with him today."

He nodded.

"What did you two talk about?" She was studying him.

"There you are!" Danny leaned and kissed Shoshana's cheek. "How do you feel?"

She shrugged, and her eyes flashed across Andy's.

Danny squinted. "Didn't mean to interrupt," he said. "Just wanted to say Andy here caught a fish for you. It's on the barbeque."

"You didn't interrupt anything."

The moment grew awkwardly silent.

"I got to use the bathroom," Shoshana said. "Too much juice, I guess." She kissed Danny's cheek, and disappeared into the crowd.

Danny didn't say anything. He just stared in the direction Shoshana had vanished.

"So, who are these people?" Andy asked. "I only recognize about half the faces."

"Prospective residents, mostly."

Danny led him down the hallway, to the bedroom, where a group of people—none of whom Andy knew—gathered in a circle. The bed was neatly made, as if no one had ever lain in it.

A shorter man with a well-trimmed goatee turned away from the circle and smiled. "You must be Andy. I've heard only good things."

"This is Trey."

Trey's face was baby smooth, and he wore a well-ironed button-down shirt. He smelled of peppery aftershave, the kind sports often wore. Andy couldn't guess his age. Certainly older than Danny, but by five or fifteen years, he couldn't tell. They shook: callous-free.

"Danny tells me you want to develop the land along Steamboat Creek?" Andy said.

"We'd rather not," Trey answered. "That creek, as I'm sure you know, is ecologically delicate. But the zoning commission leaves us little choice." Trey put his hand on Danny's shoulder.

"They won't open up any other parcels," Danny said.

"No offense," Andy said, "but I don't see why the Ipsyniho needs more McMansions."

"Sure, sure," Trey said, smiling. "The valley doesn't need any more luxury houses or condos. That's why it's so vital that we get that land."

"Better us," Danny said. "They want to put in a golf course." He shook his head. "Imagine all those herbicides washing over the spawning gravel."

"Development is development," Andy said. "Like you said, that watershed is delicate."

Trey raised his eyebrows and nodded. "You're right," he said. "Totally right." He took a sip of his beer. "But I think for a stream like Steamboat to survive the twenty-first century, it will need a community of compassionate people living along its banks. Lookouts, in a way. The people you see here will care about that stream's health. The White Oak people probably won't." Trey smiled at Danny. "But anyway," he said. "Tell me about this trip of yours. Danny says you went to Indonesia?"

"Micronesia," Andy said. "I should check on that steelhead on the grill."

He was out of the room before realizing Danny wasn't coming.

Outside, Bridge still worked the barbeque. People on the deck were eating the black bean burgers, green lettuce and red tomatoes squeezing out between the buns. "A good roast is worth the wait," Bridge said.

Andy checked the fillets. Fresh fish typically cooked fast, and this was no different. He plucked the cheek nuggets from the hot grill with his bare fingers, giving one to Bridge. "Try this."

Bridge blew on the fish with a precise stream of air, then popped it into his mouth. "Ah, steelie."

"Does it taste all right?" Andy still held the fin-sized nugget in his fingers.

"Well, it doesn't have much on a slice of elk roast, but I'm not complaining."

Andy took the fish into his mouth, exhaling the steam as he chewed. He owed the fish this much.

The meat, encapsulated in a crispy layer of fried fat, exploded on the first chomp. It was all there: the silky dawn, the too-hot afternoon, the salty breeze—the Ipsyniho in all its richness.

Andy slid the fillets onto a serving plate and carried them inside. The blackberry sauce had caramelized over the top just as he'd hoped. With a fork, he cracked it as if it were crème brulée, and leafed off a few ribbons of meat. Inside, the fillet was still translucent, the heat having barely penetrated that far. Ideal—but he wanted nothing of it. Smelling it left him woozy, dislocated, heavy.

Through the crowd, he saw Danny and Shoshana together, leaning against the wall. They were close enough to kiss, laughing together.

The song ended and everyone clapped. Danny grabbed a glass from a guest and a fork from another and clinked the two, the room falling silent.

"Shosh and I have an announcement," he said. Shoshana laughed with someone nearby. "We wanted all of our friends to find out at once," Danny continued.

Andy pushed away from the fish, and swam through the crowd toward the door. He made it out before Danny could say the words again.

Outside the air had cooled. The stars flurried against the blackberry sky. He knew the Umpqua Valley, a few ridges to the south, had steelhead year-round. He wondered how blackberries did there.

A voice beside him said, "Do you ever think about having kids?" It was Trey, looking up at the stars.

"Never," Andy said instantly.

"I didn't want any myself. Had too much work I wanted to do. Kids would get in the way."

Inside, everyone erupted in cheers.

Trey said, "I've been thankful for my daughter every day. Her smile makes the sunshine softer, the fruit sweeter, the stars brighter. She adds protein to my existence."

"Poetic," Andy said, flicking a pine cone from the railing.

Trey turned and looked inside. "Danny and Shoshana will make great parents, won't they?"

Andy's stomach cramped. He realized it had been cramping for several minutes, maybe since he ate that bite of fish. But now, it was balled tight.

Trey said, "They're so full of love for each other and for this place. I can't think of a better environment to raise a family."

"When did he tell you?"

"About what?" Trey frowned.

"About Shoshana being pregnant."

Trey studied Andy for a moment. Then he shrugged and looked to the stars. "Their kids will be the next generation of advocates for the place. These days, every place needs its ardent defenders."

"Yeah, it does." Andy tried to stand up straight, despite his stomach.

"I know what you're thinking," Trey said. "Hypocritical, right? A developer talking about sustainability. But *that* is the wave of the future, my friend. If we're to last as a culture, as a species, every developer needs to be an advocate for sustainability. As a culture, we need to get better at living." He looked out over the valley below. "I want you to know I've got this river's best interest at heart. I'm confident you'll come to see that."

"Help the river by hurting it?" Andy shook his head. "It's not hypocritical. It's paradoxical."

"Welcome to the twenty-first century, guy. Everything you do hurts something."

"So the hell with it, huh?"

Trey smiled. "The world has changed, Andy. You'll see. There are two shades of hurt—hurt that leads to nourishment and hurt that leads to destruction. People, consumers, are starting to realize this."

Andy walked away, leaving Trey alone with his bright stars. He followed the deck around to the grill, hoping to find Bridge sliding a knife through the roast. But everyone was inside now, toasting. His truck was just a hundred yards away. He gripped the rail, his stomach cramping again.

The yurt's door opened, and he heard Rita's voice. "Get in here," she said. "You're going to miss the toast."

"I'm not feeling well," he said, his own voice sounding distant. "I'm heading home."

"Don't be silly," she said. She took his hand and led him back inside, and as they came through the doorframe, she whispered, "What's going on?"

"I just ate some bad fish, that's all."

She squinted at him. "Bad fish?"

"Yeah, just some bad fish."

She raised her glass, like everyone else, toward Danny and Shoshana. "If you say so."

CHAPTER 4

People ducked in and out of the Co-op, the automatic door perpetually open. Old-school jazz and its tings and pings and titee-tats played overhead. Shoppers slung words like "organically cultivated" and "permaculture." Someone asked an employee, "How much post-consumer product is in this bag?"

Andy had spent most of the night sitting on the toilet, dozing off, only to be jarred awake as another round of cramps gripped his abdomen. The cramps had finally left sometime around dawn, leaving his head fogged with lack of sleep.

He needed a scone to fill his stomach. And he needed wine for the dinner at Bridge and Rita's that night. At least two bottles, a red and a white. "It'll be Italian flavors," Bridge had said when Andy asked about the meal. But money was tight. He hoped two bottles would do.

People carried cloth bags and stuffed them with local organic produce: sweet onions, purple beets, sea-green kale, vine-fresh tomatoes, lemon cucumbers, mission figs. Locally baked breads lined a long wall. An entire aisle devoted to the cheeses of the Northwest. A walk-in cooler of free-range, organic meats. Another cooler of bulk tofu and tempeh and bizarre soy "meats." A man with gray hair twisting out below his baseball cap—someone Andy had seen here before—lifted a wheel of cheese, read the label, smelled it through the plastic, and set it back down.

A placard near the lettuce read: According to a recent study by a Stanford economist, 4,021 calories of petroleum energy are used to deliver every 80-calorie serving of lettuce from the farmer in California to the storefront in New York. Buy local!

Two men about Andy's age, both wearing clean leather shoes with tucked-in shirts, plucked at the greens and spoke about which dressing might "bring out the astringent qualities of the arugala."

The Co-op had taken over the Thriftway Grocery storefront only a few years before. Andy used to stop at the old establishment on his way back from the river, to grab jo-jos from the deli, and maybe a cup of their bitter coffee if he was fading. Every year since the switch, the Co-op had expanded, adding solar panels to the roof, a community garden space across the street, and now, the biofuel pumps in back. He couldn't imagine what Danny's parents would say about the place if they still lived nearby. Most of the holdouts from the logging days drove the forty-five minutes to Roseburg or Cottage Grove to get their groceries. "That new place charges three times as much for the same thing," Andy had heard a bait fisherman say one day as he drifted by the Hatchery Hole. "A working man can't spend sixty dollars for twenty bucks worth of food."

Now, Andy moved to the long wine aisles. A few people stood hunched, cloth bags on the floor, reading glasses on their nose tips, studying bottles. He swam between them, moving to the local section. He found pinot noir from the Ipsyniho Vineyard, a family-owned winery that sat in the hill country fifteen miles downriver, and tucked it under his arm. The owner had once traded half a case of pinot for a pair of big hatchery steelhead Andy caught. Whites were tougher. But he soon found a pinot gris from a small vineyard near Portland, and turned toward the scones.

There, halfway in the bulk salsa bin, was Shoshana. She held one flip-flop in the air, balancing her torso as she leaned over to get a scoop at the bottom. She was wearing what must have been her gardening jeans—red dirt colored the knees.

For a moment he froze, and a woman who'd expected him to keep moving bumped into him with her cloth bag.

"My mistake," she said.

"It's nothing," he said.

Shoshana lifted her head from the bin and turned. A dab of salsa was on her cheek.

"Hi," he said. He tucked both wine bottles under one arm and stuck his free hand into his pocket. The gris slipped free and he had to lunge to keep it from crashing to the floor.

He didn't know what to say. "You have salsa on your cheek."

"I was saving it for the chip aisle," she said, wiping it off.

"Are we ever going to talk about what happened?"

"No," she said, looking around. "Old news. Please. Can we please just move on?"

"We have to talk about it."

"Why did you come back, Andy?"

"This is my home, Shoshana. You really expect me to leave?"

"If you cared about him, you would." Before he could form a reply, she pushed past him and was walking away.

He called after her, the only thing he could think of, "We can't leave things like this."

But she kept going.

Back at the truck, he reached for the radio. The familiar, buttery voice of Downtown Deb, the host of "Dead Air" on Eugene's public station, warmed the cab. He started to turn the dial—the voice fading into snow—but then turned it back.

"A little number from the show at Oregon State Prison, in the year nineteen hundred and eighty-two. One show I didn't attend."

He pulled onto River Road as the song "Reuben and Cherise" filled the cab.

Andy spent the afternoon alone, tying flies, the warm air slipping through the open windows. A gray squirrel worked diligently outside, sitting atop a stump, both hands holding a seed to his little teeth.

On the table beside the vise sat a small square of scrap paper: Meredith's number. He had dug it out and laid it there an hour ago, examining it occasionally.

After finishing a half-dozen General Practitioners, he set out the materials for his most trusted skating pattern, the Wobbler of Mass Deception: moose hair, deer hair, grizzly spey hackle. To be successful, it needed to resemble the large caddis species that hatched in fall. But more importantly, the design needed to allow the fly—when fished across a broad pool—to convey a sense of urgent vulnerability. Skating patterns, more than any other tie, required a synergistic blend of realism and impressionism.

It wasn't that he necessarily wanted to start things back up. He didn't need a relationship right now, not while trying to get settled back in the valley and all.

He clipped a clump of moose hair and combed out the underfur. With the hook firmly secured in the vise, he brought the clump to the shank and wrapped two loose coils of thread around it. Tension had to be applied at the precise moment or the whole pattern would be lost. He positioned the clump, and tightened in a motion that accelerated as it progressed—the fur fanned evenly, the hairs rigid like the needles on a porcupine.

What would have happened if he hadn't come back? Shoshana would be happy—the events at the dam would be safely buried. And maybe in the long run Danny would be happier too.

Given enough time down there, he might have come to like it, not Micronesia but Chile. Maybe he would have started his own outfitting company, or opened a lodge along one of the still undeveloped streams.

What was he thinking? That would never have worked out. When he was there, every day had gotten worse. Only movie cowboys found happy endings by fleeing south. The expats he had met were anything but happy.

He whip-finished the head of the fly, cut the thread, and grabbed the phone. 4:30. Meredith would be arriving home from school.

Meredith's high, bouncy voice answered, the same as always. She was out of breath. "Hello."

"Hey," he said. "It's me. Andy."

There was a long pause, then she said, "Andy?"

"You might remember me from such debacles as that night I spilled wine all over your mother's dress. Or the afternoon I threw a stick to your new puppy and hit her in the head and we had to take her to the vet for stitches. How is Valentine anyway?"

"Oh, you mean the self-involved Andy with old-girlfriend prob-lems?"

"No. I'm the dweeby looking Andy with a drift boat."

"One and the same," she said. "Andy Trib."

They spoke for a few minutes, laughing about safe subjects like work and mutual friends. She told him about the new principal and about the layoffs last summer, about how she barely kept her job. "Stinking Oregonians would rather suck dry their schools than pay a few cents in sales tax." She asked where he was—she had heard he was never coming back.

"I'm back now," he said. "Took my old place at the Kepingers."

"Oh," she said. "So you're here? In Ipsyniho?"

"Yeah." He held his breath and went for it. "And I was curious if you might want to, you know, have dinner or something."

"Dinner?" she said. "Ah, that's really sweet of you to ask." She didn't say more.

He waited, and the silence grew. "So what do you say? Wildfire tomorrow night?"

"Actually, Andy, I'm with someone." She waited. "But maybe we could do coffee one afternoon, or something. It'd be nice to catch up a little, wouldn't it?" A man in the background said, "Who is that?"

An engine idled down his driveway. "That would be nice. Hey, someone just pulled up here. I'll give you a call and we can set some-thing up."

He hung up and heard the truck shut down out front. A cloud of dust drifted in the open window. He stepped outside to see Kepinger creaking shut the cab door.

"Howdy, Trib."

"Mr. Kepinger. What can I offer you? Is it too early for a beer?" Andy knew the man would say no. He was here to ask after the rent.

With a sweep of the hand, Mr. Kepinger waved away the beverage offer, then looked toward the river. He wore the same clothes he always did: dusty jeans, a tucked-in flannel shirt, and a red baseball cap that sat too high on his head. A thin stick protruded from his mouth like an oversized toothpick. And a cell phone was holstered on his hip. "Some weather we're having," he said. "Ninety-nine days now without a speck of rain."

Not a single cloud was in the sky. Andy realized he hadn't seen a cloud since returning home.

"Imagine this ain't kind on the fish," Kepinger said.

"Really?" Andy asked. "Ninety-nine days is it?"

"Longest streak I've seen. Course I only been here since about the time Jesus sprung from Mary." Kepinger didn't laugh—he never laughed—but he glanced at Andy to see if his joke had been appreciated. Then he spit.

Andy smiled and said, "Blackberries are behind schedule. I wonder if there's a connection."

"I reckon when it comes, it'll come fierce. Listen, son," Kepinger said. "I don't mean to ride you or nothing, but the wife's starting to ride me, if you know what I mean."

Probably a lie. He had used that one before. "You need the rent."

Kepinger nodded.

Andy had two hundred and twenty-seven dollars. He'd had two hundred and fifty before buying the wine that morning. "I've got half of the rent," he said. "After next week's trip, I'll have the rest. I'm real sorry about this. I've had some trouble rounding up clients. On account of the weather and all."

Kepinger chewed the stick. "Half now will probably settle the wife."

"You think Mrs. Kepinger could settle for a third? I could use some gas money. With these prices and all."

The old man spun slowly until he was looking back up at his house. He tossed the stick into the orchard and turned back to Andy. "Pay what you can. I don't want to drive you onto welfare or nothing. Drop the bills by the house tonight."

"No problem," Andy said. "Thank you."

Kepinger nodded. "But Trib," he said. "Let's not make a habit of this. I got to live too."

Back inside, Andy recounted his bills. The trip next week would finish off the rent, but then how would he cover food and gas until he managed to find another trip? He'd been desperate like this before, twice, both times in the winter when trips were scarce. But never in the fall. Before, he'd called his father and asked for a loan. Both times the man had consented and transferred funds into Andy's account at the Ipsyniho Credit Union. Never had he asked to be repaid. His father liked to wield money, especially over his son. It was a chance to wordlessly say "See, I told you so." Andy could have gone into corporate business or state politics or medicine. But instead he'd "dropped out," as his father called it, and become "just" a fishing guide.

Screw it. He'd worry about money tomorrow.

Rita and Bridge lived in a section of dense woods a mile up a gravel side road, along a small tributary to Steamboat Creek called Echo Spring. Echo splashed over white stones and through caves of overhanging limbs before leveling into a marsh of beaver ponds near its confluence with Steamboat. Andy had hiked that section repeatedly, helping fisheries biologists add woody debris to Steamboat, and each time had watched young steelhead dart in and out of the shadows. He frequently wondered if he might touch one of those young fish as an adult, in three or four years.

Their house sat on a bench in the steep slope, overlooking both Steamboat Creek and the Ipsyniho River. A dense forest of Doug firs and ferns grew behind the house, hiding it. As you came down their driveway, the house appeared first as a wall of windows. On a good day, they mirrored the vista below. Then as you parked, the house's roof revealed itself, and suddenly, those windows looked more like the opening to a cave. The roof itself contained the same grasses as the hillside behind it. "Organic insulation," Bridge called it. He had built the structure almost thirty years before and claimed the natural roof locked in more heat in the winter and kept the house cooler in the summer. The only drawback was that twice a year Bridge had to summit his creation and uproot the yearling blackberries that were determined to take the thing over—"Let those buggers stay and some morning we'll wake up to vines tickling our faces." Sometimes, Andy imagined what would happen if they left the house to the land, how long it would take the blackberries to bury the house, and then how invisible the place would be.

Time spent there felt like time spent in a different dimension, a fairy tale's rabbit hole. After what felt like fifteen minutes, he'd look at his watch and realize two hours had passed. The house was like the river in that way, a reality outside the herding dogs of time.

But now, as Andy drove down the driveway, he realized something was profoundly wrong. Most of the forest surrounding the house was gone. Only a thin veil of trees remained along the property line. Between their trunks, the brown remnants of a clearcut baked in the sun. A fresh cut, probably from last winter. A war had exploded in Bridge and Rita's backyard.

Bridge sat on the tailgate of his truck, looking down the steep hill at the valley below—as if he didn't notice the expansive devastation behind him. He wore a blue flannel shirt. "Perfect timing," he yelled, a wide smile across his face.

"Picked you some river berries." Andy walked over and hopped up on the tailgate. The Ipsyniho sparkled miles below. He could just barely make out Missouri Bend, the afternoon sunlight sparking off the mansions' windows. "What the hell happened?" he asked.

Bridge didn't look at the hillside behind the house. Instead, he popped a berry into his mouth and studied the distant river.

The front door swung wide and Rita emerged, not in any of the flowing skirts Andy had always seen before, but in a pair of well-worn work pants.

"The boy brought river berries, babe."

"I don't think he qualifies as a boy any longer, dear," Rita said, kissing Andy on the cheek and at the same time taking a berry from the bag. She bit the fruit in half and chewed slowly. "You always have the cush blackberries, don't you?"

"It's the little things," Andy said. "What happened to your mountain?"

Rita didn't look at the clearcut. "That's the thing," she said. "Wasn't our mountain."

Most of the land on the hills and ridges along the Ipsyniho was public, either National Forest or Bureau of Land Management. In fact, the river itself was technically public property, state land up to the top of the river channel.

Bridge put his massive hand on Andy's shoulder, a smile on his face. "Got a proposition for you. A little change of plans."

"Don't pressure him," Rita said.

"We need to make a run up the ridge before we can have dinner."

Andy followed Bridge's eyes to the bed of the truck, to a pair of back-packs there. Between them was Bridge's bow, a stick and a string with a four-arrow quiver attached to the side—only three arrows remained. "Did you catch something?" Andy asked.

"Fishermen catch," Bridge said, "hunters shoot. No sense hiding the reality."

"Yes, he caught something," Rita said to Andy. She had been trying to convince Bridge to give up meat since Andy first met them. And he assumed, based on how old and worn their vegetarian cookbooks were, that she had been trying for years before that.

"I went veggie one time," Bridge had said once. "Thinned out so bad, I nearly blew away in a wind storm."

"So what's your proposition?" Andy asked.

Bridge told of how he had snuck up on a bull elk in the heavy forest along the ridge. As the bull trotted past at ten yards, chasing another elk, Bridge released an arrow and watched it disappear into the animal's side. The bull kept going as if nothing had happened, vanishing down over the ridge. They needed to find it and get the meat off the ground before the bears got to it during the night. "Sorry to spring this on you," Bridge said. "I tried calling, but I guess you'd already left."

"Bears?"

"You're welcome to come with us, or we could reschedule dinner," Rita said.

Andy imagined his empty house, the ticking clock on the wall.

"Or," Rita said, "I could point you to some chanterelles."

"No, let's do it," Andy said. "I'd love to help."

They piled into the pickup and drove up the road from the house, Andy riding in the middle seat with both his legs tucked with Rita's in the passenger's well, leaving room for Bridge to shift gears. The road used to be a tunnel through the thick forest, but now it was entirely in the sun-beaten open. They kept the windows down to stay cool.

Andy tried to imagine what an elk looked like up close. He'd only seen the animals at the end of a distant field or swimming across the river several hundred yards ahead of the boat. Even at that distance they looked enormous. He'd heard that a mature bull stood five feet at the shoulders. And they looked strong—when one walked, you could see its muscles flexing through the hide.

But one image proved stronger than the rest: the image of a bear lifting its head from a bloody carcass, its hawk eyes narrowing into a menacing stare. Andy studied the bow in the bed of the truck. It looked delicate enough a six-year-old could bust it over a knee. "You all done this before?" Andy asked, wiping a glaze of sweat from his forehead.

"Once a year."

Near the top, they stopped at a gate and parked off the side of the road. "Has there always been a gate here?" Andy asked.

Bridge nodded. "It's just never been shut before. They closed the roads because of the drought. The fire danger, you know."

They stood out in the middle of the open, the sun impossibly hot without the trees. A grasshopper leapt into the wind, clattering as it zipped past. To the west, the craggy Cascades clawed at the skyline, their sides still hoarding thin bands of snow. The peaks were visible only because of the new clearcut. In all four directions, yellow stumps protruded like warts from the dirt. Below, maybe a mile, Andy could see his own truck parked in the yard of the house. The house itself remained invisible because of the roof.

"This is where they put the Skagit crane," Rita said. "Ran a cable all the way to that ridge over there. I came up when they did it. Watched them cut away the mountain's skin." She rubbed her forehead. "The sight of it still makes me ill." And yet, there was nowhere else to look.

Ridges extended for hundreds of miles to the south, each rise increasingly grayed by the distance. Mount Shasta's bulbous top shimmered on the horizon. Closer, the ridges were quilted by square clearcuts, yellowed brush, and dead stumps. Andy didn't remember so many fresh cuts the last time he'd come up this high, probably two years before.

Bridge studied the hillsides, his beard blowing out before him. "Sustained yield, my ass," he said. "Every time I come up here, I want to slap the shit out of the guy who signs the permits."

"What happened while I was gone?" Andy asked. "I don't remember so many cuts."

"D.C. decided to up the board-footage cut from public lands," Rita said. "They bypassed the normal process in the name of 'emergency fire prevention.' Trees can't burn if they aren't there."

To the north, long plumes of red smoke lifted east. There looked to be a half-dozen fires burning.

"They're treating the fires like WMDs, using them as an excuse to do whatever big business wants," Bridge said. "Pretending fires aren't natural and necessary."

"No sense in getting worked up over this again," Rita said. She looked toward the coast and the sun hanging above the peaks. "Only got a few hours of daylight, anyway."

"The real issue is the soil," Bridge said. "If they keep cutting like this, the minerals won't have time to rebuild. It's just a matter of time before the land won't grow trees anymore. Somehow these dipshits missed lesson one of crop science."

Rita touched Bridge's elbow. "We've been having a hard time," she muttered.

Bridge grabbed his bow and the backpacks from the pickup's bed. He gave Rita one of the packs and slipped his arms through the other one, buckling the waist strap tight.

"I can carry that pack," Andy said to Rita.

She buckled the waist strap tight. "Why didn't you offer to carry my man's?"

"Uhh . . ."

She winked at him. "Here you go." She handed him her water bottle. "You can carry this."

They set off down the bare ridge, toward a fence of uncut trees. As Bridge walked, he pulled a small GPS unit from his pocket. He had an obsession for the things. Once Andy found him in the Co-op's parking lot trying to input the store's location into the little device. Why, he never figured out. "He's down there eighteen hundred meters," Bridge shouted over his shoulder. Andy had to trot to keep up.

Between the stumps, no brush grew. Skeletons of blackberry vines and bracken ferns and cluster maples sat frozen in the wind, strafed with herbicide from company helicopters. The new "crop" of firs would grow in faster if it didn't have to compete with other plants. Andy wondered if Rita and Bridge had been home during the spraying—he hoped not.

But the fish had been.

Once, Andy had found scores of dead juvenile steelhead stacked against a beaver dam on Steamboat. He had reported the fish kill to Fish and Wildlife, who had told him it was probably the result of a recent herbicide "application" in the drainage. "We'll document your sighting."

When winter brought the monsoons, the rain would soak the barren soil, turning it to slush. With no hardy roots to hold the muck together, it could slide, dumping mud into Echo Creek. Eventually, the sediment would work its way downhill, to Steamboat—and suffocate the steelhead eggs tucked in the gravel.

"Who did the cutting?"

"Cherry Creek Timber. Who else?"

Cherry Creek was one of the mega-conglomerates that, during the spotted owl hoopla, had bought out little mom and pop logging operations around the country, and since had decimated watersheds from Oregon to Maine. Bridge had bitched about them frequently. The headquarters of the company, according to signs Andy had seen on their log trucks, were in Chicago. The people running the show never had to see what their business did to the land.

Finally, they stepped into the shade of the forest, and within a few hundred yards, were out of the heat of the clearcut. Jade colored moss carpeted the ground and ferns grew up to their waists. Trees decomposed all around them, the wood chipping off in red chunks. Wild rhododendrons blossomed, the pink flowers hovering like ships in a sea of green. Beams of sunlight splintered through the canopy, and Andy realized he could only see fifty feet in any direction.

"Those chanterelles are over there, three or four hundred yards," Rita said.

"That's okay," Andy said. "I'll stick with you guys."

"Over here," Bridge said, stuffing the GPS back in his pocket. He examined the trees, the disturbances in the moss. "I was right there, and the bull came through here." The elk had been within spitting distance.

"How'd you get so close?" Andy asked.

Bridge put his finger to his lips. "We should whisper from here on out. Same as fishing. Just got to know the spots."

Rita went to work, her eyes on the ground. And Bridge followed along behind, his bow at his side, his eyes scanning the surrounding woods. Andy imagined a bear standing up in front of them. And then he remembered the gory picture on the front page of *The Oregonian* years before, "Mountain Lion Mauls Hiker." "Are there cougars here?" Andy whispered.

With dire seriousness, Bridge said, "Lots. But don't worry about me. They like to eat the guy in the back of the line."

Behind Andy, the ferns still shook from his passing.

"Here's some," Rita muttered. "And some more."

Bridge pointed to a fern, to a tiny pin drop of red on the green leaf. Andy touched it, and the blood smeared over his skin like blackberry juice. It was thinner, redder than fish blood.

Rita kept going, guiding them a hundred yards or so through the brush, connecting red dots. And then she found half an arrow. Bridge snatched it up and held it in the light, a professor reading an important passage. "Do you see how the blood is frothy? Means the arrow passed through both lungs," Bridge said. "As painless and lethal a hit as possible. He probably wasn't on his feet for more than ten seconds before he went down."

Without a word, Rita and Bridge traded places. Bridge went first, an arrow now on the string—in case he walked headlong into a bear or cougar? Rita stayed back, moving slowly, trusting the trail of dots. When the blood showed he had taken a wrong turn, she would whistle and correct his course with a nod of the head.

"Why didn't Bridge find the elk himself this afternoon?"

"He's color blind," Rita said. "Can't tell the difference between green and red."

"He needs your help to hunt?"

She nodded. "Although he'd never admit it."

They heard a yell from up ahead and busted through the ferns toward the sound. The hillside turned steep, cliff steep. While standing straight, Andy could touch the slope by sticking out his arm. Down on a bench in the slope, he saw a wide patch of yellow, the flank of an elk, red slime on its side. He slid his way down the slope, and hit the flat with a crash.

Bridge kneeled at the elk's head, its antlers black as sticks. He looked like a child beside the massive animal.

It had been walking and eating only a few hours before. This animal had been alive when Andy woke up this morning.

But now, ticks crawled out of the fur onto the nearby ferns, abandoning the body. The smell of musky urine hung like smoke in the air.

Andy walked a few yards down the bench and sat in the ferns, facing the opposite direction. He remembered the quivering of the broken steelhead, the panic in its eye the moment before Andy delivered the rock to its skull. He remembered standing there in the mist of the dam, alone, her smell still there. And it all felt new.

Rita laid her hand on his shoulder. "I know how you feel."

"You want to pick mushrooms?" Andy asked Rita.

She shook her head. "Got to help debone the meat, if we're to get it done before dark." She pointed at the water bottle. "Agua will help."

Over the next couple of hours, Bridge and Rita cut the hide away, spreading it over the ground like a tarp. They cut thick blocks of muscle from the bone, dropping the meat into cloth bags, and tying the bag shut when it contained as much as they could lift. Andy forced himself to help, to hold open the bags as they dropped in the meat, and later, to carry the bags from the animal's bones up the slope to the tree in which Bridge was busy rigging something. Helping was a step toward atonement.

Two ropes were laid neatly on the ground. To the first rope, Bridge tied a blue pulley. "Hold this," he said to Andy, handing him the end of the rope. Bridge tossed the pulley up and over a wide limb and caught it before it hit the ground. He fed the second rope through the gears, tying one end to the bags. Andy pulled on his end until the pulley dangled just inches below the limb, and then tied it off—as Bridge guided him—to the tree. Moments later, they both heaved the meat up into the air, until it dangled fifteen feet from the ground.

"At night, the breeze runs downhill," Bridge said. "Any bear that hits that scent will come trotting up the slope. Hopefully, he gets too full on the guts to bother climbing into the tree."

"Are we just going to leave the hide and all those bones?" White ribs stuck into the air like fingers, the meat between them cut free.

"I'll take the femurs tomorrow for soup stock," Bridge said. "But the rest stays here. In six months, it'll all be gone. First the bears and coyotes will have their fill, then rabbits and deer and even other elk will eat the bones for the minerals. They make better use of it than I would."

Rita stuffed one small bag of meat into Bridge's backpack, maybe five pounds worth. "Let's get those chanterelles and get back to the rig before dark," she said.

She led them to another bench on the slope, only a few hundred yards away. Once there, she pointed out a tannish-yellow mushroom growing from the moss. Its edges were wavy like an oyster shell.

"This is what we're looking for," she said. "There isn't anything dangerous that looks like it."

They spread out and walked down the bench, peeking through the ferns. Bridge caught Andy watching him. "What's on your mind, Trib?"

"Nothing," Andy said, turning back to the search. But there was something. "What do you feel after that?"

"Sore," Bridge said.

"That's not what I mean."

Bridge stood up, a soft chanterelle cradled in his hand. "It's fucking heavy," he said. "But that's the point." He laid the mushroom in a paper bag. "Forces you to pay perfect attention, to see the world without all the fluffy lingerie people attach to it." He reached for another mushroom. "You know how it feels. You kill fish."

They arrived back at the house as the sun disappeared over the horizon. Bridge shut down the truck, and another car could be heard revving up the hill. A Volvo appeared, and without hesitating, parked beside Andy's truck. Trey stepped out, all smiles.

"Fresh steaks tonight," Bridge bellowed. "Glad you got the message."

"Dinner after dark tastes better anyway," Trey said. "I brought wine. But the guy at the Co-op didn't know which reds would go with elk. So I brought a cab, a merlot, and a malbec just to be sure."

Trey hugged Rita, then Bridge. "You guys stink." He offered his hand to Andy. "I was hoping you'd be here." He was grinning like they were old buddies.

Inside, the house felt the same as it always had. Smart, secluded, and strangely technologically advanced. On the wall, a digital weather station monitored the conditions both inside and out. Bridge touched the computer's mouse, and an image reappeared on the screen: a map of the Pacific Ocean, distant storms marked in various shades of red. "Still no rain," he said.

A collection of obsidian arrowheads hung in a frame on the wall. Andy remembered Bridge showing them off the first time he'd come to their house. "I find one or two a decade, usually on the ridge tops." Each came from the Ipsyniho, remnants of the Calapooia people.

"Will we go a hundred days without a drop?" Andy asked. Nobody could predict the weather like Bridge. Sometimes in the winter, when the difference between a shower and a drizzle could make or break a steelheading day, Andy would call for a prediction.

"Might go a hundred and twenty at this pace." Bridge clicked the mouse and a different image appeared, this one in various shades of gray. "I just worry it'll slam us when it comes."

"I heard the Northwest's summers are going to get longer and our winters more catastrophic."

"Global warming should be good for the wine industry," Trey said. "Grapes like a warm fall."

"Bad for the fish." Andy turned his attention to the bookshelves.

One contained hundreds of books on birth and pregnancy and parenting. The books were worn, frequently read. Another shelf contained various how-to books, mostly construction and bow-building texts. And, of course, Bridge's treasured copy of *Trask*. He'd lent the novel to Andy years ago, during a bad winter when the river stayed unfishably high for a month straight. Andy hadn't been able to put it down.

Bridge put on some music, something twangy, and he and Rita disappeared into the back, to take a shower and clean up. Andy headed for the door, for the solitude of the deck. But Trey stopped him.

"A little vino before you go," he said, pulling two glasses from the cabinet—he knew exactly where to find them. Trey filled each glass with dark wine and handed one to Andy. "Cheers."

Andy nodded.

"I like to look at their books too," Trey said. "Such a collection. But my favorite," he set his wine down and grabbed a book from the shelf, "is this one. Have you seen it?"

Midwifing a Community: A Study of Midwifery and Village Life in Central Mexico. "No," Andy said, "never seen it." Then he read the byline: Rita Ortiz. Rita was an author? How did Andy not know that?

"Never?" Trey acted surprised. "She's working on a new one, you know. About the culture and practice of homebirth in the Northwest." Trey pushed a button on the stereo—and the music shifted to the speakers outside. He pointed toward the door. "Shall we?"

Outside, the sun turned the sky's only cloud—a piddly cirrus puff—fluorescent orange. Could the fall rains simply never arrive? Might the river wither until only a dry gulch remained?

"Terrible," Trey said, nodding at the clearcut behind the house.

Andy sipped his wine.

"In a strange way," Trey continued, "that clearcut is responsible for me coming to the Ipsyniho."

Fitting.

"Bridge and I always talked about retiring together, building a community of just our friends, and living the good life. But deep down, I figured Bridge and Rita would never leave this place. A great house in the middle of a great forest? Why leave?"

A beep sounded from Trey's pocket. He extracted a black cell phone, looked at the screen, and put it back.

"Bridge called me the day they started sawing the trees. I came right up."

"How did you meet Bridge?" Andy asked. If they were such good friends, it seemed strange that Bridge had never mentioned Trey.

"Friends of friends." Trey sipped his wine. "Once I got up here, we starting looking for available land. Got word that Mr. Willis had plans to sell." Trey swirled his wine and chuckled. "That clearcut got the ball rolling."

After just a few sips of his wine, Andy already felt tipsy. He hadn't eaten enough today, and the hike had dehydrated him.

It was Trey's smile he didn't trust. Too friendly, the smile of a salesman at work. Danny probably didn't notice it—he couldn't read people as well as he could read a river. "How'd you meet Danny?"

"Bridge introduced us. D and Shosh were newlyweds, living in an apartment in town. Cute kids." Trey smiled. "We built their house, you know."

"I knew Bridge built it," Andy said.

"Bridge ran the show. I just pounded nails where he told me to."

"Expensive place," Andy said. The first star had appeared, a shard of silver against the pastel sky.

"Figured we needed something nice to woo investors," Trey said. "All the houses in the community will be similar to that one."

"Must have cost a fortune."

Trey shrugged. "That's the nice thing about business expenses. They don't feel like real money."

"So you paid for it?"

Trey looked back at the sky. "We're going to need a lot of help between now and the time construction starts. If you were willing to lend your time, the business might help build a place for you too."

Why had Danny and Shoshana been lying about the wedding money?

Another beep sounded from Trey's pocket. He pulled out the gray phone—hadn't it been black? Did he have two phones?

"I better take this," he said. He left his wine on the porch and walked toward his car. He spoke quietly into the phone—Andy couldn't hear a word, especially not over the speakers' music.

Were Danny and Shoshana embarrassed to admit they had taken money from Trey? Or was it something else?

Trey hung up and said with a shrug, "A realtor's work never ends."

"I bet."

Rita appeared on the porch, wearing a wool sweater and jeans, her silver hair wet. "You boys need a refill?"

"We'll come in," Trey said. As they stood, he put his hand on Andy's shoulder. "Think about it," he said. "We could use another pair of trustworthy hands."

"Rita? How come you never told me you'd written a book?"

She smiled up at Trey, who said, "Sorry, I couldn't resist."

"It was a long time ago," she said.

"But I hear you're writing something now?"

"I'm failing to write something now," she said. She turned and looked at Trey. "Last time I tell you a secret."

Trey winked. "Some secrets demand to be told."

Bridge was at work in the kitchen, chopping vegetables, his hands working slowly but precisely. No one could cook like Bridge. Andy had once joked that PBS should hire him on as a TV chef. *The Wilderness Gourmet.*

The unprepared ingredients lined the counter—the meat, a pair of soy sausages, a roll of polenta, the chanterelles, various herbs—all awaiting metamorphosis. Andy tried to imagine the finished meal, but couldn't. Up until the final garnish was laid, Bridge's vision always remained mysterious, just smoke and steam, splashing and frying—an orchestra tuning up. But no matter how convoluted and disorganized things might seem, Bridge, the great conductor, would always deliver a symphony.

His mouth worked continually too. "The strangest part about having boys, grown-up boys, is now they have grown-up nads," he said. "The last time I saw them sans briefs was before they were in middle school—pre-pubes even. Up until this past month I still thought of them as having little-boy nads, I guess. But in elk camp this year, there was no hiding secrets. We camped at Hash Point, you know. Had to bathe daily in the creek to keep our scent down. I stumbled down there when it wasn't my turn, and let me tell you—Neil has some real stones," Bridge chuckled. "Although that icy creek does do a number."

He took a break from the stove to refill Andy's wine glass and to grab one of his own.

Andy poured river-cold water over the yellow chanterelles, grabbing one and rubbing at a dirt spot vigorously. Trey and Rita laughed in the other room.

Why would Trey want Andy's help? What could Andy offer that a hundred other guys in Ipsyniho couldn't? It's not like he had any construction experience, outside fixing a few things around Kepinger's place.

Bridge rubbed rock salt into two foot-long sections of meat. Then he pressed in mashed jalapeno peppers and garlic gloves, and completed the rub with a crust of cracked black pepper. Andy watched as he carried the meat outside and stashed it in a barbeque filled with chunks of smoldering wood.

In the dining room, Rita laughed at something Trey said.

When Bridge returned from the barbeque, Andy asked, "So, how do you know Trey?"

"Known him for years," Bridge said. "We met through an old client of mine. Good guy, isn't he?"

"Yeah," Andy said. "Real personable."

"You should see him work a deal."

Finally, the meal was ready. "Perfecto," Bridge yelled, throwing his apron across the room. On each plate sat a yellow polenta base, a layer of fried red and green vegetables, and a creamy white sauce poured like cursive over top. Beside it, on a bed of green and purple salad greens, rested thinly sliced elk backstrap, topped with chanterelles, and garnished with shredded mint greens. Rita's plate differed only in that golden soy sausages replaced the meat.

Trey raised his glass in a toast. "To the chef."

"Cheers," Andy and Rita said in unison.

"To the elk," Bridge said, tapping his glass against the others. "Let's remember who we're eating."

"And, of course," Rita said, smiling, "to D and S and their soon-to-be!"

"Here, here."

Outside later, wrapped in fleece blankets, the four of them sat in wooden chairs, their necks cricked back. The fall night was as crisp as any of the year, the distance between the earth and the stars seemingly condensed by the clean air. A shooting star cut across the sky, and its flash illuminated the night.

The slivered moon appeared over the distant ridge, a white claw projecting from the black forest. It looked massive when it was close to the land. Andy had heard in an astronomy class that when the moon first formed—following a catastrophic meteor hit that blasted millions of tons of earth dust into orbit—the moon had been closer to the earth. In its infancy, the moon had taken up a third of the sky, a huge rock hovering just overhead. With each orbit around earth, the moon slipped farther and farther away. Now, as fate had it, the moon and sun appeared to be the same size. A magical time, maybe, for planet Earth.

"The night my daughter was born," Trey said, watching the sky, "I brought her to the hospital window. She looked up with wide eyes. We had a full moon that night, and it reflected in her pupils. When she looked at me, the sky looked too."

"The two greatest highs of my life," Bridge said, "came the first time I held each of my boys."

"Better than LSD?" Andy laughed—he was the only one—though Rita offered a charity smile.

Bridge and Trey continued on about their children, each story sparking another, and Andy felt the immensity of all he was missing. An entire galaxy existed right here on earth, a galaxy he knew nothing about.

He leaned closer to Rita. "Can I ask you a birth question?"

"Of course."

"What causes a miscarriage exactly?"

She shook her head. "Some babies just aren't meant for this world."

"Sure, but something must cause a miscarriage, right? It can't just happen spontaneously."

She leaned toward him, and in a quiet voice, said, "Actually, it can. A body will flush an embryo for countless reasons, most of which we don't completely understand.

But once that embryo becomes a fetus, odds are good the body will carry it to term. Why do you ask?"

"Just curious." Bridge and Trey were laughing. "What kind of events might make a miscarriage more likely?"

"Traumatic ones, certain illnesses, chromosomal abnormalities, certain pharmaceuticals, the list goes on. There's even some evidence suggesting that hypertension can increase the risk. But Andy—"

Bridge suddenly stood up, looked downhill, a watchdog on alert. In the distance, Andy heard an engine.

"Who would be driving around here at this hour?" Rita said, standing up.

"Might be a poacher," Bridge said.

Slowly the engine got louder, and Andy could tell by the evenness of the shifting that it was an automatic transmission. But the engine also sounded deep and smooth, a truck for sure, and gas powered. No one he knew owned such a vehicle.

Lights flashed through the trees overhead as the truck turned down the driveway. And before they could even see the vehicle, Bridge said, "It's Carter."

"What's the sheriff doing here at this hour?" Andy asked. He knew that Bridge and Carter went way back. They'd grown up in the valley together, and had both been on the high school wrestling team the year it won the state championships—back when the Ipsyniho was a valley of loggers. But now Andy's pulse quickened and he steadied his hand on his knee. Had someone seen him bash that fish to death? A hatchery employee maybe?

The big white police truck stopped in the driveway, blocking the only exit, and Carter got out, leaving the truck running. He always left the truck running, as if he might get a call so urgent he wouldn't have time to start the truck on the way. He put on his hat and walked toward them, his leather holster creaking with each step.

"Everything all right, Cart?" Bridge called.

Rita put her hand on her hip. "Carter, what's going on?"

The sheriff stepped out of the moon shadows. "What? A friend needs a reason to stop by? Is that what this valley's coming to?"

Rita said. "Is it bad news?"

Carter stepped up on to the porch. He still had his Magnum PI mustache, although it had grayed a bit in the last year. "Everybody is fine. Nothing like that. Don't get your knickers in a bundle."

Bridge asked Carter if he wanted a beer, and he said, "Do babies want the boob?" Bridge disappeared into the house, and Carter noticed Andy. "That you, Trib?"

"Yes, sir."

"Didn't know you were back. Rumor had it you skipped town the night before Danny's wedding." Carter waited for Andy to say something, but when he didn't, Carter turned to Trey and stuck out his hand. "David Carter," he said. "I don't believe we've met."

"Trey Turner. A pleasure." Trey sat straight when he shook the sheriff's hand.

"Is that your Volvo there?"

"Yes, sir."

"California man, huh?"

"Yes, sir."

Carter sucked air through his teeth. "I don't have nothing against you folks, myself."

"Save it, Carter," Rita said.

"I don't mean no disrespect," he continued. "Just a lot more of you guys around than before, that's all."

The truck rumbled in the driveway. Andy was trying to think of something to say when Carter focused on him. "You're an Oregon boy, ain't you, Trib?"

"Upstate New York, actually, if I had to pick one spot."

"Hum," Carter said, looking to his feet and sucking at his teeth again. Finally, Bridge returned with a beer. Carter took the bottle, downed a gulp, and said, "Thanks for this, Furry."

"No problem," Bridge said.

"I don't mean to crash the party," Carter said. "Stopped by because I heard something today that I thought might interest you." A cloud of exhaust drifted over the deck, and Rita coughed. Carter didn't seem to notice. "Stopped by Willis's place today. He's had some trespassers in there, cutting across his property to reach the Steamboat Pool. They're tossing bait and hauling up wild fish. So, I stopped in to see if he had seen anybody in there lately."

"Good of you," Andy said.

"It's my job, son," Carter said. "Willis told me he'd found his buyer. The Eugene realtor for those White Oak guys made him a big offer this week."

Trey leaned toward Bridge. "I thought he said he wouldn't make a decision until December."

Carter eyed Trey, then turned to Bridge. "He in on this thing with you?"

Bridge asked, "Has Willis signed anything yet?"

Carter shrugged. "Not sure. But he told me they offered one point six."

Trey and Bridge shared a concerned look.

"Anyway," Carter said, "thought you'd want to know. Personally, I'd rather that land get bought up by locals—or mostly locals," he said, looking at Trey—"than see it turn into another shit heap of summer homes." He tipped the beer and drained the rest. "Well, I better get. Crime to stop and whatnot."

Bridge walked Carter to his truck. They shared a laugh and then shook hands. As Carter snapped his seatbelt, the red brake light illuminating the dark forest, he yelled out the window to Bridge, "Where will you be at Carnival?"

"Up along Long John Creek. You?"

"Running the drug prevention booth again. I'll come by with a cooler and we'll catch up." The truck reversed down the driveway, and then accelerated down the hill. They listened to it disappear into the distance.

Trey muttered, "One point six. Can you talk to Willis?"

"I'll drive down there tomorrow morning," Bridge said.

CHAPTER 5

Two hundred and twenty-seven bucks wouldn't get him to the end of the month. He needed work, so Andy spent the morning calling every fly shop from Ashland to Portland, any place that might send a client to the Ipsyniho. Each manager gave him the same story. "Everybody knows the river isn't fishing well. Not with this dry weather. No trips to give."

And so Andy called the Ipsyniho shop. Gordon answered.

"Now you want trips?" Gordon said. "You skip out on me without a day's notice, and now you want trips?"

"I'm sorry, Gordon. It was a tough time." Andy grabbed a pen from the kitchen table and flipped it through his fingers. "I'm back and ready to make things right."

"You left clients waiting at the ramp, Andy. You can't skip town and not tell the outfitter."

"I'll make things right."

"How?" Gordon asked.

"I'll work the rest of the season at 75% pay."

"Well," Gordon said. "That'd be a start."

"And I'll work any trips you want—even corporate trips—without complaining."

Silence. "Well, Andy, I'd like to get you back on the books. I really would. But the truth is I just don't have enough work. We've had bad press all summer. The sports are picking different rivers." Gordon cleared his throat. "Maybe this winter."

"Look, Gordon, I'm desperate. I'll do anything. Maybe I could close for you a few nights a week."

"Sorry, Andy. You know what, no, I'm not sorry. We all get what we have coming."

A minute later, the phone back on the wall, Andy paced the house. Even in Chile he'd found work whenever he needed it. How could he be so desperate in his home valley?

He picked up the phone and dialed his father's number. The time had come.

"Andrew?"

"Hey Dad."

"Jesus, son. I've been worried about you. Your mother called and said you were on some island?"

He had been waiting outside the Guam airport actually, using a phone booth to dodge a thunderstorm, the raindrops splattering his bare legs. She had been leaving the next day on a three-month cruise with her new boyfriend, Burt. After twenty timid years of loving a man who had left her, she was finally taking her life back, acting on a whim. He had called to say, though in different words, that he was proud of her. "I'm back now," Andy said.

"And not a phone call in a year and a half? You could have called collect."

Andy tangled his arm in the phone cord. Now the man cared? "How are Elizabeth and the kids?" Elizabeth was his stepmother. They had married the summer Andy turned thirteen. She had insisted they go on a "family" vacation together, a trip to "make us a unit." So his father stole him off his grandfather's farm for a stale tour of the West's national parks. Andy passed the time reading shitty westerns in the backseat while Elizabeth, overcome with "the nature," snapped photos of mountain goats licking antifreeze.

"Fine, fine. William Junior is fourteen now," his father said. "He saw you in that fishing magazine and now he's taken to fly casting in the backyard. He reminds me of you at that age."

When Andy was fourteen, he had been living with his mom somewhere in Pennsylvania. After the divorce, he often wasn't sure of which city he was living in. But even if he couldn't remember the location's name, he could clearly remember the details of the nearest stream, its width, its color, the timing of its hatches. He had spent his fourteenth year a short bike ride from a severly urban, severly diseased little creek, a trickle of brown water that riffled down a formless cement channel. The creek's few fish, an especially active type of chub, congregated near a roaring highway, in a pool beneath a culvert's waterfall. He had once caught a condom there on a dry fly.

"William Junior tried calling you a few times, wanting to connect with his big brother, but your number was disconnected."

"Hey, Dad, I wanted to ask you—"

"So what were you doing on that island?"

"I did some traveling, some guide work," Andy said. "But I'm back now. That's actually why I'm calling. I'm having some trouble finding work."

"Of course you are," his father said. Whether he intended it as a burn or not, Andy couldn't tell. "It happens a friend of mine in Portland is opening a new realty firm, high-end stuff. It seems your rural land prices are booming. He's putting together a team of realtors now. While you don't have any experience in sales, I'm sure you could slant your guiding experience. You know the clientele. You'd have to pass the realty exams, but that shouldn't be a problem. And of course my word would go a long way. This guy owes a favor."

"That's awfully kind, Dad, but realty isn't my type of gig."

"Your kind of gig? Andrew, you're not a twenty-year-old anymore."

Andy walked to the window. In the distance, the sun glistened off the blackberries.

"Eventually," his father said, "you'll have a family of your own and you'll need something a little more substantive. Surely you realize this by now?"

Just this side of the berries, a red-tailed hawk dove headlong into the grass. "Things are different out here, Dad."

"America is America, and capitalism works the same no matter which coast you live on."

"Capitalism is the reason I'm calling." He sat down at his fly tying bench. "Dad, I could use a loan to help get back on my feet."

A moment passed, and his father said nothing.

"Just a little loan."

"Well Andy . . ."

"A couple hundred bucks," Andy said. "Guiding work has been tough to come by."

"I don't think so," his father said. "Not this time."

"I'll pay you back, Dad. It's just a loan."

"Not this time, Andrew. This 'gig' of yours has consequences, and I'm sorry, but you need to learn to face them. I should have been firmer before. I realize that now. I'll be firmer with William Junior." His father cleared his throat. "I knew you needed money. You only call when you need money."

"That's not true."

Silence.

Of course it was true.

"I'm going to send you a gift certificate to Whole Foods. Do you have Whole Foods out there? I can't have you going hungry. Do you have Whole Foods?"

"We have a Whole Foods." There was one about an hour away.

"I'll have Elizabeth pick one up and drop it in the mail. Do you still live on that farm?"

"Orchard, yeah."

Two minutes later, the rods were in the truck and he was heading up river.

Five miles up River Road, preparations for the Cascadia Carnival were well underway. In a yellow rye field, an old one-ton pickup bounced over the broken ground. In the bed, a mound of hay bales swayed back and forth, and a man wearing a tie-dye shirt and a straw hat kicked free a bale. Another man on the ground dodged the bale's initial bounce then lifted it by twin cords and kneed it into place. Two long rows of rectangular bales extended behind them, about two car widths apart, the edges of a makeshift road. In a couple days, the yellow field would disappear under a skin of parked cars and trucks, their hoods and windshields silver scales in the hot sun. Then, everything would be easy.

Andy rolled down the window, but it didn't help. How long could he survive without money? How long until Kepinger threw him out? His heart was pounding in his neck, much too fast, like he was sprinting—he could hear each beat. He should never have gone to the dam that day. He should never have gone to Chile. The walls of the truck squeezed tighter. He should never have come back.

But in fifteen minutes he would be fishing. Everything would be fine. He could concentrate on the swing of the fly, the troughs in the bottom—eat some blackberries.

But Danny's reflection would be looking up from the water, watching him. His own reflection would be there too.

He slid the truck to a stop along the shoulder, breathing too hard to see straight.

How fucking pathetic, begging his dad for money. Sleeping with his best friend's wife. Trying to pretend it never happened.

A log truck blew its horn as it passed, rocking the pickup in its wake.

No. This wasn't right. This was not the way to live, running and hiding like this.

It was time to make things right, no matter the consequences.

He gassed back onto River Road.

Danny's truck was parked at the shop, backed in as always. He would probably be at the counter, checking fish counts and weather predictions—hunching his shoulders and squinting his eyes like he always did when he looked at the computer screen. Andy parked and checked his face in the mirror. He had to do this.

Gordon and Danny were both tending the counter, laughing at the joke of a customer who stood before them in loafers and khaki shorts. Danny nodded at Andy as he walked in, without interrupting the flow of his fake laugh.

Andy milled around the picture board, waiting, trying not to think too much. For the first time in years, the individual pictures caught his attention. Nearly every grip-and-grin shot on the wall contained either him or Danny, and some chrome steelhead cradled inches above the water. In only one picture were they together, a shot taken by Gordon, a rare trip when they fished with a third person. Andy held the steelhead, one of the biggest he had ever caught, a thirty-nine-inch winter buck, its shoulders thick and deep, the adipose fin like a sail on its back. Danny's smile was even wider than Andy's, his arm around Andy's shoulder. From the angle of the picture, it was hard to tell if Danny was smiling at the fish or at Andy.

"Trib!" Gordon slapped Andy on the back. "Glad you stopped in!" Gordon's moustache was as neat as ever, his hair perfectly parted. He went to Eugene once a month to have it cut. Probably the prettiest hair in Ipsyniho. The customer stood beside him, a pair of sunglasses dangling from his shirt pocket. "Andy, here," Gordon said to the man, "is one of our finest guides. He's been working in South America for the past year."

The guy offered his hand. "A pleasure," he said sternly, without giving his name—as if Andy should already know him.

"Mr. Arnold," Gordon said, "is hoping to move to the valley."

Still at the counter, in the blind spot behind the men, Danny flipped the guy the bird.

Mr. Arnold nodded. "Places like this are too perfect not to enjoy full-time."

Andy didn't respond when he should have, and the silence sprawled into awkwardness.

Gordon chuckled, even though he had no reason to, then placed his hand on Mr. Arnold's shoulder and guided the man out the door. The bells rattled as the door shut behind them.

"Douche bag," Danny said. "Thank me for taking that trip off your hands."

"That was the sport?"

Danny nodded. "I stayed in the hot tub last night until Shosh had to drag my corpse from the bubbles."

Andy watched Mr. Arnold step into Gordon's SUV. "Let me guess, he's part of White Oak."

"Not only is he part of White Oak," Danny said, "he's the jerk-off who had the idea. Did the same thing in Montana a few years back. Making a shitload."

They watched Gordon's SUV pull onto River Road and accelerate away. Acid rose in Andy's throat. "You want to do a drift?"

Danny shook his head. "Want to and able to are separate things. Gordon will be right back." Danny looked out the window at Andy's rig. "I see you're headed upriver."

"Thinking about it."

For a moment they were quiet. Andy knew what he needed to say but the first words eluded him. This would be the worst moment of his life.

He heard himself talking about Carter, about Willis accepting the offer. Danny already knew about it. He had talked to Bridge that morning. "Willis hasn't signed yet. Bridge is over there now trying to convince him to give us a little time."

A little more time. Andy scratched his head. "How the hell could the three of you top an offer for one point six million?"

"We've got investors," Danny said. Then he laughed, "You should have seen that douche bag try and cast! I had to tape my ears to the side of my head to keep from losing them." He shook his head. "I knew I was in for trouble when he insisted we stop for an expresso on the way upriver."

Danny was trying to change the subject, to dodge questions about money. "It's es-presso," Andy said.

Danny continued, "Get your fucking expresso before meeting your guide, right? Isn't that in the Sport Handbook? We missed the prime fifteen minutes of light on account of that dingle-berry's double hazelnut."

"Es-presso, not ex-presso."

Danny checked the door.

The wall clock counted the seconds. Why did he say that? For ten years he had disregarded Danny's casual vernacular. In truth, he found it ingratiating, a form of local authenticity.

Danny's eyes narrowed. "What's your problem? Ex-presso, es-presso. Same shit. You know what I'm talking about."

This isn't what he wanted. But instead of saying what he needed to, he brought his palm to his chest and said, "My problem? You're the one fucking lying."

"Lying?"

"Wedding money? Give it up. You're a terrible liar. I know Trey paid for your house. The real question is why you lied about it. Lied to me, no less."

Danny's nostrils flared. "I don't know what you're talking about."

"Bullshit."

"This is how you want to play it?" Danny asked. "Then fine. I'm going to ask you something, something that has been bothering me a long time, and I want a straight-up answer. No bullshit this time."

"Answer me first."

"Look me in the eye," Danny said, "and tell me why you left when you did? Did something happen, something between you and Shoshana? I know something did. She . . . she . . . I know something did."

So this was it. His moment to come clean. At least, then, it would be over.

"I already told you." Andy leveled his best glare. "Do you need me to write it down? You know what Danny? I think you have some trust issues."

He couldn't. He just couldn't. Not here, not now. He would tell him later. When they were on the river.

Danny's eyes narrowed.

"You know what you're like?" Andy said. His knee, concealed behind the counter, was shaking.

"What am I like?"

"You're like, you're like," Andy dug for something, anything, "like Kesey's Hank Stamper." The hardheaded and violent patriarch from *Sometimes a Great Notion*.

Danny blinked, and for just a fraction of a second his eyes flinched to the fly rods on the wall. But that was enough. When he tried to level them back on Andy, he couldn't maintain the glare. The allusion had fractured his confidence.

"Tell me why you lied about the house. Why you're lying to me."

A horn honked out on the road, and Danny glanced out the shop window. He continued to watch the distance long after the car had passed. "All right," he said in a whisper. "But first, just look me in the eyes and tell me. Tell me nothing happened between you two." This time, when Danny looked at Andy, he was begging.

Andy focused at the freckle on the bridge of Danny's nose and heard, "Nothing happened between Shoshana and me."

Danny released a breath. He was either broken or relieved. Finally, in a barely audible voice, he said, "Okay. I just needed to hear you say it."

And Andy felt his legs go weak. He steadied himself with a hand on the counter.

"It's just," Danny stuttered, "I just started, you know, thinking about why you would leave like that. I thought about it too much. You know how I get. My runaway mind."

"Sure, sure," Andy said. "You just over-thought it."

"I shouldn't have gotten in your face about it, though," Danny said. "I should have trusted you." He looked to his feet. "I've been working on things. On trusting people more." He nodded to himself and looked up. "I should have trusted you."

"Forget about it."

Danny leaned his weight on the counter.

"Your house," Andy said.

In a small voice, Danny said, "I . . . I haven't been straight up. But I can't tell you everything right now. We're at a crucial moment."

"A crucial moment? In what?"

"In exchange for my help on a project, they're helping pay for the house. If we can pull the thing off, we'll be able to buy Mr. Willis's land for the community."

We could use another pair of trustworthy hands. "They? What kind of project? What's going on?"

Danny said, "Last night, Trey asked you something. Do you remember?"

"Yeah."

"You should come on board," Danny said. "We need your help. And if you were working with us, I could tell you everything. No secrets."

"Why do you have to keep secrets? It's not like I'm friends with any of those White Oak people, if that's your concern."

"That's not the concern," Danny said.

Not the concern? Then why lie? Something about this whole project was way off. He remembered Trey answering Sheriff Carter's questions the night before, saying 'yes, sir.' It had struck him as odd at the time, almost as if Trey were nervous. He whispered, "You doing something illegal?"

Danny glanced over the shop, as if someone might have slipped in unannounced.

"Is that it?" Andy asked.

Danny smiled.

That was it.

"I can't say any more," Danny said. "I shouldn't have said this much."

"What has Trey sucked you into?"

Danny laughed, but didn't say anything.

"What's so funny?"

"Come on board and we'll tell you everything."

"Does Shoshana know what's going on?"

"Get involved," Danny said.

What did he offer that others in the valley didn't? "Why me?"

"Don't worry about that. Just say yes. We don't need you to do anything super illegal. Just one day's work, really. Besides, you're not going to be able to guide enough this winter to stay afloat. Bridge says it'll be another winter like last year—enough rain to keep the river flooded all season. And with these run counts, trips are already few and far between."

A customer walked through the door.

"I can't say any more," Danny said. But before turning his attention to the customer, he said, "If you say yes, they'll take care of you."

Andy raced up River Road, the engine screaming and the boat bouncing on the trailer. He didn't know where he was going or what he was doing, just that he was in motion. He only had a quarter tank of gas.

Trey. He had conned Danny into this, whatever it was. If Andy saw him walking along the shoulder, he might swerve and say it was an accident. Do the valley a favor.

Obviously the guy was right—if the zoning commission decided to open the land to building, then environmentally-minded people should get the property. But Trey wasn't about building a community; he was about manipulating people, using them to do his bidding. In the end, this was about him, about his profit, not about the Ipsyniho. Sustainability. The only sustainability he gave a shit about was his own.

And he didn't give a shit about Danny either. That much was obvious. Whatever they were up to, if they got caught, Danny would be the one getting in trouble. Danny would be the fall guy.

As he passed Millican Ramp, the back of a brown Chevy appeared in front of him, driving slowly. It was Bridge, probably heading home from Willis's. Andy followed him up Steamboat Creek, and then up Echo Spring. They parked at the house, and both trucks fell silent.

"Howdy, speed racer," Bridge said, pointing at the boat. "Last I checked, the river was down there."

Andy shut his truck door. "I was headed fishing when I ran into Danny."

"Oh, yeah?" Bridge said. "What did he have to say?"

"Enough," Andy said.

Bridge raised his eyebrows. Whatever was going on, Bridge knew. Bridge always knew. "Can I offer you a cup of joe?"

He waited on the porch while Bridge disappeared inside. The white game bags hung in the shade of a Doug fir along the edge of the yard. Brown blood stained the bags. Even from forty yards away, he could see flies fighting futilely to get at the meat.

A few minutes later, Bridge appeared with two cups of steaming coffee, and they settled into the wooden chairs on the porch.

"Rita," Bridge said blowing steam off his cup, "has prenatals all day."

Andy pointed at the meat. "Still hanging?"

"Has to cure," Bridge said. "I'll cut it first thing tomorrow."

"How did you meet Trey again?"

Bridge passed his fingers through his beard and looked out over the valley. "Friend of a friend. We go way back. What's Danny up to?"

He couldn't expect Bridge to be as forthcoming as Danny. Locals of his generation could be extremely tightlipped. "He's at the shop." But the right question might start him talking. "What kind of realty does Trey do exactly?"

"I guess I don't really know. Realty's realty to me." Bridge laughed. "Just between us, no matter what type, it's still dirty. I'm trying to convince Trey to get out of the biz, do something else. He's too good to be pimping land." Bridge studied the boat parked in the driveway. "How's your cash situation? Danny tells me you're having trouble finding guide work."

"Times are tight," Andy said. "But they've been tighter before." He sipped his coffee. "I'm good at getting by cheap."

"You know," Bridge said, "if you're looking for work, I might be able to help out."

"Thanks," Andy said. "But construction isn't my thing." Mr. Kepinger. A quarter tank of gas. "What kind of work?"

"Errands, really," Bridge said. "Like today, for instance. I've got an order of supplies arriving in Eugene, Pirate's Lumber. But I can't get down there. Got to check on a job site. You'd be doing me a big favor by running down and picking the stuff up." He pulled his wallet from his pocket. "What do you make for a half-day of guiding?"

"$275, but I'd never let you pay me that much. Those are sport prices."

"$275 it is. Plus your gas, of course. I'm not one to take advantage of a friend."

"I can't take your money, Bridge. Pay my gas and I'd be happy to help you out."

"Nonsense. You need a little cash boost and I need these supplies picked up. Friends helping each other out." Bridge counted out bills from his wallet and stuffed them into Andy's shirt pocket. "That's going to make my day significantly easier. I appreciate it. You're a life saver." He stood and walked to the edge of the deck, his coffee in hand. "You know Andy, Joel's death hit this whole valley hard, but it decimated Danny. He hardly talked for a year afterwards."

Andy rubbed his fingers over the bulging pocket. Bridge had just bought him another couple weeks.

Bridge continued, "Doesn't hurt nothing for Danny to have another friend nearby."

Andy stood beside Bridge. "Don't take my curiosity about Trey the wrong way. I'm glad he and Danny have become friends. He just strikes me as a bit off, and I hope he's not doing anybody wrong, that's all. Especially Danny."

"I stand behind him," Bridge said. "I'm vouching for him. He's a good guy. Flawed as severely as the rest of us, but he and Nikki will make a stellar addition to the valley. Trust me on this. You trust me, right?"

"I trust you."

"All right then." Bridge checked his watch. "I should get to work. Big thanks for running into town for me. I'm indebted. Any chance you could drop those by tonight? Feel free to leave your boat here and pick it up when you get back from Eugene."

Andy was to River Road before he checked the money in his pocket. Two counts revealed the same total: $400.

His grandfather had once been duped too, suckered in by a couple of smooth talking strangers.

They had been fishing all morning and were just getting back to the farmhouse when a maroon Suburban rolled down the long driveway, a car that no Upstate farmer would drive. A city man's truck. His grandfather went rigid, and laid his thick hand on Andy's shoulder. Thunderstorms were building and the air was as murky as the tannin-laced farm pond in the corner of the property.

Later, Andy would learn the government had immigrated his Opa after the war, wanting him for his knowledge of the Nazi's weapons program. They figured since he had filmed all those blasts, maybe he knew something valuable about Germany's still enigmatic nuclear program. In exchange, they helped him finish college and find a job. Despite the help, his grandfather harbored a precise fear: that the government would change its mind and deport him just as effortlessly as they had immigrated him. But on that day, when Andy was still just a boy, he knew none of his Opa's fears, none of his sufferings.

Two men stepped out of the Suburban, clean clothes, city clothes, clothes like his father wore. The driver smiled and said, "Howdy."

His grandfather waved, hiding his voice. Andy talked for him, "Do you need directions?"

"We're from the Department of Natural Resources."

The old man pointed at the chairs, smiling now. "Coffee. Andy, get some coffee for these good people. Also, get the doughnuts too."

But the men refused the offer. "We don't want to take up much of your time." The taller man did all the talking.

The Department of Natural Resources wanted to buy a truckload of soil, "a special soil" that existed only around streams such as the one that flowed across the farm. "We need it for an agricultural research project on nitrogen and corn production. Interesting stuff. Should help farmers just like you." In exchange for the soil, the government would pay three times the market rate, $15 a yard. "$750 total. Whatcha say?"

"Of course," his grandfather said. "Anything I can do. Just give it a name."

The quiet man extracted an envelope from his pocket. Later, Andy would watch his grandfather count the bills on the kitchen table, $750.

A truck and cat arrived later, a black tarp already pulled tight over the truck's bed. While the men worked—the roaring of their digging echoing over the farm—Andy and Opa occupied themselves in the shop, building a wood duck nesting box. Later, Andy would attach it to a beech tree, a stone's throw from a fish rearing pool they had built along the stream the summer before. "The entrance hole must be the same size as a grapefruit, so the mother duck can get in." Every measurement, every pencil mark traced with the blade of the jigsaw, made this afternoon feel like every other. But then, while attaching the hinge for the box's lid, his grandfather missed driving a screw. He wiped his bleeding finger on his shirt and said, "What's taking them so long?"

The roaring finally stopped after dark. They watched as the trucks drove away, their red lights narrowing down the highway. His grandfather grabbed a flashlight and said, "Get your boots."

The heavy machinery had left a barren patch of soil on a small rise above the creek. The flashlight revealed only one slice of the damage at a time, but still it looked more like they had buried something than taken something.

His grandfather blinded him with the flashlight beam. "Back to the house."

That night, suspended from sleep by the thunder outside, he heard the back door creak. From the window, he saw the hunch of the old man, a shovel in one hand and a lantern in the other, the rain turning the yard to a lake. Andy threw on his pants and slipped out the back, following the swinging lantern through the beech and hickory.

He found the old man in the ground, his shovel feeding blackness to the night behind. Mud drops streaked his face. Snot ran freely from his nose. He was wet and whimpering and this was not the Opa he knew.

Andy sprinted away from the hole, into the invisible limbs of the forest. Eventually, he hit the hedgerow and traced it back to the porch light. He laid awake until the backdoor creaked and he heard Opa kick off his boots.

The next morning, he found the old man at the kitchen table, eating his white toast with butter and salt and watching the morning news—as if nothing had happened. But soon after, a knock sounded on the door. Through the window, he saw his father's dark hair. He must have driven through the night to make it. Andy ran upstairs and locked himself in the bathroom. He wouldn't leave. The summer wasn't over. It wasn't fair. He hadn't meant to see Opa like that.

Then he heard their voices on the porch.

"So you saw a body?"

". . ."

"Then how do you know?"

". . ."

"I'll call the police, then."

"No, no police."

"Then what am I supposed to do?"

The three of them went back to the hole, and his father took the shovel this time.

"Why would you let these people onto the property anyway?"

"They were from the government," Opa said.

"Did you see any identification? Of course not. Don't be so naïve." His father threw a shovelful of soil to the side of the hole. "Besides, you don't have to let the government onto the property unless they have a warrant. This is the United States. Citizens have rights." He was using that tone, the one he frequently used when he spoke to Opa—as if the old man was a child.

"They paid Opa," Andy said.

"It's true."

"How much?" His father stopped digging.

"$750."

He went back to digging and muttered, "And you let them destroy a quarter acre of land?"

Opa touched Andy's arm, and nodded toward the forest—he wanted him away from that hole. And then the shovel scraped metal.

Opa rushed to the edge. "Stay back," he said to Andy.

But Andy stepped forward too and saw the next shovel-load reveal a flat piece of rusted metal.

Eventually, they would uncover a barrel, and his father would insist they call the EPA. Later, men in yellow suits would find ten more barrels like the first. It had been a busy a summer for these men; barrels were turning up on farms all over Upstate.

After the canisters were removed, a pit remained along the stream, a hole in the otherwise even hill. It was still there the last time Andy walked the property, the afternoon of his Opa's funeral.

River Road met I-5 fifteen miles downstream from the town of Ipsyniho, and Andy veered right onto the northbound exit. He'd be in Eugene in thirty-five minutes.

Obviously Trey wasn't ditching industrial waste, but what was he doing? It had to be something lucrative.

Up ahead, a billboard read:

> *Prestige Homes*
> *Easy Commute*
> *Easy Mortgage*
> *The Good Life*
> *(Starting at $69 a Square Foot)*

Maybe he knew some way to milk money from real estate transactions. Maybe he was selling properties that he didn't own. But then why would he need Danny's help? And why Andy's?

Another billboard:

Power Hummer!

Shock and Awe!

Go Big, Go Hard, Or Stay Home!

Andy passed the South Eugene exit, picking his way through the dense city traffic. The car in front of him swerved into the shoulder, and as he passed, the driver lifted a muffin to his mouth while shouldering a cell phone to his ear.

Danny did seem to have plenty of weed these days. Though Trey seemed too uptight for ganja.

Billboard:

Escape It All At

Eagle Feather Casino

A towering sign like an electrified totem pole, the message flashing:

Gateway Mall

Sale Sale Sale

Support Our Troops

A new Dodge pickup roared past, a chrome ladder extending a couple feet down from the passenger door. Below the trailer hitch swung a plastic scrotum, faux testicles an inch off the pavement. On the polished bumper, a sticker:

Nuke 'Em.

Be Done With It.

Finally, he made it north of town and took the Beltline Road exit. Pirate's Lumber sat just a few hundred yards from the McKenzie River, the stream that had spawned the design of the drift boat eighty years before. It was a good looking river, no doubt, with the intoxicating aroma of licorice. The McKenzie Valley wouldn't be a bad place to make a stand—it grew sizable blackberries—but it's run of wild steelhead was already extinct.

Andy arrived at Pirate's Lumber just before noon. The attendant at the counter—a lanky kid with blond hair and a wad of sunflower seeds in the corner of his mouth—loaded the boxes into the back of the truck and strapped them tight.

"Do I need to pay?" Andy asked.

The kid looked at the computer printout in his hand and shook his head. "Already covered."

"Does it say who paid?" Andy asked.

The kid spit out a shell while keeping one eye on Andy. "Just says 'paid cash.'"

"Thanks."

He drove off the lot and started home. But something stopped him. He pulled off onto the shoulder. Four hundred bucks was too much.

With his knife, he slit open the plastic tape locking each box. In the first, he found heavy containers of "flat-butted" screws and a massive device that looked not unlike a vise—maybe a jig for burying those screws. The other box was no more provocative. Inside sat three green, individually packaged "area tarps." The packaging read, "100 feet X 100 feet." Beneath the tarps he found two 300-foot lengths of nine millimeter nylon rope. Just about what a person would need to keep a stack of lumber from getting wet during the winter rains.

What had he expected? Silver briefcases filled with heroin?

Andy dropped off the boxes just as the ocean breezes pushed the afternoon warmth over the Cascades. After hitching his boat and driving home, he found a message from Danny on the answering machine. "Shosh and I are taking you out. Wildfire. 7:30. And brother," Danny said, "shower up."

When Andy arrived, he found three people at the table, Danny, Shoshana, and a woman with night-black hair, green eyes, and deeply-tanned skin. Her silver earrings shook as she laughed.

"Ah, there he is!" Danny said, kicking out a chair.

"This is Jasmine Turchi," Shoshana said without looking at him, "an old friend from New York."

Jasmine offered her hand. She wore a bracelet, green and turquoise stones in a silver setting—something from South America. "I've heard about you."

"That can't be a good thing," Andy said. "Where in New York? Upstate?"

She laughed. "No, the city."

He ordered a tequila and turned to Shoshana. "How do you feel, with the pregnancy and all?"

"It comes and goes."

"Jasmine and Shosh traveled together after college," Danny said. "Can you picture these two hitchhiking across the Sinai?"

"Sinai?" Andy said. He knew Shoshana had traveled through Israel and Turkey after college, but the Sinai conjured drastically different images: endless deserts, bombed-out tanks, AK-47s.

"Naïve kids," Jasmine said. "Luckily the Bedouin were there to keep us safe."

"Now Jasmine's a big-time writer," Shoshana said.

"Hyperbole," Jasmine scoffed.

The tequila arrived, and Andy downed it and asked for another, "Do you write any fiction?"

"Nah," Jasmine shook her head. "If it's not real, what's the point?"

Danny interrupted. "Andy was in a magazine a couple years ago. 'Expert guide Andy Trib releases a feisty steelhead.' They thought he was more photogenic than me, I guess."

"But it was your phone number they listed."

"And I haven't had a day off since," Danny said.

It was almost true. That article had doubled Danny's trip load. Andy dipped a spring roll in a dish of peanut sauce. "What brings you to Ipsyniho?" he asked Jasmine.

"Carnival," she said, cutting a spring roll in half. "Doing a piece on it for a friend of mine."

Shoshana still hadn't looked at him. Her hair was down and she wore makeup, just a little mascara—maybe she was feeling self-conscious about the dark circles under her eyes. She was obviously exhausted.

Danny and Jasmine laughed. Andy had missed a joke.

"Excuse me." He headed for the bathroom.

Danny came through the door behind him. "She's hot, isn't she? I thought you'd like her." He was obviously stoned.

Andy shrugged. "I'm not looking to get tangled up in anything right now."

"Right," Danny laughed. "Neither was I that day at Saturday Market."

Andy shook his head. "I'm too busy now. And who knows where I'll be in six months."

"You're thinking of moving?" Danny asked, his laugh fading.

Andy washed his hands. Before this moment, he hadn't considered leaving. The phrase had just popped out. This was his home. But what choice did he have, really? Shoshana was so clearly right. If he cared about Danny, he would leave and never tell him anything.

"Where would you go?" Danny asked.

A sign on the soap dispenser read:

Sanitary Pleasures
Denver, Colorado

"Durango, maybe."

Danny stepped to the urinal. "Colorado. How long have you been thinking that?"

"A while," he said.

Danny studied the porcelain. "Durango?"

Andy dried his hands. "Or Bozeman."

"Montana?"

"We'll see," Andy said, avoiding Danny's eyes. "I've been fighting the itch to hit the road."

Danny contemplated this. "God, I guess I figured you'd stay around, be an uncle to—"

"Sometimes it's time to move on."

"Yeah, I guess so."

Shoshana and Jasmine spent dinner consumed in laughter. Each story would spark a laugh in the listener, which in turn would spark a laugh in the teller, and soon the story would be paused while Shoshana and Jasmine turned various shades of red. This was their symmetry.

Then Danny told a story. "Shosh and I went camping on the coast last May."

"Not this story," Shoshana pleaded. "Nobody wants to hear this."

But Danny continued anyway. "Everyone else in the universe was camping that day too—took us hours to find a spot. It was almost dark by the time we got the tent up. And the spot was shitty, smack-dab in the middle of a bunch of tents. No privacy.

"With all the stress of finding a place, we were feeling a little frisky by the time we got the tent up, so I lit a candle lantern and we ducked inside."

Andy called for the waiter. "Can we get the check?"

"Anyway, we're inside for maybe forty-five minutes."

"Twenty-five," Shoshana muttered, mostly to Jasmine.

"Twenty-five times two." Danny nudged her in the shoulder, smiling. "Either way—that's not the point of the story—either way, our campsite was so close to other people that we had to be really quiet.

"When I finally emerged to go take a piss—almost an hour later—everyone was looking at me. At first I thought it was in my head. 'Everyone knows.' But then I saw people actually pointing and laughing. Maybe we'd been louder than we thought.

"Anyway, as I left the bathroom and started back to camp, I saw our tent glowing in the night. And inside, I saw Shosh's silhouette, plain as day, as she put on a shirt!"

"I wish you wouldn't tell that story," Shoshana said.

Jasmine laughed. "You'd put on the best shadow show this side of Vegas!"

The bill came and Danny reached for it. But Jasmine was faster.

"No, no, no," Shoshana said. "Our treat."

"Bullshit," Jasmine said, extracting a credit card. "A business expense. Let somebody back east pay."

Shoshana suddenly fell still and starred blankly at a pitcher of water on the table.

"What's wrong?" Danny asked.

Shoshana's lips pursed as if she had just tasted something horrendously sour. The color was draining from her face.

"Again?" Danny asked, pushing back his chair. "You shouldn't have had Pad Thai."

"Uuo, don't say it!" Shoshana stood and looked toward the bathroom—a line waited by the door. She darted for the front door, Danny just behind. Other patrons turned toward the commotion. A moment later, while crossing the parking lot, she vomited onto an Audi.

"Poor thing," Jasmine said, handing the bill to the server. "This kid thing looks overrated. Nine months of vomiting followed by eighteen years of headache. It's a wonder the human race didn't peter out a generation after birth control."

"Oh, for Christ's sake," a man said. He stood, wiped his mouth on his napkin, and abandoned his date. He was headed outside.

"Shit."

"What is it?" Jasmine said.

"This isn't good." Andy rushed toward the door.

By the time he arrived, the man was already shouting and pointing at the hood of his car. "Unacceptable. You can't just puke on a car!"

Danny opened the passenger door of his truck and helped Shoshana climb inside. She spoke with a little vomit still on her chin, "I'm sorry. We'll clean it."

But the man didn't seem to hear. "The acid is burning the paint!"

Danny ignored him, unrolling Shoshana's window, then carefully pressing the door closed. He wiped her chin.

"The acid is burning the paint!" the man shouted again, trying, it seemed, to get Danny's attention.

Andy touched the man's arm. "We'll clean it right now."

The man yanked his arm away and took a step toward Danny. "Hey, I'm talking to you."

Danny stopped and leveled his eyes on the man.

"We'll take care of it," Jasmine said. "I'll go get towels."

But the man paid no attention. He pushed his glasses up his nose and nodded toward Shoshana in the cab. "I've got your license plate number, and your drunk girlfriend won't get away with this. You have no idea who I am."

Danny took half a step toward the man, but then stopped himself.

"Danny," Shoshana said. "Take me home. Leave it be."

And he probably would have left it, he probably would have climbed into his truck and driven off, but the man muttered, "Dumb-shit hillbilly."

Andy rushed forward, but was too late. Danny already had the guy by his shirt collar and was driving him backward. When they collided with the Audi, Danny released his grip and the man slid over the hood, through the vomit, and onto the pavement on the other side. He landed with a sickening crunch—bone on pavement.

Danny extracted a key from his pocket and, as he walked back toward Shoshana, ran it through the Audi's paint. "We'll see you and Andy back at the house," he said, climbing into the truck.

Jasmine and a blond woman—the man's date—were already beside the guy when Andy came around the car. He was sitting against the tire, vomit plastering his hair. No blood was visible.

"I'm calling the police," he said, nearly in tears. "I'm calling the fucking police."

A server appeared with a bucket of water and a pair of towels, and Andy used them to clean the hood of the car. The job was done in less than a minute.

"They can't get away with this," the man said, struggling to stand.

"She's pregnant," Jasmine said, "not drunk."

The blond woman said, "Do you hear that, Ronny? You just yelled at a pregnant woman."

"Where's my cell phone?" The man patted his pockets, dazed.

But there was no need. Sheriff Carter's truck pulled into the lot, lights flashing. The wait staff must have called. Carter tapped the sirens, broadcasting his own royal arrival. "What's the story?" he said, stepping out of the truck, his hand on the holstered pistol.

While the man recounted all the ways he'd been wronged, Carter sucked his tooth. When the man was done, he glanced at the Audi's license plate—which was from Oregon—and said, "You're not from around here."

"Ashland," the man said.

Jasmine whispered to Andy, "It's the regular wild west around here."

The lights from the idling police truck flashed over the parking lot. "This isn't normal," Andy said.

"Yeah," she laughed. "It's a bit northwest of anything normal."

A few minutes later, Carter nodded to Andy, and together they walked across the parking lot until they were out of hearing distance.

"Tell Danny I'll take care of it," Carter said. "Good of him not draw any blood."

Andy nodded. "I'll let him know."

Carter spit a brown streak of tobacco on the pavement. "I'm thinking about taking the grandkid trout fishing tomorrow. Got any suggestions?"

A few minutes later, Andy and Jasmine followed River Road upstream.

"I never fancied Shosh the type to end up with a macho man," Jasmine said.

"They have important things in common," Andy said.

River Road contained more cars than normal, people already arriving for the Carnival. He passed an RV, then had to slow down as a little buck trotted across the road.

Jasmine cracked her window and Andy caught a whiff of something sweet, maybe honeysuckle. He realized he'd been smelling it all evening.

"I got the sense they were trying to pair us up," she said. "Danny, anyway."

"The old double-third-wheel maneuver."

"Breeders," Jasmine shook her head. "Don't worry, though. You're not my type." The light from the dashboard glowed against her skin and earrings, and her black hair blended with the night. For a moment her face seemed to hover above the passenger seat. "Breeders are always proselytizing," she said. "They don't want to see us having single fun. Though this may be more complicated than simple evangelicalism."

"More complicated?"

"Well," she said. "Considering your and Shosh's entangled history, you're a ticking bomb as long as you stay nearby and single. Put yourself in Danny's shoes."

Andy shifted into third gear and accelerated through a corner. "You think so?"

"Please," Jasmine laughed. "Feigning naivety is so valley girl."

"You know our history then?"

"Ten months traveling together is a long time. You get past the mundane by month two. By month six, you're waist deep in the heavy shit." She opened her purse. "You mind if I have a smoke?"

"Go for it. Have you guys talked much lately?"

"We haven't seen each other since before the wedding. I was out of the country." Jasmine lit her cigarette. "I just don't get these long-term couplings."

"Marriage?"

"Relationships are like pop songs. At first, you're into them because they're new and peppy. But soon that bounce wears thin and they become drab and predictable—kitschy even. Why would people hog-tie themselves to kitsch?"

"You paint a dark picture of things."

"I have no illusions." Jasmine laughed. "But then again, what do I know anyway? I've yet to have a relationship survive a fiscal quarter, although I have written several articles on monogamy."

"'Ten Ways to Keep Your Man?'"

"Close. 'Ten Ways to Keep Your Man Kissing Your Feet.'" She exhaled a stream of smoke toward the cracked window. "No one buys simple monogamy anymore."

When they arrived at the yurt, Danny was helping Shoshana to bed. Jasmine disappeared into the house and suggested Andy come inside. But he declined, figuring he would just say his goodbyes to Danny and head home. A few minutes later, Danny appeared on the porch, three open beers in his hands. "Where's Jasmine?"

"Bathroom, I think," Andy said.

Danny offered the beers.

"Nah," Andy said.

Danny scoffed. His breath smelled of whiskey. "What? You going home like all the other sports? Take the beer and stay awhile."

Andy snatched one of the bottles and took a swig. "I'm no sport."

"Whoever named it 'morning sickness' don't know shit." Danny chugged half his beer, then burped. "Shosh is pissed I tossed that guy."

"Carter didn't seem too concerned."

Danny laughed. "Fucking Carter! I love that guy."

For a minute they drank their beers, the night cold and clear.

Then Danny asked, "What do you think of Jasmine? She's a smart one, no? Grew up dirt poor but ended up at Harvard or Yale or some shit. An Ivy League school." Danny finished his beer. "There's no bullshit with her."

"She's cute," Andy said, "maybe a bit presumptuous."

"That's what I like about her. She calls it likes she sees it."

The light from the yurt cast an orange glow on the surrounding forest. The sign above the garden gate radiated: *Arousal From Below.*

The door opened and Jasmine appeared in a two-piece bathing suit, her eyes on the beer. "I hope one of those is for me." She had pulled her hair back into a ponytail. A tattoo encircled her belly button, ocean waves or the sun maybe.

Danny handed her a bottle. "It's an IPA from a brewery downstream. Not bad, eh?"

"A bit hoppy for my liking. But good beer is good beer." She looked down the deck at the hot tub and burped. "What do you say?"

"Why not?" Danny finished his beer and stepped toward the house. "I'm going to grab another," he said. "Y'all want anything."

He only said 'y'all' when he was drunk. "I'm good," Andy said.

"Aren't you coming in?" Jasmine asked Andy.

He shrugged.

She poked him in the shoulder. "If you're not careful, you might get a reputation as a sourpuss."

"A sourpuss?"

She shrugged. "The best I can do. It's been a long day."

Danny appeared in his trunks, a beer in each hand. "You're coming in," he said. "It's my house. I insist."

Andy stripped to his boxers and followed them to the blue lights and bubbling water. Jasmine climbed in carefully, settling herself against a jet. "Did you find any hot springs in Chile?" she asked.

Andy nodded. "I worked at a lodge that had three springs within a mile walk. At night, while the sports got shitfaced, we'd sneak up the trails by headlamp. The manager insisted we stop, that the springs were for the sports only, but we went anyway. What could they do? Fire us? Not likely. Guides are worth their weight down there."

"What is it like down there?" Danny asked.

His appreciation of the place, its rivers, its cultures, had been soured by a single, inescapable fact: He'd been worse than a sport while in Chile—he'd been a leech taking a job that a local could have had. It was impossible to be there and forget that. "They don't like us down there."

"They don't like us anywhere anymore," Jasmine said.

"Just seems like a good place," Danny said. "Like here, just more wild. Not that I'll ever leave here."

Jasmine set her beer on the rail of the tub. "I went to Chile maybe three years ago, wrote a piece on the ballooning eco-tourism industry. Chile is America's new playground. The new Hawaii."

"Mexico is the new Hawaii," Andy said. "Costa Rica is the new Mexico. Chile is the new Costa Rica."

"You've thought that one out, haven't you?"

Andy finished his beer. "I don't have a television."

"Fucking tourists," Danny said. "I won't go on vacation. I refuse on principle."

Jasmine laughed. "So, you're going to spend your whole life right here? What does Shoshana think about that?"

Danny looked at the dark sky. "She understands."

"Sure," Jasmine said. It was impossible to tell if she was being sarcastic.

"When do your parents show up?"

Danny stood, sending water splashing over the sides of the tub. He dried his hands on a towel and opened a brass tin sitting on the railing of the deck. "They said they'd show up sometime around dinner tomorrow." He extracted a joint and put a match to it. "But they'll probably be early." He passed the joint to Jasmine.

"So this is the stuff I've been hearing about," she said, studying the pot.

"Best in the world," Danny said.

Jasmine let the joint burn between her fingers, her earrings dangling within an inch of the water. "Is the rumor true, Carnival started as a harvest celebration?"

"That's the rumor," Danny said. "Are you going to hit that?"

Jasmine delicately put the joint to her lips and drew a small breath. She exhaled straight up like a cigarette smoker in a crowded bar. For a moment she stared into the blue fog of the tub, then shook her head and giggled. "Fuck me," she said. "That shit is for real!"

Danny laughed. "The west is the best."

"Why is that?" Jasmine asked, clearing her throat. "What does this place have that Kentucky or Florida or Guatemala doesn't?"

"Dope culture," Danny said, slipping back into the water. "It's a long story."

"I don't mind long stories," Jasmine said. "That's why I'm here."

Danny shrugged. "It's the hippies. They made dope socially kosher in the Northwest. At barbeques and shit, people are just as likely to pass around joints as they are beers. People smoke at weddings, at parks, on the city street. The other day I saw an old lady with a walker hitting a joint. The cops don't care."

"That's not true," Andy said. "Ethan got a ticket."

"Who's Ethan?" Jasmine asked, passing the joint.

"A guide who moved away a few months ago," Danny said, turning to Andy. "A state cop gave him that ticket. Those fuckers cite people for jaywalking. But the real cops, the local guys, they don't give a shit about dope. It brings in too much money for the economy. Besides, we're all libertarians around here—what right does the government have regulating a plant?"

Jasmine asked, "So there is still a lot of pot being grown in this valley?"

Danny smiled. "Definitely."

"You know this firsthand?" Andy asked.

Danny didn't answer.

"But my question remains: why is the stuff in the Northwest better than elsewhere?"

Danny studied the end of the joint. "Indoor was invented here. In Eugene, in the seventies. Once growers started growing year round, they started getting four or five harvests a year instead of just one."

"Okay," Jasmine said, nodding. "Which meant they could increase the speed of the plant's evolution?"

"Exactly," Danny said. "The dope went from being average to being the poop overnight. And nobody outside Seattle or San Fran started growing indoors until the eighties." The joint smoldered between his fingers. "The better the Northwest's dope got, the more entrenched the dope culture got. The more entrenched the dope culture got, the less the cops cared. The less they cared, the more people started growing. Now, not even the shit from Amsterdam compares."

Danny had always been a stoner, but he'd never known so much about dope. For ten years, he had been buying little bags from an old high school buddy. Somebody—Trey?—had given him a history lesson.

"Do you think I could ask you more about this tomorrow?" Jasmine asked. "Maybe over coffee?"

"Sure," Danny said. "Off the record or whatever."

She laughed. "Definitely. Shosh would kill me if I cited her husband as my pot expert."

Danny chuckled, combing his fingers through the blue water. "Do you want another joint?" he asked Jasmine.

But she was lost studying the boiling surface of the water.

Danny waved his fingers in front of her face. "Do you want another?"

"Christ no!" she said. "I'm thoroughly toasted."

But Danny took another from the tin can anyway.

Jasmine stood from the tub, water glazing her skin, and stepped over the side. Another wavy tattoo sprawled across the small of her back. Then it was gone, lost behind her towel. "That's it for me, boys. I'm still on right-coast time."

"Wrong-coast time," Danny said.

"Maybe," she said, "but nonetheless, I need some shut-eye." She puffed out her chest like a movie cowboy. "Think I'll roll out my sleepin' things and tip the ol' hat over the ol' eyes." She finished her beer and stepped inside.

Andy turned to Danny and went for it. "So, Trey's got you growing for him?"

Danny laughed. "Hardly."

"You sure seem to know a lot about this shit all of the sudden."

Danny shrugged and passed the joint. But Andy waved it away.

"What did Bridge send you to Eugene for?" Danny asked.

"A couple boxes of building supplies. He overpaid me."

Danny was staring at him. "A little money to help you move to Colorado."

Andy splashed water over his face.

Then Danny said, "Have you called your daddy yet? He'll be stoked you're finally leaving this place. Maybe he'll buy you something real nice." He toked so hard that he broke into a cough, a cough that sent seizures through his body—the hand holding the joint dove underwater. After he regained his composure, Danny saw the soaked roach and flipped it over the railing. He turned to Andy, his eyes hidden behind a red glaze. "What were you saying?"

Andy sat up on the edge of the tub. "Why are you smoking like this?"

"Like what?"

"Like your dad drinks?"

"What do you care?"

"I care about you."

"Fag."

"You don't have to be a dumbass."

Danny's jaw locked and his eye twitched.

"You can talk to me," Andy said. "Whatever it is."

Danny didn't respond.

"I'm just confused because—" Andy said.

"You would be," Danny said. "You're the same. Wouldn't know the real world if it ran you over. Just a sheltered rich kid. There's always someone ready to save you. People like me, we don't get a safety net."

"Looks like you've got a nice safety net now," Andy said, pointing at the house. "Nicer than me, anyway."

"And," Danny shouted, splashing a wave of water onto the deck, "we don't take shit from pansy-assed Audi drivers. He's lucky I didn't smash his head through the windshield and carve out his tongue with a shard of glass. Fucking, I could of."

"Calm down."

"Fuck you. Judging me. You're just a fucking tourist like the rest of them." He snatched his beer and heaved it. Glass shattered in the driveway. "You're just here until you've taken all you can, then you'll be gone. Just like them."

Andy jumped out of the hot tub and laid a towel between them. "Calm down, Danny. You're talking crazy."

"Fuck you," Danny said again. "All up on your ivory horse. At least I don't have to beg for money. At least I don't have to call my fucking daddy and get an extension on my allowance. At least I can fend for myself. Hank Stamper, my ass. You act all smart, but you don't know shit."

"Danny, calm down," Andy said, backing away. It was time to leave.

Danny rose from the water, pointing toward the trucks. In the blue fog, he towered like a statue. "Sure, leave!" he shouted. "That's what you do best." He looked ready to leap from the water. "I don't need you anyway."

Andy retreated down the deck, grabbed his clothes, and crossed the black driveway to his truck. As he opened the door, the ball of his foot spread abnormally wide—and wouldn't accept his weight. He pulled himself up into the truck, using the steering wheel for support. In the yellow glow of the cab light, he saw the blood, and under closer examination, the meat of his foot—a shard of glass had razored him open.

He started the truck and reversed into the night, without so much as glancing back.

CHAPTER 6

Around four in the morning, he awoke, the sheets soggy in the darkness. In the half-consciousness of waking, he thought the river had flooded and was lapping over the bed: the apocalypse had come.

But when he snapped on the light, a red stain crawled over the sheets. Blood oozed continually from the two-inch wound.

The emergency clinic in Ipsyniho stitched the cut and charged him $250 for the service. Dr. Campbell told him not to wade the river for at least a week. "I'm serious about this, Andy. You need to treat this laceration delicately."

On the drive home, the morning sun just cresting the eastern ridge, he couldn't stop worrying about Danny. He shouldn't have left him in the hot tub. The hot water could have gotten the best of his drunk mind and pulled him face first into the bubbles. He'd always worried Danny would die in an accident, and something about this scenario—the tenor of the newspaper headline: Area River Guide, Drunk, Drowns in Hot Tub—seemed too tragically possible.

Mr. Kepinger was on his porch as Andy drove past, and they shared a wave. The old man started every day on that porch, watching the sunlight flood the valley. This time, however, he pointed down the driveway and shrugged.

Danny's truck was parked next to Andy's house, and even from a distance, he could see the silhouette of someone sitting in the cab, waiting. The person looked too short to be Danny—was it Shoshana?

He pulled up behind the truck and stalled the engine. The silhouette didn't move. This was the moment. It had happened.

But then Danny's wide forearm pushed open the door, and Danny's utterly alive red hair stepped into the morning light. He gave a tentative wave, his eyes squinting against a hangover.

"Morning," Andy said as coolly as he could, keeping the door between them.

"I don't particularly remember last night," Danny said. "I know that sounds like an excuse, but I don't mean it to be. I ended up drunk, and nothing good happens when I end up drunk." He stepped toward Andy. "And this morning I found a broken bottle and a smear of blood in my driveway."

Andy stepped gingerly from the truck, walking on his heel to keep the stitches off the ground. "It's nothing," he said. "I just stepped on that broken bottle while I was leaving."

Danny came over and gave Andy his shoulder. "Don't walk on it," he said.

"It's nothing. Just a little cut. Doc Campbell stitched it up. My own fault."

Once inside, Danny saw the bloody sheets. He looked absently out the window. "Before those beers, I drank some whiskey. More than some, actually. Andy," he turned. "I'm sorry for whatever I said. I didn't mean any of it."

"Forget it."

Danny rubbed his eyes. "I can't drink any more. Not with a baby coming. I won't be a drunk for a father."

"You won't be. You care. That's more than a lot of dads."

Danny snorted and shook his head. He laughed at himself and fingered his eye like he had something in it. "Sorry, I don't mean to sound all poor me."

"You don't. You know I'm here anytime you need an ear."

Danny picked up a picture from the table—a picture of a big steelhead being released. Andy had taken it seven or eight years before, on a winter day when the river was in perfect condition. Danny was the one releasing the fish, though only his hands were visible. "I just want to be good at being a father," he said.

"You're good at everything you do. I'm sure parenting is a skill like any other. You'll get it wired."

Danny didn't seem convinced.

"It probably isn't that different than fishing, really. You've got a creature and you want to provoke a certain reaction, in this case happiness I would imagine, and you've got a vest-load of techniques to try, and the trick is figure out which one—"

"I don't think it will be anything like fishing," Danny said, "but thanks anyway."

"What do I know anyway."

Danny walked into the kitchen. "Can I make you anything? Some breakfast?"

"I'm good."

"What did the doc visit set you back?" Danny pulled out his wallet.

"Nothing."

"Bullshit. I know you're tight on funds now. What did the doc set you back?"

"Nothing," Andy said. "Besides, I cut my own foot."

"Fine," Danny said. "But I'm making you some breakfast." He opened the refrigerator and pulled out the eggs.

"Really, Danny, I just ate. There's no need."

Danny pulled a pan from the wall and clicked on the stove. "I'm going to tell you something," he said, dropping a dollop of butter into the pan, "something that has to stay right here. No bullshit."

"Sure," Andy said. "No bullshit."

"Bridge and Trey can't know that I've told you anything. Nobody can know that you know. Scrambled or over easy?"

"Over easy, if you're making it."

Danny cracked a pair of eggs and tossed the shells into the compost container beside the sink. "I started helping as soon as Trey came up here last winter," he began. And he continued, explaining how the three of them had found a wet, south-facing slope up in the headwaters of the Ipsyniho, a place only accessible by following a maze of old logging roads and how they had trucked in three hundred planting buckets, a hundred and fifty yards of organic planting soil, and three hundred marijuana starts. "We put in a holding tank up the slope on top of the spring, and we rigged drip lines to all the plants." Danny shook his head and laughed. "The real deal. Took us three weeks to set it up."

"You're joking," Andy said.

"No joke." Danny shook his head. "Do you realize how much a hundred and fifty yards of soil is? That's a semi-truck load. Of course, we moved it in six dump truck trips. Bridge knows a guy."

He had been expecting something like this, but even so, he couldn't believe it. This was too much. "A semi-truck?"

"If you're going to do it, you might as well do it right. Can't trust the soil up that high to be any good." Danny flipped the eggs. "Trey and Bridge have been taking turns checking on the plants all summer. They're getting close." He turned off the heat, letting the eggs finish on the residual heat. "But we've run into a hell of a dam. Do you have any coffee?"

"In the freezer. Does Shoshana know about this?" Why would she sit idly by and let Danny take such enormous risks? Especially now?

"Well," Danny said, "that's tricky. She knows a little bit."

"A little bit?"

"Listen," Danny said, "you can't say a word to her. Andy, I'm serious about this. You can't say a word. She knows that I'm helping, but she thinks I'm doing legit logistical work, stuff I couldn't get busted for."

"Why would Trey give you a house for simple logistical work?"

Danny frowned. "Trey wouldn't. But the house is more complicated than that. They're trying to get investors. They need a show house if people are to commit. That's how I sold it to Shosh. Plus, we're making payments." He smiled. "Of course, once we harvest—if we harvest—" he knocked on the wooden cabinet, "the house will be ours outright. I'll explain it to her then."

"Does this seem like a smart time to be getting into this kind of thing? I mean with the baby and everything."

"There's never been a better time. Start his life off right, you know?" Danny flipped the eggs. "I'm doing this one time and that's it. We'll be set. Between my guiding and Shosh's art, we'll have a comfortable life.

A safety net. Everything the baby needs to grow up healthy and happy. A good house is the key to it all."

"But you could end up in prison."

Danny shook his head. "People have been growing dope in this valley forever, good people, people you know. When was the last time you heard of a bust?" The water pot hissed, and he poured its contents over the coffee at the bottom of the French press. He walked to the front window and stared at the blackberries in the distance. "Everything will be fine, if we can overcome this one problem."

"Trey wants me involved because he thinks I can solve this problem?"

Danny shrugged. "Well, yeah, that's why we came to you."

Andy scoffed. "You know, maybe I'm a bit square, but three hundred plants? It just seems too big, too much risk."

"Don't be a sally. The road we've been using to access the zone— that's what we call it, 'the zone'—was closed to vehicles last week. Fire danger. All the back roads were closed. BLM and the Forest Service locked their gates."

"Bridge told me," Andy said, "when we went after his elk."

"We're talking about 900 pounds of dope here. We can't carry 900 pounds twenty-two miles. Not without an army of sherpas." Danny looked Andy in the eye, on the verge of saying something more.

"What?"

He turned and walked back into the kitchen, grabbing a pair of plates from the cupboard. He flipped an egg on each plate.

"What are you suggesting?"

Danny delivered the eggs and a bottle of Tapatio. "We'll have to wait on the coffee."

"Hell with breakfast," Andy said. "What are you talking about?"

"We can't carry it," Danny said, busting the yolk of his egg, "but we can boat it."

Danny drove them up river, a travel mug of coffee in his hand. As the truck squealed around the corners, he explained the proposal. "Boating it was my idea. The zone is at the top edge of the Wikkup Canyon.

Nobody runs that section, so we could move all the dope without seeing anybody."

Andy examined the man beside him. "Nobody boats it because that canyon is unrunnable."

Danny chuckled. "Don't be so dramatic."

"I'm not being dramatic. You're talking about the Wikkup Canyon on the upper river?"

"The one and only."

"It can't be run."

"Sure," Danny said, "you wouldn't want to run it in a typical drift boat. But I'm not proposing that."

Andy gripped the dashboard as they powered around an especially sharp corner. "Do you know how many kayakers have died on that section?"

"That's not the issue."

"It's entirely the issue!" Andy shouted.

"But we're *entirely* not going to run it in a kayak," Danny said. "At first I thought heavy water catamarans because they're so stable, but they're too wide for some of those tight squeezes. So I talked to some boat builders and figured it out: sixteen-foot river dories with a complete hull cap. You could dive one of those things headlong into a standing wave and not get an ounce of water inside. But they feel like a drift boat when you're oaring one and are plenty narrow enough for the canyon water."

His foot throbbed like the skin was about to split open. He shifted in his seat, trying futilely to find a position that lessened the pain. "This is impossible. Not even Prince or Preacher dared run Wikkup." Prince Helfrich and his preacher buddy Veltie Pruitt—two old-time McKenzie guides who'd built early drift boat prototypes and treated them like saddles for the river's broncos—claimed Wikkup was a death trap. "And those guys ran rapids that even modern raft guides rope around."

Danny scoffed. "But Prince and Preach oared board-and-batten boats with square sterns. If they were alive today and had modern river dories, they'd run it."

"You've lost your mind. Does Shoshana know this part?"

He turned to Andy. "You promised not to tell her anything." When the truck tires touched the shoulder's gravel, he gave his attention back to the road. "Besides, we really don't have any other options. Either we boat it out or it'll mold up there before the roads reopen."

"It just might have to mold."

"And give Steamboat to White Oak? Not a chance."

Andy shook his head. "I'm not doing this. I'm not taking a boat through Wikkup. You're not either."

Danny straightened in his seat. "Thanks, mom." The tires squealed around a corner. He accelerated and shifted from third to fourth. "Fine," he said. "Then I'll run it twice."

The only thing more dangerous than the two of them running Wikkup Canyon would be running it alone. If the boat ended up pinned against a midstream rock, or trapped in the trough of a large wave, another boat would be needed to free it. And if one boat were to tip— god forbid—another would be needed to pick up the swimmer and get him out of the canyon. "How can you even get a boat to that section?" Andy asked. There were no ramps above Wikkup. Kayakers carried their boats to the water.

"The highway touches the river one last time before going the long way around Wolf Mountain. That's where we're headed now."

"And if a person survived the descent, where would they take out?"

"Altitude Ramp," Danny said.

But Altitude was just a one-way ramp, a put-in that required a drift boat to be winched down a forty-five degree slide. "You can't take out there."

"Sure you can," Danny said. "Just attach a tow cord to the bow and drag it up with the truck. Easy. I tested it."

They'd already passed Moonshine Creek and were now flying along the upper river, a section of mostly plunge pools and fast rapids. Here the river rocked and rolled, attracting hordes of rafters during the summer months. Few fishing guides with their hard-sided boats dared run this section—and this was still miles below the canyon. Up there, the river would be smaller, and dropping at a much steeper gradient. Andy shook his head, trying to imagine what such water would look like from the oarsman's seat.

Twenty minutes later, Danny pulled off the road and shut down the truck. Above them, the craggy faces of the mountains cut the wind, producing an endless low-pitched howl. A snow drift remained tucked in a crevasse on Wolf Mountain. While not the highest of the Cascades, these mountains were certainly the most radical in the entire range, made so by the sharp river that gouged them open.

Here the road abandoned the Ipsyniho, choosing to go south around Wolf Mountain, following an easier route into the high desert of central Oregon. Andy opened the door and delicately applied weight to his foot. The air bit at his face, artic cold even at nine a.m. No other engines could be heard.

"This is where I thought we'd put in, on the day in question." Danny pointed over the edge. Goose bumps textured his arm.

The river raged fifty feet below, already churning, white and violent. "You're insane," Andy said.

Danny smiled.

On the way back downstream, they pulled off into Mamma's Diner, the highest outpost of civilization on the river. It was a single-room operation, frequented by rafters mostly, and had earned a reputation for its homemade blackberry pie. The rafting season was all but over, and theirs was the only truck in the parking lot.

The server, maybe Mamma herself, looked up from a library copy of *Housekeeping* as they walked through the door. "Hey, boys," she said, her gray hair held back by a bandana, "take your pick of tables." They chose a corner booth, under a bear head that protruded from the wall.

They'd just started looking at the menus when the woman appeared beside the table. She flipped over their coffee cups and snuck a glance at Andy's foot. "What did you do there, hun?"

"Stepped on a piece of glass," he said, aware again of the throbbing.

"Let me guess: a busted beer bottle?" she asked.

Andy nodded. "I was barefoot and climbing into my truck."

Two RVs roared past the diner, their engines screaming to get up the hill. The first vehicles they'd seen since coming up this high.

The woman looked from the RVs back to Andy's foot. "Probably some out-of-state wanker who busted that bottle," she said. "Too busy sunning himself to take his leftovers to the recycle bin." She examined both Andy and Danny, rubbing her forehead. "You boys from town, right?"

"More or less," Danny said.

"Figured as much. You got river tans and rowing muscles. Fishing guides?"

"Spot-on," Danny said.

"What drags you up this high? Rare we get fishing guides. Mostly the splash and giggle crowd."

"Just up sightseeing," Danny said a bit too urgently.

She raised her eyebrows, then poured coffee into the cups. "Wasn't my business to ask anyway."

A moment passed and she said, "You know, I see that cut as meta-phorical. A symbol, you understand, saying something in a roundabout kind of way. Those tourists come, they break things, and then us locals get hurt. It's been that way around here since the dawn of time. Don't figure it'll change anytime soon." She pushed her glasses up her nose, bringing her gaze back into the room. "Course my book circle thinks I'm a bit of a semiotic."

"Nothing wrong with that," Andy said.

"I'll do a BLT," Danny said. "Shosh won't let bacon within a half-mile of the house."

"Sure thing, hun. Aged cheddar or regular sharp?"

"Regular sharp."

Andy ordered a prosciutto and rye. As she collected the menus, Danny asked for two blackberry pies to go. "For tonight," he said to Andy.

"Good choice," she said. "But the pies won't be perfect. Berries are running a bit late this year. I'm stuck using last year's fruit."

"No worries," Danny said. "Still the best fruit pie in the valley."

"In the state." She smiled and headed back to the kitchen.

A clean and new pickup pulled into the parking lot, and of all the empty spots in the lot, took the one next to Danny's truck. A pair of binoculars sat on the dashboard. Two men stepped out, wearing nearly matching clothes: clean military boots, green Carharts, and long-sleeve camouflage shirts. One was clean shaven, the other had sideburns and scruff. They weren't the same age, maybe ten or fifteen years apart. And they didn't look like the kind of guys who would be friends, one a biker type, the other a golfer maybe.

Danny corrected his posture.

The two walked in, nodded at Andy and Danny, and sat down in a booth on the opposite side of the diner. When Mamma appeared beside their table, they ordered without looking up from the menus.

"DEA," Danny whispered.

"What?"

"Feds, for sure."

Both the men had removed their baseball caps. "I don't know."

The older one looked up and caught them staring.

Andy nodded as casually as possible.

The man raised his eyebrows and went back to his menu.

As Mamma walked by, Danny signaled her. "Yes, hun? More coffee?"

Danny said, "Can we get our order to go?"

She glanced at the guys in the booth, then said, "Sure thing."

A few moments later, she appeared with two paper plates covered in tin foil and a pair of heavy pie boxes. She placed them on the table and looked at the order pad in her hand. "That'll be thirty-three sixty-five."

Danny pulled two twenties from his pocket. "Keep it," he said.

She leaned over and whispered, "They're here every day. Same time. I asked what brought them up this high, and they said elk hunting. But elk season closed two days ago and they're still coming in." She shrugged. "Symbol search that one."

Danny grabbed the pies and his plate and walked out the door. By the time Andy caught up, Danny already had the truck running.

They arrived back at the yurt and found Shoshana and Jasmine sunning themselves on the porch, each slurping a glass of orange juice through a twisty straw. "Endless summer," Jasmine said, her eyes hidden behind sunglasses.

Shoshana pulled her sunglasses down her nose, looking at Danny. "Where'd you go? You left the boat."

"Scout a new drift," Danny said.

"Which drift?" Shoshana asked.

"High up," Danny said, turning to Jasmine. "We should have rain by now."

Shoshana squinted, looking from Danny to Andy, then back to Danny.

Jasmine yanked her sunglasses from her face and studied Andy's bandaged foot.

"It's nothing," Andy said. "Cut it on a little glass."

Shoshana cringed. "You should let Rita look at that."

"Doctor Campbell stitched it up. It's fine."

"Yeah, but Rita knows her shit," Shoshana said. "Herbs that might help. Wouldn't hurt to get her advice. Doctors don't know everything."

"Did my folks call?" Danny asked.

Shoshana finished the rest of her orange juice. "Showing up around four," she said. "Your mom is bringing baby clothes."

"Already?" Danny said.

"Tell me about it. I don't have a belly yet and she's already counting the grandchild."

"She's just excited, that's all," Danny said. "No need to be hard on her."

"This is what mothers-in-law do," Jasmine said. "A new baby is coming into the family. The redux baby. Their chance to be perfect." She sucked up the remainder of her orange juice through the straw. "It happened to my sister's mo-in-la when she got knocked up."

"At least you'll get free stuff," Andy said.

"It's not like my parents have any extra money," Danny said. "I hope they're not using credit cards again."

"It's just bad juju, that's all," Shoshana said.

"Just seems nice to me," Andy said.

Jasmine yawned. "You boys interested in a little foray to the hot springs? Shosh and I are going."

"Hell, yes," Danny said. "Which hot springs?"

"Which one was it Shosh?"

"Lion Springs."

"We're there," Danny said. "Right, Andy?"

New blood was on the bandage, probably from all the walking. The doctor had told him to spend the day on the couch. "Nah, I should—"

"Of course you're coming," Danny said.

"I think Andy is afraid of water," Jasmine said. "He tried to dodge the hot tub last night too."

"He doesn't have to come if he doesn't want to," Shoshana said.

"What the hell," he said. "Doc's crazy if she expects a person to waste a perfectly good day on the couch."

They piled into Jasmine's rental car, a new electric Toyota, and drove the twenty minutes across the valley to Steamboat Creek. Lion Springs sat high in the headwaters, a stream that appeared from a crack in a cliff wall, then cascaded twenty-five feet to a pool below. Hundreds of years before, the Calapooia had built rock tubs below the waterfall, each big enough to seat six or eight people. The water in the top tub was almost scalding, while the water in the bottom was room temperature.

The Ipsyniho Valley had a reputation for plentiful hot springs. People drove from as far away as Portland to spend the day soaking at various pools and tubs. Enough people came to support a small resort up Bracken Springs—a cluster of cement pools hidden in a grove of imported bamboo. Despite all the tourist pressure, a few natural springs remained off the maps. Lion Springs was one, known only to select locals. Bridge had taken Danny and Andy there one night a few years back, before Shoshana. "If you let this secret out," Bridge had half-joked, the full moon behind him, "the river will drown you both."

"Don't write about this," Danny said as they parked at a nondescript wide point in the road.

"I can keep a secret." Jasmine scanned the surrounding vegetation. "How did this place get its name?"

"Mountain lions," Andy said.

Danny tossed a towel over his shoulder. "Supposedly, cougars hang out here in the winter. Our buddy Bridge has seen them sleeping beside the pools."

"In winter?" Jasmine asked.

"Probably in summer too." Danny smiled.

"Don't worry about it," Shoshana said, rolling her eyes. "These Oregon guys like to scare you with lion this and bear that. I've yet to see hide or hair of either."

"And Bigfoot," Danny said. "Got to watch out for all the Bigfeet."

"I'll have my camera ready," Jasmine said.

Danny helped Andy hobble up an overgrown trail to the base of the falls, a distance of nearly half a mile. Once they arrived, Andy sat on the first flat rock, a boulder the size of a car that overlooked the pools. Steamboat Basin sprawled out in the distance. On the far ridge, below a massive clearcut, sunlight shimmered off a large window—Bridge and Rita's place. The house danced in the hot distance. Then, for a moment, the image stabilized, and Andy thought he saw the silver sheen of Trey's Volvo in the driveway. But before he could be sure, the image gave way to the heat.

"Let me help you the rest of the way," Danny said.

Jasmine and Shoshana were almost to the pools. "Why would Trey be at Bridge's right now?"

Danny squinted into the distance, then shrugged. "Why wouldn't he be?"

Andy imagined Trey patting Bridge on the back, smiling that smile. "Come on," Danny said. "Give me your hand."

"My leg is pretty cramped," Andy said. The bandage had browned with dust and blood. "I'm going to rest a few."

"Suit yourself," Danny said. "Holler if you need a hand." He trotted down the trail.

Jasmine, her back to Andy, stripped and dropped her clothes onto a rock beside the second pool. Her olive skin seemed to glow, contrasting with the drab rocks, and her hips possessed a symmetrical curviness, their outer edges just wider than her shoulders. As she turned, a long scar appeared on her thigh, then the fluid rounds of her breasts, the nipples small and black. She tiptoed into the water and sank until only her head remained visible. She said something, but the breeze devoured the words.

Shoshana grabbed her shirt, about to pull it over her head, then stopped and looked uphill toward Andy. Before her eyes could find him, he looked up—to the water freefalling from the cliff. An eagle or a vulture circled high above, its silhouette occasionally disappearing behind the rock wall.

"Get down here," Jasmine yelled, her voice echoing against the cliff. "Nobody gets a free peep show."

"My foot," he shouted. "I won't look."

"Come on," she yelled. "That foot is no excuse. Don't be shy. We're all built from the same blueprint."

"I better not," he said.

Danny was in the water now, whispering with Shoshana, their bodies lost under the surface's sheen.

"Well," she yelled, "at least come down here so we don't have to scream."

He pushed himself up and hopped, slowly, down the stone path to the pool. Soon he stood by the water and was about to sit when Jasmine said, "Now that you've made it this far, drop your damn drawers and get in the water."

Danny and Shoshana were engrossed in each other, and Jasmine turned her back, giving Andy privacy. "Drop them," she said.

But he needed to keep his foot dry, doctor's orders. He pulled up his pant leg and sat, lowering his good foot into the boiling water.

"Oh, come on," Jasmine said, turning. "At least get naked. It's more fun that way."

He pulled off his shirt and dropped his pants. Jasmine smiled as he sat back down beside the pool, the rocks warm on his cheeks. "You have nothing to be shy about," she said.

Shoshana took a brown stone in her hand and dunked it in the water. "Rita says the minerals in these stones are good for your complexion." She rubbed her finger over the stone and a tan paste appeared.

He could only see her shoulders above the water, but he remembered their width in his hands, their softness. These were not thoughts he wanted. "You think steelies have ever made it up this high?"

"Not with this water temp."

Jasmine wiped paste on her cheeks. "Hippie Noxzema," she said. Soon all of their faces were obscured by the stuff.

He found a soft and warm rock just under the surface and rubbed it until the paste appeared. He painted a mask over his own face.

Jasmine rubbed the muck down her arms. "Were you guys yelling last night? I thought I heard yelling."

"We were joking around," Danny said. "Guy stuff."

Shoshana squinted at Danny. "Is that when Andy cut his foot?"

"Yeah," Danny said.

"Name the book," Jasmine said. She had covered herself in the paste, including running it through her hair. The edges of her body bled into the nearby stones. Only the green of her eyes remained, two points of color. She raised her hand as if holding a spear.

"*Lord of the Flies*," Shoshana said.

"Ding, ding, ding." Jasmine splashed Shoshana.

Shoshana splashed back, then cupped her two hands together and forced a splash at Danny—hitting him squarely in the face.

He blew the water from his lips, then slapped at the surface, blasting spray over all of them.

The water drenched the bandage on Andy's foot. But whatever, he needed to change the bandage anyway. He collected a load of paste from the rock in his hand and painted an "A" over his heart.

"Is that your name tag?" Danny asked, already painting a "D" on his own chest.

Shoshana just stared at him.

And Jasmine's eyes flashed between both of them.

Danny's parents were sitting on the porch when they returned from Lion Springs. Nancy had a romance novel in her hands, Jon a Milwaukee's Best.

Nancy rushed toward the car, her dyed red hair frozen with hairspray. As Shoshana stepped out of the car, Nancy was there whispering to Shoshana's bellybutton.

Jon swaggered off the porch. "There she is! The new mamma." He kissed Shoshana's cheek and rolled his eyes at Nancy. "Don't mind her. She'll settle down in eight or nine years." Then he saw Andy. And his face fell straight.

He had aged five years in the last one, the skin of his face sagging under his jaw. His nose glowed red, and as he approached, the red became laced with blue, thread-like veins. He stopped an arm's reach away and sucked his tooth.

"Howdy, Jon."

A smile broke Jon's glare, and he offered his colossal hand, a mitt made lumber-hard by years working saws. Andy took it and the man pulled him close, slapping him on the back. "Goddamn," Jon said. "We thought you were gone for good." He stepped back, but continued to hold Andy's hand. "Nance, you see the shithead I got hold of?"

She turned. "Andrew?"

"Yes, ma'am."

She hurried around the car, and stopped just short of a hug, glaring. Finally, she poked him in the shoulder. "That's for missing my baby's wedding." Then she poked him in the stomach. "And that's for not calling to tell us you were okay."

Inside, Andy, Jon, and Danny watched from the kitchen as Nancy unpacked a suitcase of baby things. Shoshana sat on the couch, taking each item as it was handed to her, saying over and over, "You shouldn't have." Jasmine took the blankets and diapers and onesies and baby socks and baby hats as Shoshana handed them to her. "This should be illegal, it's so stinking cute," Jasmine said.

"I bust my ass all day to make my eighty bucks, and that one over there," Jon nodded toward Nancy, "goes to the mall and spends a hundred and sixty in twenty minutes." He shook his head. "At this rate, we'll be broke before this baby gets himself born."

"We've got some money," Danny said. "We don't need you buying us this stuff."

"With you boys," Jon said, "we didn't spend one sixty in the entire first year. Babies are cheap, if you let them be."

Danny crossed his arms and looked into the distance. For a moment, he was gone from the room.

Jon touched Andy's elbow, and whispered, "She's finally getting that third baby. I think my wife reckons Shoshana's womb to be an extension of her own." He wiped his nose, "Is it whiskey time yet? A toast to the new McDonald?"

"Goodman," Danny said. "And maybe we should wait for every-body else to show up before busting into the hard stuff."

"Nonsense," Jon said. "The more toasts, the healthier the baby." He opened a cabinet and reached for the tumblers on the top shelf. "You sure about that? About Goodman? Of course, it's your choice."

Danny dipped a chip in the bowl of salsa.

Jon touched Danny's arm and muttered, "I just mean, you wouldn't want to close any doors on the kid. Life's hard enough. It's the Jews they come after first, you know."

"America ain't the place it used to be," Danny muttered. "This ain't 1951."

Jon glanced to Shoshana, then back to Danny. "In 1951, they said 'this ain't 1939.' In 1939, they said—"

"We know, Dad."

"Think about it. That's all I ask. The Jews don't offer anything that the Methodists don't."

Danny yanked his arm free. "We have thought about it. We're Jews, and we're proud of it, and that's what it offers. I'm not ditching my peo-ple just because it might be easier."

Jon's jaw locked tight and his eyes narrowed. "I never ditched nobody."

Danny shrugged. "I'm just saying."

Jon swiped the whiskey and a tumbler off the counter and headed for the door. A moment later he was on the porch, spitting over the edge.

Nancy yelled from the living room. "You two butting heads already?"

"It's nothing, Ma," Danny said. "Dad just needs a cig." Then to Andy, "And some therapy, paranoid old fart."

On the porch, Jon leaned against the railing, a cigarette in his hand.

Nancy appeared beside them, her hand on Danny's arm. "Get out there," she said to her son. "I don't want him moping the rest of the day just because you two got in a tussle."

"Come on," Danny said. "I didn't do anything."

She tipped her head ever so slightly—a look worth a thousand lec-tures.

"Fine," Danny said, already heading toward the door.

"And Dans," Nancy called after him, "get that bottle away from him."

Years before, Danny had talked about his dad's drinking. "He's not a real drinker. Not like those lushes at the Woodsmen, warming the same stool day in and day out. He only needs it to help him sleep."

Nancy watched the two of them out the window. "You like this with your father, Andrew?"

"We don't talk much," he said.

"I think it's hard on sons to see their fathers slow down. Makes them realize the world is built flimsy."

Out the window, Danny reached for the whiskey bottle, took a sip, and pointed into the distance. As Jon turned to look, Danny sat the bottle beside the hot tub.

"We women seem to know that from the get-go."

"Seems about right."

"I remember one time," Nancy said, "must of been when Danny was twelve maybe. His voice hadn't made the man-switch yet, and Joel was still with us. Danny's aunt and uncle were in town from Redding, showing off their new baby, Olivia. She was getting handed from person to person, everyone cooing at her and ogling. When Jon held her, she broke out crying and wouldn't stop. But little Danny whispered something in her ear and she stopped. Just like that." Nancy smiled. "He's such a tender soul. The first time he ever held a baby, I think."

She touched Andy's arm with her finger tips. "You know, Andrew, Danny didn't do too well with you gone."

"Seems like he did pretty well," Andy said, gesturing toward the house around them.

"Money-wise, maybe. Although god knows where they got this money. I don't want to know nothing about it. No," she looked at her son outside. "Once a little brother, always a little brother. Danny needs somebody around, somebody he can tell his secrets to, somebody he can look up to."

"He's got Shoshana." Shoshana and Jasmine laughed on the couch, their shoulders touching.

"A wife isn't the same," she said. "Not for Danny, anyhow."

Once Bridge and Rita arrived, Danny fired up the barbeque. From a cooler filled with ice and microbrew, Bridge extracted a glass bowl containing two thick roasts in marinade. Nancy smelled the meat, and asked after the recipe.

Jon shouted to Rita, "Any births lately?"

"Actually," she said, "a healthy little girl at 5:12 this morning."

"You angel," Nancy said. "You must be exhausted."

A Volvo appeared shortly after, and Trey stepped out with a cloth Co-op bag, smiling of course. He shook Jon's and Nancy's hands, saying he'd "heard only great things."

"Andy," Trey said, crossing the porch. "Great to see you."

"Isn't it?"

Danny appeared from the house, and he and Trey exchanged a hug. "I've got something we need to discuss," Danny muttered.

Trey nodded. "Later."

After dinner, Andy sat on the porch, resting his wound. He would need to change the bandage first thing, once he got home. Rita, Nancy, and Shoshana stood a few feet away.

"How's your energy?" Nancy asked. "You seem to be kicking along better than most first-trimester mammas."

"I've got my moments," Shoshana said. "I puked outside Wildfire last night."

"Ah!" Nancy said, tossing her arms into the air. "I've been there!"

Rita sipped a glass of wine and laughed. "When I was pregnant with Cammie, we were living in a tent, and Bridge was finishing the house, and I was stuck peeing outside all the time."

"I remember this," Nancy said. "I used to bring the boys over."

"Wasn't bad until my tummy started getting in the way," Rita said, cradling an imaginary belly. "Whenever I squatted, I had to make room for this gargantuan thing. Had to completely take off my pants. Imagine that, me squatting in a clump of ferns, nude from the waist down!" She laughed. "I remember one day, Bridge was up on the roof pounding away, and I had to pee real bad. One of those urges that comes out of nowhere—you'll get them later. I barely made it to the ferns. It was such a relief, you know, I got a little lightheaded, and when I tried to stand back up, I got a Brackston Hicks. That cramp had me!"

"How did you get back up?" Shoshana asked.

"I didn't. I fell over!"

"Did Bridge come help?"

"No. I hollered to him, and you know what he said? 'One sec, babe, I'm taking a piss.' And he was! He was standing up there peeing over the edge!"

Shoshana laughed. "What is it with these Ipsyniho men and their need to pee outside? I can't convince Danny to use our perfectly functional bathroom."

"That's Jon's fault," Nancy said. "He potty trained the boys outside."

"It reassures them of their freedom." Rita puffed out her chest—her best impression of Bridge. "Look, I'm swinging my thing around and nobody can stop me!"

Shoshana rubbed her belly. "Maybe this one will be a little girl."

"We can hope!" Nancy said.

"Whatever it is, I'll be happy. Just a healthy baby, that's all I want."

"Once you've got them," Nancy said, "the hard part is letting them out of your sight. The world is a dangerous place."

The three of them stared at different points on the deck. Rita broke the silence. "All that talk of pee. Excuse me."

As Rita headed into the house, Nancy focused on Shoshana. "This house will be a great place for a baby. You'll want to put chicken wire along the railing of the deck, of course. But I'm sure you already thought about that."

"Uh-huh."

"You should have Danny build you a gate by the steps, while he's at it."

"Yeah."

"Just so you know, I'll come up anytime. If you need a few hours with your friends, or if you and Danny want to go camping. Jon and I will be glad to take the baby. Think of it as 'our baby,' if that lightens the load—I know how overwhelming a first child can be." Nancy glanced back at the house. "It just occurred to me, where are you putting the crib?"

"We're not using a crib. The baby will be in bed with us."

Nancy laughed, as if it was a joke—then realized Shoshana was serious. "Oh. Of course."

Jasmine climbed the deck stairs from the dark driveway, dropping a cigarette butt in a beer bottle. Jon was right behind her. They were laughing. Shoshana called to her friend.

Andy hobbled the other direction down the porch. He hadn't seen Trey or Danny in some time. Halfway around the house, he heard their voices. They stood near the fish-cutting table. He leaned into the roof's moon shadow.

"How would they have found it?" Trey asked. "Assuming they did."

"From an airplane maybe?" Danny said.

"We should tell Bridge."

A hand appeared on Andy's shoulder. He spun and found Bridge's dark shape. "Jesus!"

"Sorry," Bridge said. "I have some bad news. I couldn't get you a pass."

"A what?"

"To Carnival."

Andy had always gotten a pass to Carnival. He was a local. Locals always got passes.

"The Entrance Committee is made up of new people," Bridge said. "People I don't know. I told them we needed another pass, that one of our members hadn't received one, and they refused." Bridge sipped his beer. "To be honest, they were jerk-offs about whole thing. Like I was putting them out by asking."

"A new committee?"

"Yeah," Bridge said, sighing, "part of the great Carnival coup. It's no longer the Ipsyniho throwing a party for the world. It's the world throwing a party in our backyard and maybe we can come, if there's room. I pulled every string and couldn't drum up a ticket."

Jasmine was telling a story on the other end of the porch, and everyone laughed.

"Am I out then?" Andy asked. He couldn't be out.

"I say fuck 'em," Bridge said. "Sneak in and we'll hide you in the booth."

Trey touched Andy's elbow. "Just the guy I wanted to talk to." He raised his beer for Andy to clank.

Andy brought his beer to his lips.

Trey took a sip and said, "Have you given any thought to what we talked about?"

Danny's silhouette appeared beside Trey's.

Bridge whispered, "We're talking about one day's work. A boat trip. That's all."

"It'll be a well paid boat trip too," Trey said.

"Why the secrecy?" Andy asked, chuckling. "You guys are acting weird."

Bridge was straight-faced. "Technically, what we're talking about is a felony."

"But," Trey said, "it's a minor one. And with little chance of being caught. You'd be helping everybody: the valley, your friends, and yourself. And I know you could use the money right about now."

"But," Bridge continued, "there's very little risk."

"A minor risk with a big reward," Trey said.

Andy shook his head and laughed. "I don't think I'm your guy."

"We're prepared to pay you a year's wage for twelve hours of work," Bridge said.

Trey smiled. "Imagine. You could put a down payment on a place along the river. Or set yourself up any place in the world. Montana, maybe."

"I know we're springing this on you and you're a relatively straight guy, but we need an answer soon," Bridge said. "We're in a serious pinch. You'd be doing us an epic favor."

Danny crossed his arms, the bottle dangling from his fingers like an oar at rest. He would never survive that canyon alone.

Andy chugged his beer. "Is this all some huge joke, like you're filming me right now or something? Some prank to get even with me for not being at the wedding?" He laughed.

But he was the only one.

Bridge said, "Andy, we'll give you $50,000 for twelve hours. That's how badly we need you."

"Say that again?"

"You heard me. Fifty Gs. Well, a percentage on the end. Should work out to be about fifty. Got to get the stuff out, cleaned, and to the buyers first."

"Fifty Gs for a simple boat trip," Trey said.

"A boat trip with a few hundred pounds of weed as your passenger." Bridge smiled. "And I promise weed will make a better sport than Rich-Bob and his dingle-berry golf buddy."

Jon appeared on the deck. "There you all are." He sensed that he had interrupted something. "Sorry, just letting you know the ladies are cutting into the pie." He looked at Danny.

"We were just coming inside."

As they walked toward the house, Bridge held Andy back. "Whatever you decide, let us know soon, definitely before the end of Carnival. We're probably looking at next week, maybe the week after, if the weather holds."

In the kitchen, Danny cut one of the pies while Jasmine grabbed plates from the cupboard.

"To Carnival," Rita said, raising the glass into the air. "And to our two Carnival virgins!"

Trey raised his beer. Jasmine grabbed a stray bottle from the counter and the two of them shared a smile.

"Prepare to get your gaskets blown," Jon said.

CHAPTER 7

Drums echoed up the river, reverberating between the ridges—the endless samba call of Carnival. The drums wouldn't stop for four straight days and nights, maintained by a cycling troop of enthusiastic volunteers.

Andy dropped the boat off the trailer, this time loaded with camping gear instead of fishing rods, and pushed off downstream.

He was eager—if a bit anxious—to see Carnival again, see how it had changed. Since its conception, the event had been the social apex for the valley, if not the state. What had begun as a party for locals had swelled over the decades into a major festival, attracting people from the world over. The Ipsyniho's residents had always run the event. The old hippies worked side by side with other, more conservative folks to put the thing on. There was a lot of fun to be had—and money to be made. Some Ipsynihians made their year's income in these four days. But each season, as the profit from the event attracted bigger business interests, governance of the Carnival had slipped further and further from local control.

But he also needed the Carnival's respite. It was a place outside of places, a time outside of times. Four days spent wandering through the music, the dancing, the utter chaos could lift you from reality, only to redeliver you later with a new set of eyes—eyes enhanced with critical lenses, eyes capable of bringing the real world into sharper focus. The place, the event, conjured the words of a philosophy professor he had had years before: *Dionysus forces us to step past ourselves—so that we may look back and see ourselves in a clearer light.* He liked Carnival for the same reason he liked novels.

On day three, he would need to guide those clients of Stream Born's. But a lot of Carnival existed between now and then.

Everyone else was already there. Danny, Shoshana, and Jasmine, Jon and Nancy, Rita and Bridge, everybody. Their overnight passes allowed them to simply park and walk in legitimately.

The river carried the boat into a rapid, a short plunge with one move at the bottom. He pushed in, cocked the bow, and pulled hard on the oars—nailing the move in a single stroke. His arms owned the oars, the veins riding high over the muscles. For the first time since he returned, the boat felt a part of him. Its control demanded no more thought than his hands did. If he wanted around a boulder, the boat went around the boulder. No translation between the language of his mind and the language of the oars was needed.

But these rapids were a far cry from those of the upper river. There, the moves would come fast, one on top of the next. The waves would be high, much higher than the boat. And gaps between rocks would be narrow, narrow enough he would have to ship both oars and squeeze through. One missed stroke anywhere and the boat might swing out of control.

As the boat drifted by Long Tom Creek, the eastern boundary of the Carnival grounds, he worked the oars, slowing to a stop in the heavy current. The bank of the river had been severely eroded since he had last been here. The winter flood had left only tender walls of black loam, and no place to anchor the boat. He pushed on.

Just as the volume of the drums peaked, Andy spotted a cavern in the bank where the flood had undercut the roots of an ancient oak tree. The tree still stood, but now a cave big enough to hide a boat existed underneath. No one would ever find the boat there. But he would have to watch the weather—if on the errant chance the river rose, the boat might become pinned. Of course with this endless high pressure system, the odds of that happening seemed nil.

He backed into the cave and dropped anchor.

Overhead, a gap in the roots just as wide as his shoulders revealed blue sky. He shipped the oars and tucked his camping gear under the seats—he would come back for it once he found everybody. After double-checking the anchor and tying off the bowline just to be sure, he grabbed the roots and pulled himself into the tunnel.

That morning, he had wrapped his foot in a thick layer of gauze. The bandaged foot wouldn't fit in a shoe, so he wore his wading sandals. Now, climbing the roots, the foot ached. The sandal's limber sole allowed each step to bend. The doctor had said he would feel some relief after twenty-four hours. But thirty-six later, the cut hurt worse than it had at any point before. Once he found camp, he would elevate the foot and give it some time to heal.

The tunnel emerged in the middle of an especially fertile blackberry patch. Wide berries hung in grape-like clusters overhead. Fruity driblets lay scattered over the ground. Already, black juice stained his knees and palms, the smell heady and sublime. He followed a raccoon path.

And emerged into chaos: Red pumpkin-sized orbs floated by, hovering on the shoulders of people clad in black tights. Behind them, long ribbons of purples and blues corkscrewed through the air, then in unison, changed direction and did circles around their puppeteers.

A silver man—every centimeter of his naked body painted chrome—appeared in Andy's space. "Drop a top, my friend?" In his hand sat a sugar cube with a pink dot on it.

"Nah," Andy said. "I've learned my lesson."

He was in a crowd of dancers, each wearing a costume. A huge monkey spun, bumping Andy with his long tail. A green wood nymph leapt and shook, sticks and leaves barely covering her not-so-private private parts. A long Chinese new year dragon snaked by. Ahead, a pair of full-size jackalopes hopped. And Ronald Reagan waved to the crowd.

Booths lined the path, cubbies in the forest constructed of wooden frames. Many contained handmade clothing, musical instruments, paintings. One sold leather purses. Another, silver jewelry. Food booths: teriyaki and jalapeño wafting over the trail. Each booth acted like an eddy in a river, places a person could spin out of the main current and go nowhere for a while. In a booth that sold drums, a woman with dreads to her knees kept rhythm on a large djembe. Her beats were lost to the

Carnival's roar, her palms landing without sound. She looked at Andy and smiled.

Around him, peach colored dust hovered to waist level. Ronald Reagan wore Birkenstocks, his toenails painted neon red.

A girl, twelve maybe, her purple hair electrified.

Moldy body odor. Barbeque smoke. Patchouli.

In the first-aid booth, a stethoscope dangling over a Bob Marley T-shirt.

Andy gave himself to the music, to the crowd, skipping to the rhythm, and the former president slapped him on the back, nodding madly.

Sometime later, he spotted Rita sitting at a booth talking with a shirtless woman. On the table in front of her lay a miniature model of the Steamboat community and a list on which people could write their name if they wanted to receive more information. A banner read: Green Living Along the Ipsyniho. On the walls of the booth hung pictures of Danny and Shoshana's house and laminated blueprints.

Rita looked up, saw Andy, and smiled. "They're in the back," she said, tossing a thumb over her shoulder.

Behind the booth, sheets hung from cords that bisected the trees. They acted as walls, walls tie-dyed in oranges, reds, and greens. Andy followed the gaps between them and suddenly emerged in an enclosure.

Danny, Bridge, and Jon sat around a stone fire pit, a pile of coals smoldering. Danny wore a tiger-striped skirt, Bridge a kilt, and Jon a shirt that read: Been there, done that. When Bridge saw Andy coming, he thrust a bottle of Jack Daniels at him. "Ah, there he is! The great smuggler!" The bottle was warm in Andy's hand, the fluid inside nearly gone.

Jon pushed himself up from his chair and swayed over to Andy, faking a punch to his stomach. "Remember when Danny first dragged this kid off the river?"

"A bit green, wasn't he," Bridge said.

"He's nothing but a drifter now," Danny said, his eyes deeply stoned.

Jon's gaze dead-centered the Jack in Andy's hand. "Take your pull and pass the bottle, son."

Andy brought the liquor to his lips, and took a long pull. "Lava," he said.

Jon slapped him on the back and laughed, stumbling back into his lawn chair.

Andy turned to Danny. "Where's Shoshana?"

"At her booth," Danny said.

"Heard they wouldn't give you a pass," Jon slurred. "Fuck them. Every year they've got some new law. Barely gave Nance and me passes. Said we weren't locals no more on account of living in Eugene." He shook his head, his eyes more shut than open.

Bridge spit in the fire. "There ain't a whole lot of community spirit left in the show."

Jon screwed the lid on the bottle and tossed it over the fire. Bridge missed the catch.

"Now it's about bossing people around," Jon said. "Telling them what they can and can't do. Fascists!" Jon yelled.

Bridged laughed.

Jon continued, "Now it's about making us all into sandal-wearing yuppie wackos. You can't go nowhere without seeing a goddamn recycle station."

"Come on, Dad."

"I saw like five booths handing out pamphlets on saving trees! *Trees!* As if their own booths weren't made of lumber." Jon raised his hand toward Bridge. "Toss me back that bottle, Furry."

Bridge tossed the whiskey. "The real problem is the industry. Look at it. It's nothing but a fancied-up strip mall."

"Shoshana makes more money here in four days than she does in four months at Saturday Market," Danny said. "The real problem is the fucking sports."

Andy nodded. "Take, take, take."

"Fucking environmentalists," Jon said. He tipped the bottle back, searching for the last drop. "Goddamn it, Furry. You drank my juice."

"You boys man the fort," Bridge said, nearly falling. "We've got work to do."

Bridge wrapped his arm around Jon's neck and the two of them staggered toward the front of the booth.

Danny was rolling a joint. "They started a bit earlier than normal."

Andy stirred the coals with a long stick. "Carnival. That's what it's for."

They sat around the fire, listening to the drums and talking about the coming run of winter steelhead. Last year, the river had only been in shape long enough for Danny to run eight trips. Normally, he ran closer to thirty in the winter. "Counts were down too. In May, Shosh and I walked Steamboat for Fish and Wildlife and counted half as many spawning pairs as the year before. World's going to shit faster than ever."

A rustling came from the tents behind them, then a prolonged zipper sound, and a woman emerged up from the largest tent in the group. She shouted something back into the tent.

"That's Nikki," Danny said, "Trey's lady."

She was tall, taller than Trey, her blond hair pulled back in a pony tail. As she stepped out from the cluster of tents, a smaller version of herself appeared beside her leg, a little girl, maybe four or five years old.

Danny hid the joint. "Hey, Nikki."

She obviously didn't want to stop and talk, but she paused to be polite, and the little girl collided with her leg. "Hi Danny."

"This is Andy. You've probably heard me talk about him."

She looked across the fire and smiled. "Nice to meet you." She wore a tank top and yoga tights and Nikes. "Chloe and I need to get some food. Is Shoshana around?"

"At her booth," Danny said. "The corner of Peach Path and Kesey Street."

Nikki shook her head. "This place is dumbfounding."

"That's sort of the point, I think," Danny said.

Chloe tugged on her mom's pant leg.

"I thought I'd grab Shoshana a sandwich or something. She's got to be starving out there."

"What's your favorite part of Carnival so far, Chloe?" Andy asked.

The little girl smushed her face into her mom's leg. Nikki answered for her. "So far we're both totally overwhelmed."

146

"You might try the Kids' Kettle," Andy said. "Over on the west end. It's a playground with clowns and square dancing and stuff. More mellow than everywhere else."

Nikki sighed. "A world where clowns seem mellow."

Trey stepped out of the tent and zipped it up behind him.

Nikki glanced toward him, then turned to Andy. "Nice meeting you." She smiled then quickly led Chloe toward the front of the booth, away from Trey.

Trey walked to the edge of the fire, scratching his head. "The pleasures of being coupled."

"Trouble on the home front?" Danny said.

"I do the best I can." Trey yawned. "I thought bringing her to a party would be the best way to give a sense of the place."

"Giving her a sense of something," Andy said.

The music became deafening—the samba train had probably rounded the corner in front of the booth.

"You want to cruise?" Danny shouted.

"Definitely," Trey shouted back.

Andy raised his arm, showing his bare wrist. Everyone with a pass received a bracelet that had to be worn at all times. "Maybe I should lay low until after dark."

"Nonsense," Danny yelled. "Put on a long sleeve shirt. And here," he disappeared into his tent and reappeared with a two-foot tall red and white striped top hat. "Wear this."

The trails had grown more crowded since Andy had come up from the river. More people with shopping bags clogged the trails—Day Trippers, as the locals called them because they came from faraway cities simply to shop for art and handmade crafts during the daylight hours. There were more Day Trippers than Andy ever remembered seeing before. Danny and Trey wedged their way through the crowd, and Andy limped along behind—the hat swaying back and forth with each step.

After the last Carnival Andy had attended, he heard that ninety thousand people had bought Day Tripping passes, which could be purchased like any ticket to a concert. Another forty thousand had been issued All-Nighter passes, including venders, maintenance crews, and supposedly, the Ipsyniho locals. Bridge claimed Carnival had grown by ten percent each year since the Grateful Dead played in seventy-nine. Before that, it was a relatively intimate affair. There had been no booths then, or vendors, or even tickets—just people camping and playing music. But once the Dead came, everything changed.

Security guards lined the paths, men and women in bright orange shirts with radios on their belts. There hadn't been any security ten years ago, but now they were everywhere. They studied the crowd as it passed, looking for alcohol, drugs, whatever. If they found something they didn't like, they might eject a person from the grounds or call the police or, even worse, revoke that person's Carnival privileges for life. Danny had been ejected for smoking a joint three or four years back. Of course, Bridge made a phone call and got Danny back in.

A giant with ten-foot legs stepped over them, the wood peg of his stilt nearly landing on Andy's foot.

Danny grabbed Jasmine's arm as she passed, a pink cowboy hat on her head, a camera around her neck. She shut off the voice recorder in her hand.

"Did you guys hear?" she shouted, the crowd sliding by her. "Darkstar is playing tomorrow night on Main Stage! Shosh will shit."

"Darkstar?" Trey asked.

"Grateful Dead cover band," Danny yelled.

Jasmine shouted, "They cover entire shows, not individual songs. Sound just like the real deal."

A man wearing a pink cowboy hat—just like Jasmine's—yahooed and Jasmine high-fived him, yahooing back. She raised her camera and snapped a picture. "This place is madcap," she laughed.

"Just wait until the sun sets."

Jasmine grinned. "I better get back to work. I've got serious New Journalism to do."

She touched Andy's arm as they passed. "I dig, by the way. Very Cat-in-the-Hat."

At the junction of two trails, a woman pushed her barista cart in front of Andy, severing him from Danny and Trey. Andy called out, but the music was too loud, and Danny didn't hear. Andy struggled to get around the cart, but the crowd had him pinned.

At the shoreline, Andy picked his way through the thickets and black-berry patches until he found the big oak under which he had stashed his boat. He took off the hat, and got on his hands and knees to follow the same raccoon path he had taken earlier. He paused to gobble berries as he went, barely chewing—he had forgotten to eat lunch.

"You shouldn't eat so fast." A little girl's voice. High. Close.

There was no one behind him, or in front. He pressed his chest to the ground, getting lower so he could look further through the brush. And still, there was no one. Had Carnival already taken his mind?

"You'll get a stomachache. Trust me," the voice said.

Again, Andy looked all around but saw no one. Slowly, hesitantly, he looked up.

"Down here, silly."

In the hole, the very hole from which he had emerged hours before, a face. A little girl, her twisted and tangled hair bleached by the sun.

"If you eat too many berries too fast, you'll have to go poop." Purple marks from the berries stained her skin. "Trust me. I know what I'm talking about."

He blinked hard, but she was still there, squinting at him.

"Do you talk?"

"Yes," he said definitively. "I talk."

"My one friend is mute," she said. "Except we don't call her mute. It's not polite. We call her Milly because that's her name."

He looked past her down the hole, but didn't see anyone else.

The little girl giggled. She picked a berry and popped it in her mouth, chewing with her mouth open. "Do you want to see my ship?"

"What are you doing out here?" he asked.

"How old are you?" she said, reaching for another berry.

He had to think about it.

"I'm eight and one quarter." She raised her eyebrows, waiting. "So? Do you want to see it or not?"

"The boat?"

"It's not a boat," she said. "It's a ship." Her head disappeared down the hole.

For a moment, he sat there, unsure of what to do.

"Come on!" she yelled. "I'm setting us free!"

Andy dropped his legs through the hole, scurrying down as fast as his foot would allow. Once below, he found the boat as he'd left it, except for the little girl sitting in the oarsman's seat. The anchor was still down, the bowline still knotted.

"You can be first mate, if you want," she said.

"Okay," he said. "Are you the captain then?"

"No, silly." She handed him a berry—an especially ripe berry—from a collection resting on the fish box. "I'm Tallulah. I'm a pirate."

The berry was the finest he'd had this season, ripe yet firm, syrupy yet musky. "I'm Andy," he said while chewing. "How'd you find this ship?"

Tallulah's eyes locked on a large insect crawling along a root overhead. She pet its wing with a careful pointer finger. It didn't take flight, instead holding still, its antennae rocking back and forth.

"That's an October Caddis," he said. "Scientists call it *Discosmoecus*." He had used his guide voice—was he showing off for her?

She frowned. "His name is Sam." She continued to run her finger down its wings, not taking her eyes from the little creature. Sam crawled onto her finger and sat. "He's one," she said. "He looks older but he's not." She hopped from the oarsman's seat to the bow, the insect tame on her finger.

"Hi Sam," Andy said.

Tallulah squinted at Andy. "Where's your kid?"

"What?" Andy laughed.

"Your love child?"

"I don't have a love child."

"Don't your special places work?"

"Lots of grown-ups don't have kids."

"They all do." Tallulah touched her finger to a nearby root, setting Sam free. "That's what makes them grown-ups."

"I assure you it's common," Andy said, "increasingly so, in fact." He glanced out over the river.

Tallulah collected her stash of berries, picked out four for Andy, and put the rest in the pockets of her dress. "Don't wreck my ship." She climbed up the hole.

"Thanks for the berries."

The river lapped against the boat.

"Tallulah?" he called. But she was already gone.

By the time sweep started—an hour-long process by which Carnival Security systematically flushed the two hundred acre festival grounds of its Day Trippers—Andy was safely in camp. He had just set up his tent when the sweep bell rang.

More people were in camp now, nearly everyone who had attended Danny and Shoshana's party the night Andy killed the wild fish. A cluster of people milled around the fire, pumping beer into red cups from a keg hidden in the bushes. As Andy walked by, people raised their cups and smiled, reciting various lines from Dr. Seuss.

Out front, Alison and Marcus—the owners of Ipsy's Wine Bar—strung Christmas lights along the booth and connected them to a car battery tucked against a nearby tree. Two young children chased each other around Rita, while she spoke to their grown-ups.

Danny stood in the corner of the booth, pointing at the pictures of his house. A shorter man with broad shoulders nodded. The guy's shirt read: Islamorada Fly Shop. Andy realized it was Ethan Malloy, back from wherever he had fled.

"Look who the winds blew in," Danny said when he saw Andy approaching.

Ethan smiled, pulled Andy close, and slapped him on the back. "We may depart," Ethan said, "but we can't stay away."

"Damn straight," Andy said. "Tell me you're back for good?"

Ethan shook his head. "I've got a good thing going in Florida, running tarpon and bonefish trips. Almost sixty last year. That's a good start for down there. And I met somebody. Another guide." He smiled. "You should see her double-haul a ten-weight!"

Ethan always had a lady friend. As long as Andy had known Ethan, he had never paid a month's rent—he went from one woman's house to the next.

"Where the hell did you run off to last summer?" Ethan asked.

Andy recounted his trip, the rivers he fished, the fish caught. He kept talking, keeping the air full so Ethan couldn't ask why he had left. "But now I'm back, and trips are hard to find, and—"

"I hear it's been a bad year. You know," Ethan said, "I could get you plugged in down in the Keys. There are always trips down there, being so close to—"

"We three should get on the river before you leave," Danny interrupted.

"For sure," Ethan said. Then he squinted and dead-centered Andy. "Why the hell did you leave, anyway? Just before the wedding and everything too."

Andy chuckled, concentrating on not glancing at Danny. "Family shit."

Ethan nodded. "Sure, sure, understand that."

Suddenly, Bridge was there, standing beside Andy. "They're searching booths for Day Trippers." He was out of breath. "You've got to hide."

"What?" Danny said. "They're searching booths?"

"Coming into tents?" Ethan frowned.

"Exactly," Bridge said.

"Shit." Ethan held up his wrist—he didn't have an all-night pass either. "I'll catch up with you guys later." He hurried away, down the trail.

"Come with me," Bridge said.

Andy followed Bridge past the fire, through the tents, and out behind the camping space. Just before they hit Long Tom Creek, Bridge stopped. "Lay down right there," he said. "Behind that log."

Andy did as he was told, tucking himself into the mossy crevice. Bridge took Andy's hat, broke a pair of heavily needled limbs from a nearby Doug fir and laid them over, then plucked a handful of bracken fern and stuffed the stems through the boughs. Andy could barely see out.

"I'll come back and get you," Bridge said, and then he was gone.

Andy watched as the last rays of sunlight summitted the nearby ridges. The moment the light left, the cool river breezes started, and in a matter of minutes the air temperature dropped from eighty-something to the low seventies. By midnight, it would probably be in the fifties.

His foot ached, a new kind of pain. It had hurt throughout the day, but now it felt hot, as if a red coal burned in the bandage. He needed to get in his tent and change the dressing. He needed to rest it.

A tiny brown bird landed on a salmonberry limb not three feet from Andy's face, flinching each time it tweeted. A second later, it ducked through the boughs and landed on Andy's hip—instantly realizing its mistake and launching into a flapping frenzy. It bounced off the boughs, off Andy's crotch, off the mossy log before finally finding a gap and escaping back into the darkening world.

Voices came from the tents, and then the sound of zippers, one at a time. Security was searching the tents. They had never done anything like this before. In years past, they had come to the front of the booth and asked if there was anyone in the back that needed sweeping. If people said no, the sweep continued to the next booth.

A few moments after the zipping stopped, feet kicked at the brush nearby. He shut his eyes, trying to slow his breathing and make himself disappear.

"They're gone." Bridge lifted the boughs and offered Andy his hand. "Fucking Gestapo."

In the tent, Andy used a headlamp to illuminate his foot as he unwrapped the gauze. The stitches were still intact, but the skin had swollen and fresh blood oozed from the wound. He needed to stay in the tent, rest the foot. Just for one night. He could read, listen to the party all around. *The River Why* was in his bag.

He wiped the wound with disinfectant, applied a new bandage, and stuck it back in his sandal. He could rest it all day tomorrow, but he couldn't live with himself if he missed the first night's lightshow. He climbed out of the tent.

People convened around the fire as evening turned to night. Bodies moved through the flame's flickering glow. Ethan and Danny were there, near the keg—Ethan was pouring for anyone who handed him a cup.

Just as Andy started hobbling toward them, Shoshana and Jasmine appeared. Shoshana leapt horizontally into Danny, he caught her in a cradle, and they kissed. Ethan turned to Jasmine, flashing his boyish smile and asking her something. Jasmine handed him her cup and thanked him with a touch to his bicep.

As always, the midnight show at Main Stage was drawing an enormous crowd. Everyone with an all-night pass—and any Day Tripper savvy enough to sneak through sweep—was laying out blankets and setting up lawn chairs. Despite arriving early, they found themselves near the back, a sea of churning bodies before them. They had walked over together, Jasmine and Ethan out front laughing the whole way.

Just as the moon emerged from a wall of Doug firs, two streaks of flame lifted from stage, mushrooms against the dark night. Everyone fell silent.

Then the purple glow of black lights illuminated the stage and a half-dozen skeletons back-flipped into view. They circled, and a moment later the skeletons began juggling skulls. They even moved in the spindly and awkward way a pile of bones should.

A camera flash overpowered the black lights—the skeletons were painted onto black tights worn by gyrating dancers. The crowd booed at the camera.

Above the stage, thousands of lasers—salmon red, sunset orange, mint green—streaked through the dusty air. Once, they froze perfectly vertical and lowered like a peacock's fan over the crowd—so close they looked to be within arm's reach. And at that moment, fireworks fractured the night and hundreds of drums opened up like machine gun fire.

CHAPTER 8

Andy snapped awake, still panting from a dream. Sweat soaked him. A fever. In his sleep, he had kicked his sleeping bag to the far corner of the tent. He unzipped the door and the cool morning air rushed inside.

Not a fever, just stale tent air.

The memory of the dream returned, its panic still immediate. A boat had tipped, Danny's boat. And the rail had split Danny's head.

The cut on his foot ached and his ankle felt a little stiff. But the sensation of hot coal trapped in the bandage had passed. He popped a pair of Advil and stepped into the day.

Ethan was there with a cup of coffee, talking with Danny beside the fire. When he saw Andy, he said, "There he is. Knew you'd be up early." He handed Andy a cup of his own, creamy coffee steaming through the lid.

"Ah," Andy put the coffee to his lips. "Woke up in heaven."

"Surprise, surprise," Danny said. "Fishing guides up before the rest of the world."

"Sleep is for sports."

Andy laid a log across the fire and took a seat. To Ethan, he said, "Did this guy tell you he wants to run Wikkup?"

Ethan turned to Danny, frowning. "Wikkup Canyon? Like above Altitude Ramp?"

"It was just an idea I had," Danny said.

Ethan contemplated his coffee. "Do you think a drift boat could handle that section?"

"He wants to use a river dory."

Danny laughed. "We were just kidding around."

"Well," Ethan shrugged, "if anybody can run it, it's you." He brought his coffee to his lips, took a slow sip. "Don't know why you'd want to, though."

They sat there, the log smoking in the morning's chill, no one talking.

Finally, Andy broke the silence. "Tell us about this tarpon-guide girlfriend of yours."

Campfire smoke blanketed the early morning Carnival grounds. On the edges of the path, people slept beside their guitars, drums, bongs. Two orange-shirted security guards cuddled under an apple tree, one of them snoring. Andy blew the steam off his coffee as he limped toward the river. He wanted to check on the boat.

The river: tendrils of fog snaked over the current and, above, smoke tinted the dawn light a supernatural red. A trout slurped—a ten- or twelve-inch fish by the contour of its rise.

The rapids rolled smooth and glided for fifty yards or so before tailing out and disappearing into another stretch of whitewater. The old guides claimed that this pool, "Long Tom Run" they called it, used to hold pods of steelhead. The fish had trusted Long Tom Creek as a spawning tributary then—just like they still trusted Steamboat—and would hold in the pool awaiting ideal ascension conditions. But something had happened in the eighties and the steelhead had stopped using the creek. No one had seen a spawning fish in Long Tom in twenty years. Guides blamed Mr. Lambardi, the rancher who owned most of the Long Tom, for letting his cattle graze right down to the water's edge. They said those cattle had allowed the banks to erode into the creek, burying the spawning gravel—much like the clearcuts did in the hills.

Again the trout rose, but this time the fish didn't descend back through the water column—it held just under the surface, its back bulging the current's sheen. Andy blocked the peripheral light with his hands, and the glare dissipated. The fish was there, like it was watching him. He blinked, and the fish was gone.

The boat was fine, except for hundreds of little muddy footprints. It seemed Tallulah had been back. He would have to wash it out before he picked up his clients tomorrow morning. But no matter.

Looking around, he wished she were here now.

Danny sat at the table in front of the booth, sullen. The first Day Trippers of the morning ambled by, eager and smiling, their cloth shopping bags empty and ready.

Andy took the seat next to him. "What's got you dour as an old hen-fish?"

Danny didn't answer.

Andy ribbed him with his elbow. "Come on."

A woman wandered up, looking at the model of the community on the table. "What are y'all selling?"

"Do you see any price tags?" Danny said.

"O-kay," she said, walking away.

"You shouldn't have said anything," Danny said. "Low move."

"What did I say? I didn't say anything."

"Ethan? Wikkup?"

Andy laughed. "That? I didn't say anything secret. Look, I'm worried, all right? I just thought hearing Ethan's opinion might, you know, convince you otherwise."

"Yeah, but Ethan?" Danny said. "I mean, he killed a man, Andy. Can you fathom that?" Danny shook his head. "I don't think you could possibly understand. No offense, but you've lived a pretty sheltered life."

Andy poked at some papers. One read: Green Living.

"And that's not even the issue. You promised not to say anything. Your word doesn't mean shit anymore."

"You're being kind of uptight about all this, aren't you?"

"Forget about Wikkup. I'll be running it alone."

"Sure," Andy said. "Kill yourself for a hull-load of dope and abandon your pregnant wife." He pushed up from the table, leaving Danny for the tents behind the booth. He needed a nap—twenty minutes would do him right.

Jasmine sat in a chair beside the fire, alone, typing on a laptop. She did a double take when she saw him walking by. "Andy! Wait a second." She was jumping up from her chair. She came close, close enough he could smell the blackberries on her breath. Purple stains covered her fingertips. "Is it true Danny is going to run some killer rapids?"

"Where did you hear that?"

"We all heard you this morning, by the fire. I had to ask Shoshana what Wikkup Canyon was. She says nobody has ever run it. Is that true?"

"Everybody?"

"You act surprised."

He needed those twenty minutes.

"So it's true? Shoshana is pissed."

"I'm going to take a nap."

"Looks like you could use it."

Andy slept and, after waking, stayed in his tent. With his head propped up with a mass of extra clothes and pillows, he reread the scene in *The River Why* where Gus pulls a dead body from the Tamawanis River.

A pair of urgent voices came from the tent next door, Trey and Nikki's tent, the voices muffled but partially decipherable. Andy dog-eared the page.

Trey said, "With all I'm doing . . . "

Nikki's voice, " . . . not for anyone else . . . "

"Someone has to support your lifestyle."

"You said you'd be insulated from any risk. I remember. You used the word 'insulated.'"

" . . . "

"Sure, but then I get out here and you're right in the middle of it."

" . . . "

"Either you're lying right now or you were lying then."

" . . . "

"I know it's for us! You could use that excuse to justify anything!"

A zipper cut the air, and a moment later, someone hurried by.

Andy unzipped the tent flap and looked toward the fire. People gathered around the small blaze, sitting in lawn chairs, laughing. Danny wasn't among them.

Sid, a rafting guide from town, and a tall woman Andy had never seen before, juggled oranges between them.

Jasmine listened, her voice recorder in hand, as Nancy explained how the valley had changed over the years.

Nikki and Rita talked privately, their chairs close together, away from the other people. Chloe wiggled around on Nikki's leg, her pointer finger buried to the knuckle in her nose.

Out front, Bridge sat at the booth's table, talking with someone who looked vaguely familiar. Only after Andy took the seat beside Bridge did he remember who the man was—Mr. Arnold, the sport financing the White Oak development.

Arnold turned his attention to Andy. "We've met, haven't we?"

"We have."

"You're a fishing guide, right?"

"You're a money-grubbing developer, right?"

Arnold retracted his smile.

Bridge chuckled and patted Andy's shoulder, as if it were all a joke. "Jack just stopped by to say that Willis is considering a third offer. Seems Cherry Creek is now interested in the property."

"Cherry Creek Timber?"

Bridge pulled at his beard. "The one and only."

"Of course," Arnold said, "I don't know what they're offering. And this could just be a stunt from Willis to force up our offers."

"Either way it complicates things," Bridge said.

Arnold shrugged. "I knew you'd be interested. I know we'd both hate to see that property stripped."

"Damn straight," Bridge said. "Enough is enough."

Arnold checked his watch. "How does a fellow get to Delta Junction from here? I'm meeting my gal in ten minutes."

Bridge gave Arnold directions as if they were old friends, and then they shook hands.

After Arnold had left, Andy asked, "Think he's bullshitting us?"

"Could be." Bridge stared blankly at the passing crowd. "If he's a liar, he's a good one."

"You think he's being straight up?"

"Whoever originally assessed Willis's timber royally fucked up." Bridge turned to Andy. "I mean royally. I've got a forester friend who claims there's at least ten times the board footage Willis advertised. You've been up that creek. Think about all that original forest along the water."

He was never good at judging land, but it seemed like a few hundred acres of huge trees extended up both sides of the creek, some as wide as cars. Those trees were most certainly the reason Steamboat still contained wild steelhead—their root structures kept the silt out of the creek and their huge trunks shaded the water from the summer's heat. "Who did the original assessment?"

"Don't know. Whoever it was might be on Cherry Creek's payroll. Undervalue the property, tip off the big company, and get a kickback after the deal goes through." Bridge spit. "If this is true, there's no way we can compete with Cherry Creek's offer."

"Which is why we can't trust Arnold's word. Might be trying to get us to give up."

"I'll look into it," Bridge said. "Either way, let's not mention this to anyone."

"Sure."

Bridge laid his massive hand on Andy's shoulder. "I mean it, Andy."

"Of course."

"So I assume Danny told you everything, if he told you about Wikkup."

"You heard about that?"

"What else did he tell you?"

"Nothing really."

"You might bullshit Arnold, or Gordon, or even Trey—but Andy, don't bullshit your friends."

"I just know about Wikkup. Danny didn't tell me anything else. This morning, that was an accident. I didn't know people could hear."

Bridge thought this over. "Besides this morning have you talked about it in front of anyone?"

"No," Andy said. "Definitely not."

"You sure?"

He thought back over the last couple days. "I'm sure."

"You know, you put Danny in a sticky spot with Shoshana. Hard to justify risks like that to your pregnant lady."

A Day Tripper said, "This isn't worth fifteen dollars." And the woman next to her said, "It was ten last year."

"Is there something else going on here?" Bridge asked. "Maybe something between you and Danny that I don't know about? Maybe something between you and Shoshana?"

Andy scoffed.

Bridge was waiting for an answer.

"No, you might have read a little too deeply into this one. I'm just concerned for Danny, that's all."

"That's why you skipped town just before their wedding? It's none of my business—until it becomes my business," Bridge said.

Had Bridge figured it right? Was it that obvious? Of course it was. Who else was talking about this behind his back? Behind Shoshana's back? Behind Danny's back?

Jasmine appeared beside them. "Howdy, men." She wore a pirate's hat, and someone had painted dragons down her shoulders and forearms. She stretched and said in a yawn, "I'm starving."

"You want to get some food?" Andy asked.

She shrugged. "If you're buying."

As he stood, Bridge grabbed his arm, and whispered, "In the long run, you can't bullshit yourself either."

Jasmine ploughed a path through the crowd, yelling "Scalding hot oil." The Day Trippers stumbled to clear a path.

"I've got a two o'clock with Carnival's executive committee," she said. "Supposed to meet them over by Main Stage. Scalding hot oil! You mind if we eat over there?"

Andy shook his head. "How does falafel sound? There's a tasty booth right off the stage."

"Hey! You don't have any oil!"

"Ideal," she said. "I've been dying for Mediterranean."

It took a half hour to cross the Carnival grounds, and when they arrived at a booth called Abba's Falafels, they found a pocket of shade under a cherry tree. They sat in the grass, their pitas steaming fresh, steel drums on stage. Jasmine took a big bite, tahini smearing her cheek.

Andy brought the food to his lips, sniffed it, but couldn't bring himself to go any further. "How's the article coming?" he asked.

"I won't write it until later," she said. "Now, I'm just sponging up everything I'll need." A man waved at her from the passing crowd, an obvious All-Nighter with dark circles under his eyes. "Shoot straight!" she yelled, and he formed a pistol with his hand and fired a round in the air. "That guy was hilarious last night," Jasmine said.

Andy set his falafel in the grass and stared toward the Day Trippers. A painted flower on a girl's cheek. A little boy with twisty dreadlocks. A woman with butterfly wings and a string bikini licking a mound of green cotton candy. "Why waste your time with those sports on the executive committee?"

"Sports?" She was still chewing. "I've heard you use that word before."

"An especially self-involved genre of tourist," he said. "They see this place as their own private paradise."

"What's wrong with a little Eden fantasy?"

"When they call the Ipsyniho paradise, they're saying they expect it to entertain them. They turn the valley into a 3D television show. They have no concern for the place, or how they might be affecting it."

She finished her falafel, balling up the wrapper in her hand. "Sports turn the place into an 'it'."

"Exactly." He wiped the cold sweat from his brow. "I think."

"They objectify it. They refuse to acknowledge the place outside its ability to serve them. For a carpenter, a hammer is an 'it'. For you," she said, "a boat is an 'it'. For me, a computer. Boobs, for a teenage boy."

"And some grown-up boys too."

Jasmine lit a cigarette. "Testicles don't have that same charm."

"But the sports, they think they understand the nuances of the place, the nitty-gritty. They would deny that they've created an 'it'."

"We all deny it," she said.

An orange shirt loomed over them, a security guard. "Carnival is a tobacco-free zone."

Jasmine rolled her eyes and snuffed out the cigarette. "So, you're a fan of Hawthorne's?"

"Hawthorne's?"

"Nathaniel? The author of an obscure little book, *The Scarlet Letter?*"

He lied, "I haven't read it."

"Huh."

"I flunked high school English."

"Really?"

"Yep."

"Shosh says you were an English major in college."

"For like a week. Who wants to do all that reading?"

"Huh."

"What do you think of these falafels?"

"You skipped town just before the wedding? Is that right?"

"I didn't exactly skip town."

"What would you call it then?"

He considered this. "A strategic withdrawal."

"A strategic withdrawal?"

"I had family stuff going on. It's two fifteen, by the way."

She checked her watch and balled up the remainder of her falafel and tucked it in her bag. "I got to go." She stood, but didn't leave. "You know, I'm no doctor, but you don't look so good."

Andy awoke to the sweep bell. He had dozed off under the cherry tree, lost in the roaring silence of Carnival.

Which was weird, because he didn't remember falling asleep. The sweep bell rang again.

He had only gone halfway back to the booth when he encountered the wall of security guards, their arms locked. "Proceed to the nearest exit," one of them shouted on a megaphone. "No getting through without an all-night pass."

He needed to find a place to hole up. Someplace the sweep wouldn't search. Shoshana's booth might work. It was closest. But he couldn't go there.

So he holed up behind a row of latrines and covered his nose against the stink. He hadn't been there two minutes when a security guard stepped around the edge and said, "Real original spot, dorkus."

"'Dorkus'? Is that the best you can do?"

"How about 'illegal'? Get your ass to the exit, and don't let me catch you again or I'll make damn sure you're charged with trespassing."

Between here and the exit, he couldn't think of a better place—a place less likely to be searched—than Shoshana's booth. It was a vendor's booth, small and busy; sweep might peek around but they wouldn't look hard enough to disturb commerce. Maybe he would just check with her, feel it out. She had hid people before, her friends from out of state.

He arrived to find her taking a man's cash, a tile mosaic of a Mediterranean cityscape under his arm. Only after the man turned to leave did she acknowledge Andy. "What are you doing here?"

He tossed a thumb over his shoulder. "The sweep started and I can't get back to the booth."

"You can't hide here," she said.

"I don't think I can make it to the river. I can't think of any other place to hide."

"Sorry." She said it without even looking at him. "There's a row of bathrooms just down Peach Path."

Boxes were piled at the back of the booth, some as large as a man. "Anything in those?"

"Andy, I could lose my permit."

"If I get booted out, I won't be able to stop Danny from running Wikkup."

She stopped sorting money. "Why is he running Wikkup?"

"Hide me."

"Tell me."

The sweep sounded from just up the trail.

Telling Shoshana might be the only way to save Danny's life. No one had a better grip on him than she did. "Hide me first."

She led him to the back of the booth, to the stack of boxes. They stepped into the dark space between the booth and a head-high wall of debris separating the Peach Path and Kesey Street. "In that one there."

"Thank you."

"Just get in. And don't come out until I get you."

Danny's called from the front of the booth, "Shosh?"

Shoshana and Andy shared a look, and without pause, Andy began crawling into the box. They couldn't get caught alone back here.

He was just halfway in when Danny came around the corner. "Hey Shosh, I . . . "

"Andy was just hiding—"

"From the sweep. Shoshana was just helping me hide from the sweep."

"He couldn't get back to the booth," she said.

"And Shoshana offered to hide me."

Danny's eyes flashed back and forth between them. For a long moment he said nothing. He just stood there. Finally, he muttered, "This won't work. If they get suspicious, that's the first place they'll check."

"He's right," Shoshana said.

Danny stared at her unflinchingly.

"You got to go somewhere else."

Danny asked Andy, "Why did you come here to hide?"

"I was stuck and they found me behind the bathrooms and I didn't think I could make it to the river, not with all these security—"

Shoshana said, "You need to go."

"If you go now," Danny said, "you can still make it to the brush behind Main Stage. I hid there once. Use a coon path to get as deep in as you can." He didn't offer Andy a hand, he didn't help him to his feet. "You better hurry, though."

Andy climbed up and left them alone, together.

He limped back toward Main Stage, pushing through the crowd.

What else could Danny think? They had been so awkward, so obviously nervous.

Behind Main Stage's massive speakers, he found a raccoon path and crawled in. The path cut to the heart of the bramble, a spot where two other tunnels met. None of the berries interested him. He lay down, careful to avoid the thorns, and was suddenly aware of a violent thirst turning him to dust.

He awoke in the dark. The Grateful Dead in front of him, Jerry and his mandolin, Micky and his drums. Phil turned and said, "You're the worst kind of liar." Jerry nodded. "You're the kind that burns long and hot."

Then he was alone.

He stood, but only made it halfway up. Ropes and fishhooks pressed him back to the dirt, snagging his skin, ripping his flesh. He tried again, frantic this time, and his ear caught something and was tugged hard. He collapsed onto his knees. He was pinned. What kind of boat was this?

He yelled to Jerry and Phil, but they were gone. Only their music remained.

This was not right. His arms weighed too much to lift—as if they had been filled with lead.

He collapsed onto his belly. Was he dying? Had he already?

Above him, just out of arm's reach, the moon quivered with the music.

The music. The stage.

This wasn't a boat.

This was just a blackberry thicket: he had crawled in, and he could crawl out.

He needed to pick a line.

In front, a gap. He pushed through and found the tunnel.

He stood into the blue glow of the stage lights, dizzy: people bouncing and spinning. Was that Danny? He staggered closer.

Shoulders, arms, hair. A foot stepping on his. "Watch it, buddy." Everybody was Danny.

The stage, a reference point. Danny singing Jerry's line. Yellow and green and Donna still ruining the song. Except it wasn't Donna.

Don't you come around here anymore.

He tried to lie down, but strange hands held him up.

Bertha, don't you come around here anymore.

"Take him to first-aid."

"No," he heard a familiar voice say. "Let Danny stay. He loves her for real."

"Bringing one in. More bad acid."

Hands under his shoulders, hands under his legs, floating. Bouncing with the current. The cool river breeze over his face. Water.

He needed water.

"Calm down, friend."

Water. He needed out of the boat now.

"Fuck, he kicked me. I'm bleeding."

But there was no water, just dirt.

"No, that's his blood."

No water left in the world. Only dry stones and dirt and dead grass. Dead fish. He reached to touch them. To tell them he was sorry.

"Bring the backboard."

"Holy shit. Andy?"

"You know this guy?"

"He's with us. He's with us. Leave him alone." Jasmine's face blue and green, then red and orange. Honeysuckle. "What happened, Andy?"

"Bad trip. We've been getting them all night. Somebody's slinging shabby acid."

Andy, look at me. Did you take something?

Sweltering. Too hot to breath. Then artic shivering. Too cold to think.

Shoshana's face: I don't think he dropped anything.

He just needs to be guided. Twelve hours or so. We see it all the time.

Pinpricks of sweaty ice. Snow flakes on his molten skin.

It's snowing.

Andy, it isn't snowing.

Tell him it's snowing. Lie to him. Pretend you see the dragons and clowns too. It's easier that way.

Danny. I'm cold. I'm sorry.

What happened?

Don't leave.

I won't leave. Tell me what happened. Did you swallow something? Get Rita! Andy, listen to me.

Ask him if it was a sugar cube. A sugar cube with a pink dot.

Red-haired Danny. The real guide. The real native. His only real family.

What did you do what happened

I'm sorry sorry sorry sorry

What are you sorry sorry for

For sleeping with her

CHAPTER 9

He unzipped his tent and found the sun low in the sky—dawn's glow. His back hurt, low, over his kidneys, and he allowed himself to lie back again.

Dreams, their residual fog, haunted him. One, in particular. He was under the flashing lights confessing again and again, Danny hunched, dumbfounded and disbelieving.

It was a dream, but he couldn't expel the image of Danny's face, the way his eyes drooped like he had known it all along but assured himself it couldn't be true.

"Drink this," Rita said. She was kneeling at the tent door. She held a red keg cup filled with green fluid, a straw poking out.

He sucked a mouthful of the fluid and swallowed. "I can't. I'll puke." It tasted like a tree.

"Drink it slowly," she said, putting her hand to his forehead. "You won't vomit. It's willow bark, Spanish lichen, rose hips, some other stuff."

"My back hurts."

"You're lucky more doesn't hurt."

"What happened?" he put his hand to his temple to quell the buzzing sound.

"A fever," Rita said, kneeling beside the tent. "Your foot got infected. You should have respected that wound, Andy. You should have seen me sooner. You let it get horrendous."

"I've got a trip today," he said. "Two clients for Stream Born."

"I think you're confused."

"No. It's today. I've got to get ready."

"Just lay back down," she said.

Andy looked west and found the sky brightest there. It wasn't dawn—the sun had just set. He had missed an entire day.

Rita pointed at the red cup. "Finish that and lay back down. If the sweep comes by, pretend to be asleep, and I'll make sure they don't harass you."

And then it was dark. A fire burned, and he watched it out the tent door.

Someone said, "Reality is more precarious than you think."

He lay there for he didn't know how long, staring blankly at the fire, and sipping water from a jug Rita had left. Occasionally, the wood would pop, sending flares into the sky.

Trey walked by.

"You're going to kill him," Andy said.

Trey searched for the voice, and upon finding Andy, he laughed.

"He'll die in Wikkup."

"As if you give a shit."

"I know your type," Andy said. "You're just using him. Everybody knows it."

"*I'm* just using him? You're crazy. What right do you have to talk?"

"I'm his friend. I know the real Danny. He's just a tool to you."

Trey laughed. "Some friend. Anyway, Danny and I are equal players in this thing."

Before Trey was even out of sight, Andy felt a new warmth sweep over him, a warmth growing into panic. What had happened? What had he done?

And where was Danny?

He pulled the sleeping bag over his head and tried to escape back into sleep, to wake up and discover *this* was, in fact, the dream.

He opened his eyes to see Bridge beside the fire. With him stood an old barefoot hippie with a beard longer than Bridge's. They spoke quietly, their beards bouncing with each syllable. From such a distance, the particular words were impossible to decipher, but then there was the word "strain." Sheriff Carter was there too, wearing jeans and a flannel shirt, a beer in his hand. The hippie handed a small jar to Bridge. Bridge smelled it and patted the man on the back before passing it to Carter. Carter scanned the camp, and smelled too. He lipped the word "wow." The hippie pulled a pair of joints from his beard and gave one to Bridge and the other to the sheriff.

And then Shoshana was kneeling by the tent, her hair held back by a red bandana. She looked ill, her eyes sunken with crying.

"Why is he running it?" she whispered.

"Does he know?"

She looked toward the fire. "He knows. Everyone knows."

People around the fire were sneaking glances at them.

"Where is he?"

"I don't know," she said. "No one has seen him since last night. Why is he running it? I think I know, but tell me."

As if any of his promises to Danny were relevant now. And telling her might be the only way to save his life. "You know what they've got growing in the hills?"

"'They?' Don't tell me he's involved in the growing. Bridge promised me, no felonies."

"Bridge."

"Who else?"

"Trey."

"Trey? That guy needs Bridge's help to tie his shoes."

"So you know about the growing then."

"I don't know what I know anymore. Don't tell me he's running dope through that canyon."

"They can't drive it out on account of the roads being closed. Fire danger."

"Damn it. He promised me."

"I don't think promises matter anymore."

"They always matter," she said.

"I told him? I told him last night?"

"Yes, Andy, you fucking told him. What about that don't you understand?"

"What did he do when he found out?"

"He disappeared." She cradled her forehead in her hands, as if she were on the verge of giving in, of sinking to the ground. But then she said, "Why is he doing this? Why? Why? Why?"

"He's doing it for you and baby. He's telling himself that running Wikkup will mean the money he needs to provide for you. A safety net."

"I work. I make money. This isn't the fifties."

People around the fire were muttering and looking at them.

"Is that place as deadly as they say it is? Can he run it?"

"No. Especially not without a second boat." He didn't recognize any of the faces by the fire. "What are they saying?"

"Fuck them." She didn't so much as glance back. "Maybe he won't run it now. Maybe after . . . this, he won't run it."

"Maybe."

"We have to assume, though, that he will. We have to talk to Bridge. Talk some sense into him."

It would have been one thing if Andy had come out and told him properly, honestly, if he had said something at the fly shop or in the hot tub or countless other times. Or if Shoshana had told him immediately. Before the wedding, even. But to find out like he did revealed all of their lies. A year of lies.

"At the dam," he said. "You came ready. Parked in the shadows. It was premeditated."

"Don't push this on me," she said. "You called me, remember?"

"I did and you came. But the . . . the act—"

"Can we not talk about this right now?" She started to stand and leave. "I have to find him."

"Please," he said. "I have to know why."

She wasn't leaving. She was biting her lip.

"You seemed not into it, you know, the act, and yet you suggested we talk in the car. You touched my leg."

"Don't pretend I started it. You called me."

"I didn't want you back," he said, "just for the record. I hadn't planned on any of that. I called, I needed to see you for a different reason."

"That doesn't absolve you," she said.

"I'm not looking to be absolved. This, this is too heavy for that."

"You want to know why?" she said, her voice quivering with anger. "You want to know why I came? I was scared, that's why. Scared of being married. Scared of marrying him. He sprung it on me so fast. And his upbringing, you know? We're different people. I was scared, and I knew . . . I don't know what I knew, but I came to the dam. And you came too."

He'd been scared too. He thought he had loved her, that he was losing his life's real love. But of course, as soon as it ended, as soon as she drove off, he realized that it hadn't been her he loved at all—he loved a person who didn't exist anymore. He loved a character from the story of his past. "We should have told him," he said. "We should have come out right away."

"No," she said. "I didn't tell him because he wouldn't have got it. It would have been just a betrayal to him. He's not a forgiving person—he can't forgive himself, and he can't forgive other people. In his eyes, it wouldn't have been any more complex than that. It was a mistake, a moment of confusion, not a betrayal, a mistake that showed me how much I wanted to be with him. But everything is so simple to him." She bit her lip. "Everything is so simple."

"What is it?"

"Nothing," she said. But then she continued anyway, her voice nearly a whisper. "I miscarried, you know. Just a week before. During the night. And as the days passed, I started to think maybe losing the baby was a sign, a sign that marrying him wasn't the right thing. A sign from God or whatever, you know?

"I wanted to come clean about what happened. I did. Especially after you vanished. I wanted to tell him more than anything. But I was afraid, afraid he'd say I lost it on purpose. That I had wanted to lose the pregnancy because I really loved you."

She stood and wiped at her eyes. "I can't lose him. Not right now." Her hand was touching her stomach. "Not like this."

"I'll find Bridge. I'll tell him about the canyon."

"Be careful," she said. "Stay away from him right now. Until I can talk to him."

People watched as she walked past the fire. She flipped them the bird and kept going.

He found himself sitting near the front of the booth, in a lawn chair, his foot up. Red light illuminated the path before him, though he sat safely in the black shadow cast by a wide tree.

It didn't take long for Bridge to walk by. He held a little device, maybe a weather radio, to his ear.

"Bridge."

He turned toward the shadows, squinting. "Is someone there?"

"It's me."

Bridge came closer and looked at the bandaged foot. "I thought you'd be gone by now." He gave his attention back to the radio at his ear.

"What is it?"

"The jet stream is slipping south and a tropical depression is rising north. We got to move the schedule up."

"He can't boat that section. Nobody can. You don't understand. Haven't you heard the stories? There has to be some other option."

"This is no squall." Bridge was still listening to the radio. "Hurricane force winds by tomorrow night. Maybe sooner. I can feel it. The barometer is already plummeting."

"I know I fucked up," Andy said. "But you have to hear me when I say this: he could die."

Bridge turned to Andy, though he kept the radio to his ear. "Danny says it can be run, and frankly, I side with him on this."

An orange-shirted security guard walked by, and Bridge stopped him. He described Danny's appearance and said there was an emergency message—Danny needed to rush back to the booth. After some convincing, the security guard finally called in the alert on his handheld CB. He was surprisingly young. He still had fresh acne.

Once he had finished, Bridge grabbed the device away from him.

"Hey, give me that back!"

Bridge fiddled with the dials. "What channel is the sheriff using?"

"You can't use that! I could get in trouble!" His voice cracked.

"What's the channel?"

"You can't—"

Bridge touched his finger to the center of the kid's chest. "Listen," he said, calmly. "You're going to tell me which channel."

"Two."

Bridge switched the channel and said into the device, "Bridge to Carter, over."

A moment later, a snowy voice said, "Furry, is that you?"

Bridge explained the storm. "NOAA says unprecedented wind speeds. You might consider closing this show."

For a moment, the radio simply snowed. Then Carter said, "No weather for over a hundred days and then we get this?"

"Are you surprised?" Bridge asked.

"Nothing surprises me anymore."

"You might tell the executive committee."

"All right," Carter said. "I'll do it."

Bridge gave the security guard his CB, and said to Andy, "You should get out of here. While you still can."

Trey appeared beside them. "I'm a little concerned about what Danny saw up there. The two feds."

Bridge guided Trey away from Andy so he couldn't hear. They whispered there together until Trey nodded. He seemed calmed by whatever Bridge said.

Bridge patted Trey on the back and said loud enough Andy could hear, "Let's find Danny. These security dolts couldn't find their dicks with four hands."

The red glow on the trail seemed like normal light now, as normal as the noontime sun. Above, even the stars seemed red.

He couldn't actually remember seeing Bridge at any construction sites. Not a one in ten years. And he had never seen him with lumber in his truck either. And he had never met anyone who pointed at a new outbuilding or a new deck and said, "Bridge made this." Anyone except Danny.

The construction thing had to be a ruse. He probably funneled the dope money through his "business" to clean it.

If he hadn't known that Bridge was a grower, what other illusions did he entertain?

In the red light of the path, a Bigfoot did back-flips.

Then he noticed the drums. For at least a day, they had existed as white noise, a steady, invisible backdrop to the fever, to the sleep, to the recovery. They had become like the breezes along the river, always there and rarely noticed. What did people say? "The fish can't tell you about the water."

"What's that?" Rita pulled up a chair, a cup of beer in her hand.

"Nothing."

"How do you feel?"

"Better. Worse. I don't really know."

"So," she said, checking the area around them, "I hear you're in the circle."

"Maybe I was in the circle."

"Once you're in, you're in. This is serious stuff."

"I know."

"Andy, hear me when I say this: one slip-up could mean the downfall of everyone."

"Sure."

"That kind of thing has happened to people we know over the years," she said. "Good people sent to horrible places."

"Loose lips sink ships."

"This isn't a joking matter. We've gotten along this far by keeping a tight circle."

"Of course. Has Bridge always been involved in this kind of thing?"

She shrugged. "It might surprise you to know who else is involved in the green industry."

"Who?" he asked.

She laughed. "Good one."

Shoshana and Jasmine returned. Shoshana was visibly distraught. The color had left her face and she was chewing her nails.

"Tell me you found him?" he asked.

Jasmine shook her head, then opened a bottle of water and handed it to Shoshana. "Where would you go, Andy, if you were in Danny's place?"

"The river."

"Where exactly?" Shoshana asked.

"Probably the beach downstream of Tamawanis Loop."

Shoshana started down the red trail.

"Your flashlight," Jasmine said.

He tossed her the light. "Stick to the trail."

She ran to catch up.

An orange-shirted security guard—a woman with piercings through her eyebrows—appeared in front of him. "Is your booth leader around?"

He shrugged.

She studied him, his wrist. "Where's your pass?"

His long sleeve shirt had been pulled up to his elbow, revealing his naked wrist. "I don't know," he said. "I must have lost it."

She looked at the booth behind him. "Are you with Bridge?"

He nodded.

The woman fingered a silver stud in her lip, and looked again at his wrist.

"Bridge will vouch for me," he said.

"I'm supposed to throw you out," she said.

"Go for it."

The prospect seemed to bore her. "Tell Bridge, Carnival is closing tomorrow night. A storm or something is coming. You have to have your booth cleared by midnight tomorrow."

"Tomorrow midnight? The storm will be here before then."

She shrugged. "I'm just relaying the message."

"Who gave the message?"

"The executive committee, I guess."

CHAPTER 10

Dawn came slowly, the light diffused by low winter clouds. The tops of the ridges had vanished, and the air smelled of rain. A breeze lifted a spiral of summer dust from the path.

Andy still sat in front of the booth, a knot in his neck. He had been unable to sleep during the night, the thought of Danny out there somewhere broken and abandoned.

The Carnival had all but died in the last hour or so, the samba rhythm maintained by a few ardent souls. Every minute or so, they missed a beat. A few people trickled toward the gate now, dust-caked refugees, their camping gear piled high on shoulders or in wheelbarrows. A little boy shivered as he passed.

"Where y'all headed?" a man shouted. He was juggling a half-dozen avocados and walking toward the center of Carnival.

A woman with pink hair turned to him and said, "The sheriff says to leave by noon. Says tonight might be too late."

"Don't buy into the fear." The juggler put one hand in his pocket— all six avocados stayed airborne. "No storm can kill Carnival."

"I got to trust the sheriff on this one," she said. "He actually lives around here."

The juggler shrugged. "To buy into the fear, or not to buy into the fear. The great American question."

Andy had finished the gallon of water overnight and made repeated trips to a certain wide tree behind the booth. Yet again, he felt the tension of a swollen bladder, and so he pushed himself up and hopped past the fire pit, through the tents, and into the mossy firs. Since his last visit, his urine had browned the tree's green moss.

A crow swooped down beside the fire, picking at peanut shells and potato chips, red cups and candy wrappers. With each hop, a puff of dust lifted into the air and wafted east.

While in midstream, Andy heard a commotion from the front of the booth. The crow heard it too and lifted himself away, up through a gap in the trees.

There was Danny rushing past the fire, Bridge behind him. Danny's eyes were narrow, his face swollen. He looked only vaguely like the Danny Andy knew.

He tore open the door to Andy's tent and rumbled, "Where the fuck is he?" He lifted the empty sleeping bag and threw it behind him. Then a book came flapping through the air like a wounded bird and hit a tree a few feet from Andy—*The River Why.*

Bridge shouted something, but Danny seemed not to hear. Again, he reached into the tent. Bridge grabbed him and hugged him tight to his own body. Danny's forearms waved wildly like little naked wings, but he couldn't free himself. Every vein in his neck bulged, and his face darkened to the color of a bruise.

Bridge dragged him out of the tent and continued toward the fire pit, Danny's legs kicking at the ground. Bridge was whispering in his ear. But still, Danny kicked. Bridge was straining—a vein in his own forehead looked ready to burst. Finally Danny shouted, "Okay, okay. Let me go."

But Bridge continued to whisper. And Danny seemed to be listening. A moment later, he said in a nearly calm voice, "Fine, then let me go."

Danny teetered there, nearly falling over, then collapsed into one of the lawn chairs. Bridge did too.

Trey said, "I wonder if he left."

A tent unzipped, and Nikki stuck out her head. When she saw Trey's face, she ducked back inside, closing the tent behind her.

People in other tents were whispering. The dim outline of faces could be seen through mesh doors.

"You've been," Bridge said between pants, "drinking . . . haven't you?"

Danny scoffed.

"You can't row . . . not in your state."

"Bullshit."

"How much have you had?"

"Fuck off. I can row."

"How much?"

Danny turned his eyes on Bridge. "I said I can row."

Bridge pulled at his beard. "Fuck, Danny. This isn't the time. We need you straight right now."

"If I said I can handle it, I can fucking handle it. Let me just find that fuck-up first."

Bridge looked at the sky, then at his watch. "All right," he said. "Let's get on with it."

"Give me ten minutes," Danny said.

"No. Either we leave right now or we do this thing without you."

"You can't do this without me. Give me ten minutes."

"We don't have ten minutes. We should already be there, should have been there at dawn."

"All right," Danny said. "All right, all right."

Bridge whispered to Trey before continuing on out of the booth.

Trey started toward his tent, but stopped before the door. "Honey? Pack the stuff and you and Chloe go with Rita back to their house. Don't waste time. Pack your stuff and go."

Andy stepped out from behind the tree.

"Were you there the whole time?"

Andy limped toward the fire. "Get me up there," he said.

"Did you see what just happened? You should get out of here while you still can."

"If anybody sees Shoshana," Andy called to the faces in their tents, "tell her Danny is headed to Wikkup." To Trey, "Get me up there."

"You're going to boat it?"

"Get me up there."

Forty-five minutes later they passed Mamma's Diner. A closed sign hung from the window, and a pair of rain drops hit the windshield.

"Good thing Bridge hung the stuff under tarps," Trey said. "Seemed silly at the time, with the weather so hot and all."

As they passed Altitude Ramp, Andy saw a U-Haul truck sitting in the parking lot. No one was in the cab. "Is that ours?"

Trey nodded. "The delivery truck."

The world had turned gray, the heat of summer gone overnight. He had never seen weather like this in the Ipsyniho. Usually the high pressure systems of summer trickled away, slowly allowing more and more showers to enter the valley, until suddenly it had been gray and drizzly for weeks and the sun seemed like a childhood memory. But this storm was different. The clouds weren't still. Their charcoal mounds rushed eastward, a steady river flowing inland.

Orange leaves swirled in the wind like snow. The car rocked with the occasional side gust. The air coming through the vents had begun to smell tangy and sweet—aerosoled Doug fir.

"I'm barely using the gas pedal," Trey said.

Blackberries lined the road, blurring as they passed.

To a drift boat, wind blowing over a river acted as a contradictory current, making the craft nearly impossible to maneuver. Under such conditions, the river ferried one way, the wind the other, and the boat became paralyzed between the two. If the wind became too powerful, it could actually overpower the river, driving the boat upstream. With a river dory's high sides, the effect would probably be magnified.

"I'm not sure about you coming up here."

Wikkup Canyon opened to the west, its expansive walls narrowing to a pinch the width of the river—all the wind would be channeled, funneled, focused.

"Danny's dangerous right now. You saw him back there."

Blackberries beside the road. "Pull over."

"We don't have time," Trey said.

He needed a moment, outside, to steady himself, to figure his plan. Two minutes, no more. He couldn't think straight next to this guy. "Pull over."

Trey slowed to a stop along the shoulder. The wind grabbed the door as Andy cracked it, peeling it open. He stepped out and limped toward the blackberries. The wind caught his baseball cap and he watched it vanish over the brush. He had owned that hat going on ten years.

The berry clusters were small, the individual fruit only the size of a dime. This patch sat on the upper limits of the berry's habitat, a frontier bush. The clusters waved violently in the wind, bouncing up and down. The ripest fruit had already fallen. He picked a few of those that remained.

He had to do this. He had to try at least.

"You're wasting time!"

If Danny came at him, he wouldn't fight back. He would go limp, totally passive, take what he had coming. Bridge would be there to pull Danny off before too long.

Back in the car, Trey accelerated.

Andy studied the six little blackberries in his palm.

Some of the berries' globs remained orange—they had yet to ripen.

"What is it with you and those things?"

"Our finest native crop."

Trey laughed. "Those are from the Himalayas."

"Bullshit."

"Nope," Trey said. "Buy a fucking book and look it up."

Bridge's pickup was parked in the pull-off where Andy and Danny had stopped a few days before. Two brand new river dories sat nested on the trailer. Rogue River sixteen footers. Their high sides would hold the wind like a sail.

Danny was nowhere to be seen. Andy opened the door.

"What are you doing here?" Bridge shouted, the wind suspending his beard. He looked at Trey. "Why the fuck did you bring him?"

"Isn't he supposed to run the second boat? I thought this is what you wanted."

Bridge eyed Andy. "You're not running this with him. Not after—"

"Danny's not running it either," Andy said.

Over the edge, there he was, kicking free rocks. He was clearing a path for the boat. Andy stepped back from the edge. "This canyon can't be run. Especially not today. He won't survive. He's drunk for christ-sake."

Bridge eyed him. "Get out of here. Before he sees you."

"You're setting him up."

"Like you did?" Bridge asked.

"I'm just telling you the reality."

"No, it has to be done and Danny can do it. If he says he can, he can. I know Danny. I know Danny's clan. Their word is solid. It has to be done."

The sound of an approaching truck, the engine gurgling—its driver trying to find a gear. Since passing Altitude Ramp, they hadn't seen another vehicle.

The truck roared around the final corner: Danny's biodiesel.

"What the hell?" Bridge said.

"Hey," Trey said. "Isn't that Danny's truck?"

The truck slowed, pulling in behind the Volvo. Shoshana and Jasmine leapt out.

A gust of wind lifted dirt from the shoulder and it pinged off the boats.

Shoshana rushed forward, leaving the door open behind her. The wind tossed her hair, and with both hands she pulled it out of her face. "Where is he?" she yelled.

"Over the bank—"

His words were cut short by a rifle's crack. A half second later, the earth shook as a tree hit the ground. The wind had busted it free. Dust and debris filled the air. Another tree snapped, this one closer, and for a moment, Andy could barely see his own feet. He gripped the ground for balance, and saw Bridge had done the same, his beard flapping wildly.

And there was Danny, his clothes sucked tight by the wind, the trees bucking behind him. He was looking from Shoshana to Andy.

It wasn't that he was drunk, though he may have been; it was that he was shattered, empty. He was the ruins of the Danny Andy knew. He had been betrayed by the two people he trusted most, and now he was left with nothing—nothing but a knife in his still powerful fist. And he was coming this way.

Andy backed away, into the wall of boats. Tears filled Danny's eyes and now he was waving the knife and Andy put his hand out and said, no not this, but Danny kept coming. It can't go like this. Then Danny was on the ground and the knife was loose. Andy could have grabbed it, but he hesitated, he didn't move. And then he had missed his chance and Danny was rising to his feet and blood was pouring from Bridge's lip and the knife was back in Danny's hand. Stop. You can't do this. But Danny kept coming saying Why, Why, Why. Andy felt his way along the boat, pushing out from it, his other hand up like a shield. Please. You have a child to think about. This is bigger than us. And at the last moment, Danny seemed to flicker, to pause, to see the silver blade. But it was too late. Andy felt the pressure of a shoulder against his ribs, the spacey feeling under his feet, the warmth of Danny's neck against his armpit—then there was the cracking of something behind him, under him, and the panic of no breath.

Holy shit, he couldn't breathe.

It was Jasmine's voice that brought him back, not her words at first, but her sounds. Then a body beneath him, writhing, pushing him off. Shoshana had broken his fall. She must have been coming up behind.

"Jesus," Jasmine said. "You're going to be okay. Can you hear me? Shit, shit. You're going to be okay. It's not even bleeding that much."

Shoshana struggling for air, gasping, her eyes wide open. Her fingers feeling—feeling for the knife in her abdomen.

Blood was soaking her shirt and the knife was angled along the ribs, crooked and silver.

It was all a dream. It couldn't be real. Danny's knife in Shoshana. This wasn't happening. This couldn't be happening.

"Don't touch it!" Bridge was beside her, his own face bloody. "Leave it in."

And Danny was there too, on his knees, looking at what he had done.

Jasmine punched at him, striking his neck, but he seemed not to notice. Then she was back at Shoshana. "You're going to be okay. You're going to be fine. It doesn't even look that bad. There's not really any blood."

"Help me," Bridge said. "Lift her legs."

But Danny lifted Shoshana all by himself. As her body draped across his arms, she screamed a single momentary burst, then fell horribly silent.

"I'll call an ambulance," Trey called.

"It'll take too long," Bridge said rushing to the truck.

Jasmine and Bridge met Danny there, and helped Shoshana onto the back seat. She was moaning now, a shaky, sickening hum.

Jasmine stepped back, the truck keys in her hand, and hurried around to the driver's seat.

"Keep her legs up," Bridge said. "Keep her legs above her heart and don't touch the knife. Water. Does anybody have any water?"

Danny looked back at them—his eyes wide and terrified. For a moment, he stood there utterly dumbfounded, the dust swirling like red smoke.

Then the engine roared to life and he climbed in and they were accelerating away.

CHAPTER 11

The first dead body he ever saw belonged to his grandfather. He had died alone, at the kitchen table, one morning in May. Andy was due to arrive on the farm in three weeks. Instead, he missed school and arrived with his father just in time for the funeral. In place of the gray corpse for which he had prepared himself, he found an utterly alive Opa sleeping at the bottom of the casket. He looked not as he had the summer before his death, but as he might have a decade prior, his death concealed by a mortician's brush.

In a year, Andy would be gone, headed to Eugene, and the farm would be sold to a large agricultural conglomerate. But in that moment, all that existed was a casket, and an eternally alive body.

"God only takes when the time is right."

"Jesus knows best."

Afterwards, as people patted their eyes and shook Andy's hand, a leatherbound book appeared before him, held by an uncle he barely knew. "He wanted you to have this."

Andy recognized it instantly. He carried the heavy book into the silence of the bathroom, away from people, and untied the ribbon that kept it shut. There it was: all his Opa's data about the weather on the farm, about the timing of the berries, about the behavior of the stream's fish. And there were notes about Andy, about his favorite pools, about things he'd said—as if he too were a player in the ecology of the property. The journal contained twenty-two years of meticulously recorded observations. Twenty-two years of insightful deductions and measured inferences. It was a key that unlocked a place.

He wouldn't notice his Opa's inscription, written in shaky print, until later that night.

> *In your own life, Andy, find a healthy place and make*
> *it an island.*
> *We weren't built for continents.*

The valley's isolated Doug firs and half-rotted white oaks—and the homes and cars beneath them—sustained the majority of the storm's damage. The next day, on the way downstream, they saw trucks pressed to the ground, houses sliced in two, horses running loose.

After Danny and Jasmine had sped away with Shoshana, an argument had erupted. Bridge, his beard streaked with blood from his gushing lip, had told Andy to man the boat. "There's nothing we can do for her, and we can still save a boat's worth." Andy had refused, insisting they follow the truck to the hospital. "Grow some balls," Bridge had said.

By the time Bridge finally relented, precious minutes had passed. They raced downstream, Andy with Trey in the Volvo, Bridge alone in his truck, only to be stopped a mile past Mamma's Diner by a tree across the road.

"We can move it," Bridge said, throwing open the door. But they couldn't. The tree was as thick as two telephone poles. Bridge kept at it, rigging a rope to his truck's tow hooks. But the tires smoked as he gave it gas.

"Do we wait here?" Trey asked.

"No," Andy said. "We need shelter."

"We can make it," Bridge said. "We can move this tree."

An especially powerful gust ripped through the trees. Limbs cracked and fell all around.

"Bridge," Andy said, "we can't get stuck out here."

Trey agreed, and as he and Andy retreated upstream, Bridge finally did a U-turn and followed them upriver.

They found Mamma in her house, a two-story cabin attached to the back of the pie shop. *Housekeeping* sat on the counter, on top of a half-dozen other library books waiting to be returned. Bridge knew her as Betsy Hindman, and Betsy insisted they stay. "Rita's hands were the first to touch my granddaughter. It'd be an honor." She gave them a fresh pie, the last one made before the storm. Every few moments, the rain's volume would increase and the house would shake against a gust.

"I thought my daughter was nuts for taking her family to Hawaii for vacation during Carnival," Betsy said. "But now, with this storm? I'd be going mad if they'd stayed. Thank the stars for a well-timed sojourn!"

That night Andy lay on the floor, watching the ceiling. He could still feel Shoshana's writhing body beneath him; he rolled onto his stomach.

Danny still had the knife as he tackled Andy, though he had clearly chosen not to use it. As Andy had been driven backward, the knife's blade must have remained out and struck her. He could have picked it up, the moment before, as it lay on the ground. He could have tossed it to the river. But he'd locked up. And now she was who knows where, hurting.

His shirt was drying over a chair. He'd found a smear of blood on the back, her blood. He'd spent almost an hour in the bathroom rubbing at it, pouring water, rubbing more. Still the stain remained.

He should have been the one. He wanted that more than anything.

Every time he shut his eyes, it was there, over and over. From his perspective, then from hers, finally from Danny's. From hers, it was terrifying; from Danny's, it was horrifying.

For the first time in his life, he wished he believed in a god. Then at least, he could help them with prayers.

Dawn revealed a calm world, the winds nearly gone, the rain still falling. The front of the storm had passed.

The fire department's chainsaws roared up the valley. The yellow rescue truck stopped when the driver saw Bridge in the parking lot. He yelled out the window. "Cleared seventy-six so far."

"What about the people at Carnival?" Bridge said.

The driver shrugged. "The ambulances ran all night. Don't know anymore than that."

On the eerie drive downstream, the Volvo's purring the only sound, they crossed yellow lines of sawdust—the fallen trees cut into rounds and rolled into the ditch.

Andy's truck and trailer sat where he had left them, at the boat ramp above the Carnival grounds. A tree had fallen across the neck of the ramp, but missed the truck. "Call if you find anything out," Trey said out the window, as he and Bridge pulled onto River Road. Their families were somewhere downstream.

Andy drove straight to Ipsyniho's hospital, the same place he had had his foot stitched a few days before. Even as he arrived, an ambulance left, sirens screaming, headed toward the bigger hospitals downstream. He didn't see Danny's truck in the parking lot, but he parked anyway.

"Are you family?" the desk clerk, a small man with wire glasses, asked without looking up from the papers before him. The phone was ringing.

Andy had only asked if Danny or Shoshana had checked in.

"Not exactly."

"Then you'll have to sit over there and wait." Another phone started ringing. A man with a cast on his leg was wheeled by. The desk clerk handed a folder to a nurse who hurried by.

"I am family. The brother, actually."

"Don't waste my time."

"I'm not asking for any personal information," Andy said. "I just want to know if they're here."

"I can't help you," the desk clerk said.

Andy reached across the counter and seized the man's arm. "You have to tell me. Please, just do me the favor."

The clerk yanked free his arm and shouted someone's name.

Thick arms wrapped themselves around Andy and a knuckle struck the sensitive place along the top of his forearm. A moment later, he was in the parking lot looking into the eyes of two large men—one of whom he recognized. An old logger buddy of Danny's dad's. They had met a couple times before, at community events.

"Earl, is it?"

"I know you. The fishing guide, right? Danny's friend?"

"Damn." Andy rubbed at his arm. A bump was already rising where Earl had hit. "Did you have to punch so hard?"

"Sorry. I didn't realize who you were. We've had a lot of Carnival crazies in here today."

"Seriously," the other security guard said. He was a couple inches shorter than Earl and seemed half as old. He stared at Andy as if staring at a landscape—without noticing, it seemed, the social awkwardness of maintaining such a gaze. Andy nodded, and the man mimicked the salutation, then continued to stare.

Andy leaned against his truck, and asked Earl, "Have you seen Danny?"

"No, but it's been a shitstorm around here. We were supposed to be off four hours ago. He could've pulled up and I wouldn't have noticed. Or he could have come before us. What's up? Is he all right?"

"Shoshana's hurt."

"Bad?"

"Yeah."

Earl spit. "What kind of world hurts a gal like that?"

"Seriously," the other security guard said.

Earl shook his head. "I've lived here a long time. This used to be a good place, a safe place, the kind of place you could raise a family. But now . . . I think Mamma Earth wants us gone."

An ambulance screamed in the distance.

The other security guard turned toward the sound, then tapped Earl's shoulder.

"Yep," Earl said. "Figure you're right." Earl offered Andy a hand. "Sorry about that punch."

"Seriously," said the other security guard.

"Just doing your job," Andy said. "No hard feelings."

Earl and the other man turned and walked back toward the hospital. It wasn't until Earl touched the guy on the small of the back that Andy realized they were father and son.

He climbed into the truck.

Roseburg's and Eugene's hospitals were both an hour away, one to the north and one to the south. He could drive and check both, but that would take the rest of the day. And a whole day had passed since he had last seen Danny or Shoshana. Maybe they were back home by now. Though that seemed unlikely. If they weren't home, the phone might be a faster way of locating them.

Up at the yurt, he found Jasmine's electric car in the driveway, but Danny's truck was still gone. He knocked on the door, despite the darkness inside. The knocks echoed through the vacant space.

Twenty-five hours after the storm hit, Andy arrived back at his own house to find the carport ripped free. Inside, he flipped a light switch but found the power out. The phone was dead too. He should have expected as much.

Clouds filled the sky, and rain steadily drummed the woodshed's tin roof. To the west, endless pillows of moisture lined the sky. For the first time since the storm, the wind had come to a complete, utter halt. If he had seen a picture of the valley in this condition, he would have figured it to be the dead of winter. But now, standing on the porch, he was sweating in a T-shirt. A stray tropical storm.

In the span of a single heartbeat, the accumulated weight of stress and exhaustion settled on him. Even breathing was too much. He needed some stillness; he needed to be near water.

He pinned a note to the door in case someone showed up, and limped toward the river.

The blackberry vines were wrecked. The green leaves had been torqued by the wind, and their silver bottoms were turned toward the sky. Only tiny red berries remained on the vines. On the ground, like mounds of bear shit, sat mushy piles of fallen fruit. The berries had rotted during the storm. Using his good foot, he stepped down the vines and made his way toward the river.

The currents had turned from emerald to mocha and had risen two, or maybe two and a half, feet up the bank. Limbs and small trees and other debris bobbed over the surface. Upstream, a large object rode the center currents. It looked to be a drift boat. But as it neared, he realized it was the top twenty feet of a Doug fir.

He had left the boat in the cave. The anchor had likely pulled free, lifted by the rise in the river. But the bow line would still be attached, although if the boat had swung into the current, the river's pressure might have worked that free too. And if the boat hadn't swung into the current, the river might have risen enough to press it into the ceiling of the cave—where it could stay until spring.

He lay in the wet, shoreside grass, losing himself to the world, losing himself in the sound of the Ipsyniho.

Sometime later, a voice cut through the rush of the river. He opened his eyes to see the world significantly darker than he had left it.

Jasmine stood on the edge of the orchard. He raised his arm to signal her, and she made her way through the vines.

"What happened?" he said. "Where are they?"

"You're soaked," she said. "Have you been sitting down here in the rain?"

"Tell me, Jasmine."

She looked out over the river. "They're at the Eugene hospital. She had surgery yesterday. They say it's a shallow wound, that she must have been turning when it hit her. She's lucky, they said. 'Lucky' was the word they used." She sat in the grass beside him.

"What about the baby?"

"I don't know."

She lifted two beers from her backpack, opened both, and offered one to Andy.

"Where are they now?"

"The hospital. When she woke up, she wanted to be alone with him." She rushed the beer to her lips and swigged.

The rain fell from the sky and dripped from the trees and punched divots in the river's surface.

The rain soaked her hair, and a drop hung from the lobe of her ear. "On the way down, every turn hurt her. The pressure, you know? No matter what I did, no matter how slow—I couldn't stop hurting her. The word 'hurt' doesn't come close. She couldn't even breath, Andy. She came up there to stop him from killing himself, to save him, and he stabbed her for it."

"It was an accident. He didn't mean to hurt her."

"I don't care if he meant to or not. He fucking stabbed her."

"Is she in pain?"

"She can't roll over. She can't sit up. She can't even get out a whole sentence." Jasmine removed the cigarettes from her bag and put one to her lips.

"Can I?" Andy asked.

She flicked the box and a butt emerged an inch above the others. She sparked the lighter and touched the flame to his first. She had done all this without looking at him. They both exhaled and the smoke hung above like a blanket.

An osprey screeched as it flew upstream. While ten feet over the river, its wing beats paused, and the bird shook itself like a wet dog—haloing mist around it. Its talons were empty.

With a pinkie finger, Jasmine brushed a wet lock off her cheek. Her skin had turned a ghostly pale. "Tell me a story."

"I don't have any stories."

"Tell me something, Andy. Please."

He sipped his beer. "With all this high water, the summer steelhead are probably ascending Steamboat Creek."

"Something better than that."

"Forty years ago, steelhead entered the Ipsyniho every month of the year—one of three rivers in the world that could claim that. The valley was famous because of it. I used to read about the Ipsyniho in old fishing books. Every little stream in the valley was used for spawning then, even Feather Creek right in town. Steelhead everywhere. But now, the only healthy tributary left is Steamboat. The Ipsyniho's wild steelhead are almost extinct."

"But there's that hatchery."

"Hatchery steelhead don't compare—a dairy cow to a bison, you know."

Jasmine sipped her beer. "So you and Danny kill rare fish?"

"We let the wild ones go."

"You hurt them for no reason? A endangered fish that you admire?"

"Welcome to the twenty-first century. You can't do anything without hurting something."

"What does that even mean?" Jasmine shook her head. "Fuck that. You take joy in hurting these fish? What is it with you people? This whole place is based on hurt."

"Anglers are the only people who give a shit! Other people, even those who claim to love all beings, won't go out of their way to protect a fish. Maybe they'll donate five bucks to the Sierra Club and get a bumper sticker, but that's it. They won't help count spawning fish or place woody debris in the water or stand up and scream when somebody wants to destroy the headwaters."

Jasmine stared at the water, swigging her beer.

"I don't mean to yell."

"Maybe you help the species," she said, "but still, you hurt the individuals."

He couldn't argue, as some did, that fish don't have pain receptors in their mouths, that they couldn't feel hooks. There was a reason a hooked fish fought so hard.

"Yeah, that's true."

"You just turn a blind eye to your cruelty."

"You let that city insulate you from yours."

Jasmine finished her beer, and he did the same. Finally she said, "I've got more booze in the car. Can I help you up?"

"Thanks," he said, taking her hand.

"Maybe we all look the other way," she said. "But maybe there comes a time when we just can't anymore."

They arrived back at the house to find the phone line still dead. The electricity was still out too, so Andy went around the house lighting candles. "Here," he said, handing Jasmine a headlamp, "you might want this."

She tightened the device on her forehead. "I haven't eaten since yesterday."

He pulled crackers from the cupboard and smoked steelhead from the now tepid refrigerator, laying them out on a plate.

"You don't have a TV?" Jasmine said, throwing a beam of light across the room.

He bunched newspaper into the wood stove. "I threw it out November second, 2004. Sank my ship to the mainland." The match flared in the dark room, and he touched it to the paper.

They ate slowly, the fire flickering against the wall. The light was dim and heavy, and rain pattered the roof.

"I remember one time when the power went out in Shoshana's dorm," he said. "It was winter break and she and I were the only people still in the building—except for a couple international students. We must have lit a hundred candles in that little room, just to see how many we could have burning at once. We couldn't get the smell of warm wax out for weeks."

"How come you didn't go home like rest of the goyim?" Jasmine asked.

He shrugged as if he couldn't remember. "My family doesn't really do Christmas." He had done Christmas with his mom the year before, and was supposed to go to his father's that December. But the man hadn't called. That fall his new son had been born. Maybe he had figured Andy was too old for Christmas.

Jasmine handed him a new beer and he put it to his lips.

"New rule," she said. "No more stories about them."

The wood burned late into the night, warming the dark house until they were forced to shed their extra clothes. Jasmine sat at the table wearing a thin T-shirt, jeans, and no shoes. As she examined the playing cards in her hand, Andy leaned back and snuck a look at her bare feet. A couple of her toes wore silver rings, and the thick pads of well-developed calluses could be seen along the edges of her foot. These feet had gone places.

She pulled them away. "Are you looking at my feet?" She tucked them up under her, sitting cross-legged on the chair. "My feet are off limits," she said. "No looky-looky."

"You might recall," he said, "I've seen you nude. Besides, if you don't want people looking at them, why wear those rings? They kind of draw the eye."

She organized the playing cards in her hand. "I slipped those on back in college, and now I can't get them off. I still had nice feet in college." She moved three hooks into the center of the table. "I call."

While Jasmine taught him to play Texas Hold'Em, they finished one six-pack and dented another. Neither of them had mentioned Danny or Shoshana in hours. And it was better that way.

He folded.

"You can't fold now!" She jabbed his shoulder. "I just called you!"

"Right, right."

"For that error," she said smiling, "you owe me your shirt."

"Silly rule."

Then the beers were gone and so was the wood, and the midnight moon sprawled across the floor.

"How long do I have to kick your ass at poker before you'll invite me to stay?" she said.

By then, he had lost his pants and socks as well.

"I'm a city girl, Andy. I can't stay in that dreadfully silent yurt all by myself. And besides, I'm sufficiently snookered to warrant taking a taxi, except," she dropped into a Texas drawl, "there ain't no taxis in these here parts."

He had been preparing himself to ask for several minutes, testing different phrasings while only paying partial attention to the cards in his hand. He was out of practice at this sort of thing, and he didn't want to sound overly eager, given how eager he was. He didn't want to be alone either.

"You should stay," he said casually. "I'll make up the bed for you and the couch for me."

Jasmine shrugged. "If that's what you want, seems a bit puritanical to me." She rested her elbows on the table, and her shirt hugged tight to her breasts. "We could share the bed," she said. "You know, for heat retention purposes."

He pinched out the candles and watched as Jasmine crawled under the quilt. She had replaced her jeans with a pair of his boxers—the fabric revealed a couple inches of that scar on her thigh.

He thought of the warmth of her legs, how they would slide against his—a candle burned him; he had forgotten to wet his fingers before pinching the wick.

She was sitting up in bed, fingering through a back issue of *Fly Fisherman*.

A strange urge overtook him. He wanted to thank her for being here, for staying. But he held his tongue. How could he voice such a sentiment without sounding severely corny?

She set the magazine on the nightstand without another look. "Thanks for letting me stay," she said.

"Of course. Better we're together. In case there's news."

She lifted the covers. "Get under. It's cold."

He kicked off his flip-flops and scooted into her warmth. The smell of June sunsets: honeysuckle blossoms and ocean breezes—and the thin smell of cigarette smoke. Her hand found his, their fingers lacing together, and the rain kept rhythm overhead.

"I'm so cold." She turned her body against his, her leg across his.

He fingered the long scar on her thigh. "Where did you get this?"

"A bike accident as a kid." She said it quickly, like it might have been a well-practiced lie.

"You might be a little shy," she whispered, "definitely a bit backwoods, too. But you're a good cuddler, Andy Trib."

"You might use your wit to remain illusive, you're definitely a bit big city, and I'm probably just some warm body to you—"

"You're not just some warm body," she snapped.

"Even if I am. You're not a bad snuggler yourself."

"When I had a car, its only bumper sticker read: I'd rather be spooning."

He kissed her hair and imagined them together in ten years, drinking pinot along the river, laughing. Maybe they would travel together, her writing, him fishing. Maybe he would start writing fishing articles about the places they went. But no matter where they traveled, they would always come back to the Ipsyniho, to their home. "Do you think you'll ever have children?" he asked.

"Fuck no. I'm far too fickle for kids. I can't even commit to a cat." She laughed. "My *modus operandi* is the whim, according to Sh . . . according to a friend."

He took a deep breath of Jasmine's hair. "I'm glad you're here. I like this."

"What about this?"

"That's nice too."

CHAPTER 12

They awoke to a single ring of the phone, both of them launching from sleep. Andy rushed to the wall but found only a dial tone.

"Is it working?" Jasmine said, pulling on her shirt.

"We're on."

After dressing, Andy looked up the number and dialed the Eugene hospital. When the desk clerk answered, he handed Jasmine the phone. She paced while she talked. "I'm the sister who was there earlier."

The power was back too, and he got dressed and started hot water for coffee.

A minute later, Jasmine hung up. "They checked out this morning. What time is it?"

The clock on the wall—the house's only battery-powered one—read 11:15.

"They could be back at the yurt," he said. His stomach twisted at the mere thought of seeing them. "Maybe I should stay here."

"Maybe you should." Jasmine wrapped her arms around him and her body pressed tightly against his. They had spent most of the night in a similar position, sleep only arriving once the eastern sky warmed. She kissed his lips and said, "You're not just some warm body to me, Andy."

A minute later, he watched her accelerate up River Road.

The call came less than an hour later. He had spent the time sitting on the edge of the bed, paralyzed between the smell of honeysuckle, the red look in Danny's eyes, and the bloodstained shirt sitting in a ball in the corner. Under the paralysis boiled a panicked urgency, a need to rush, to solve things. But there was nothing to do, nothing he could do. The phone was at his ear before the first ring stopped.

The line fuzzed—Jasmine was probably standing on the yurt's porch. "They're here," she said, her voice coarse.

"How is she?"

"The same," she said. "The same, the same."

"What about the baby?"

There was a pause. "She hasn't said and I don't want to ask."

"Is Rita there?"

"She's been here all morning. Look, Andy," Jasmine said, "I've got to go. I'll call you later. Do something, okay? Get your mind off this. Get out of the house, or something."

He hung up and walked out onto the porch—he needed some distance.

On the ridges, the clearcuts caught the light. On their edges, swaths of downed trees could be seen, long sections of windfall, the logs lying parallel.

He drove to the Carnival grounds and walked the well-worn path toward the abandoned gate.

The aftermath of the storm was still there. A row of outhouses sat on their sides, the stench thick. Clothes and paper plates and food wrappers dotted the parking lot and lay stacked against the fence like snow drift. A totem pole had fallen, catching itself in the crotch of a tree. Limbs and branches lined the paths, the muddy ground buried under a layer of fir needles and oak leaves.

At the community booth, the walls had been stripped, the pictures and blueprints scattered in the surrounding forest. Chairs sat on their sides, tables flipped on their tops. Out back, he found his tent thrown into the forest, his clothes scattered. Other tents sat upside down or wedged into the brush. One hovered six feet off the ground, drooping like a teardrop from the skewer of a tree's limb.

He collected his things and stuffed them into a backpack.

Near Main Stage, a man wandered past, his eyes lost in the distance. Dirt smeared his face and moss clumps dotted his fleece coat. He was whispering to himself.

Despite walking the river bank, he had trouble finding the cave where he had hidden his boat days before. The oak tree, his reference point, had vanished. So had the blackberries and the raccoon path.

But there was Long Tom Pool—and obstructing its currents was the huge oak. It had blown into the river, taking the bank and the blackberries and his boat with it.

He sat cross-legged on the edge. Below, the wide oak roots protruded from the murky water like fingers grasping for air. Maybe it was under those roots. Maybe it had washed free and drifted downstream. But either way, his boat—his livelihood, his life—was gone.

Tallulah. Of course she hadn't been in the boat when the tree fell. Of course she had been safely with her mother. He should have told her not to mess with it.

If she had been hurt, he'd be responsible for that too.

How could he be so fucking shortsighted?

So selfish?

Danny was right. He was just another sport.

It all blurred with tears, tears that came not from his eyes but from his throat, his chest, his fingers, his toes. They came from every spring in this watershed. He owned this, all of it, all of their misery.

He needed to leave this place once and for all. Leave them. They would all be better off without him.

He needed to leave himself.

The river sloshed over the roots, driven by the world's only consistent force: gravity. Would it be in tidewater today? Tomorrow? He stood and jumped.

Icy water stole his breath, canceling the day in a black vacuum. A root slammed his thigh—and his leg was caught. The river bent him backwards, a new gravity, pulling even his arms over his head. His shirt too. There was no fighting it. The water was roaring past, holding him flat in the current. The cold river owned him now.

So this was it. He would drown in the Ipsyniho. A half-naked body caught in a sweeper. A tourist's death.

Fitting, Danny would say.

No, this couldn't be it. Not like this. Please, not like this. But black-berries were everywhere. Thousands of them, the sun igniting in their sides, blues and reds and yellows, exploding rockets of color. And the river stopped, became a block of ice, and he saw it clearly: this was his moment. He could give in to the berries, follow them now into the sun-light and everything would be warm, or he could try one last time. But why would he? Because he would be leaving everything like this, that's why.

Andy, go slow to go fast.

First the shirt off, the arms through, mobility again. One move at a time. Next the leg, compressing toward it not bending. The root, there, impossibly slippery. But let go now and you die, there's no time for a second try. Pulling toward it and kicking—it won't come free!

Andy, you can do this.

Hold the root in the bend of your elbow, more stable and with only one arm. The other sliding down your leg, following it to the pinch. Soften the leg, relax it, there you go, let it bend where it must. Be like water; fluid carved the Grand Canyon.

And then, just like that, freedom. See? What did I tell you?

Air, dizzying air.

And the current was carrying him, and he was stiff with cold, but there was air and he could breathe it.

By the tailout, he had made it to the beach, shirtless, frozen, hot scrapes down his leg. And his foot was bleeding again.

CHAPTER 13

Jasmine called. Shoshana's mother was in the air between Boston and Eugene. Nancy would pick her up from the airport and bring her to the yurt. "Rita went home, and I'm not leaving Shoshana alone with him until they get here."

"She's the same?" he asked.

"She's the same. He's the same. Everything is the same. Nothing is going to get better, Andy. Can't you get that through your head?"

"Sorry."

"No, I'm sorry." There was a pause, and then she said, "Everything is just so goddamn wrong and there's nothing I can do about it."

"Do you want to come back to my place?" he asked. "I need to see you right now. Something happened."

"I'm catching a flight home tomorrow," she said, flatly.

"Sorry?"

"I'm leaving tomorrow. I can't be here for this. I have to go. I've got to be back in New York by Thursday. Work commitments."

"Just like that?"

"Yeah. I can't rearrange things."

He wanted to believe that was true.

"Shoshana's mom will be here. And besides, I've got to be back for work."

"Can I give you a ride to the airport at least?"

"I have the rental car."

"Right. Do you want to have breakfast or something anyway?"

"I should go," she said. "I don't want to leave Shoshana alone for too long. I'll call you."

While sitting on the toilet lid, he cleaned the new scrapes and the old cut and strapped on clean bandages. This time, he would be more attentive.

The house no longer smelled of Jasmine and no volume of music would chase away the thoughts he didn't want to have. He'd never felt so alone. So, just before sunset, he climbed into the truck and drove toward town, to the Woodsmen Tavern. The bar had been there since the thirties, the go-to watering hole for four generations of desperate Ipsynihians.

Inside, he waded through the stale smoke. The walls displayed rusty old saws and oxen harnesses from logging's ancient days. A twenty pound native steelhead hung over the bar—caught by Jimmy Stevens in 1972, according to the placard underneath. Rifles and pistols sat on mounted deer paws that had been pegged to the wall specifically for the purpose. The barrel of one rifle turned back a hundred and eighty degrees—leaving the muzzle pointed directly where the shooter's forehead would be. A sign below it read: In Good Condition. Only Shot Once.

He didn't see Bridge until he had already taken a stool and ordered a pint. The big man stood in back, in front of a pinball table. By the volume of his shouts, any stranger could tell he was hosed.

When the bartender delivered the beer, Andy asked for a double tequila to go with it. He downed the liquor and carried the pint toward the pinball machines. Already, the tequila's warmth was working its way down his arms and legs.

"Fucking A," Bridge said, without looking up. "You see this shit? Regular pinball wizard."

"Seriously."

Bridge slapped at the white buttons on the side of the machine despite the ball bouncing safely at the top of the maze.

"How long have you been here?" Andy asked.

The ball slid down one wall, and Bridge missed the save. "Bullshit!"

The score counter flashed: Game Over.

"Hey man, you got a quarter?" Only then did Bridge realize who was beside him. "Oh, Mr. New York himself!" He pushed Andy and they both nearly fell to the floor.

The big man used the machine to gather his balance. "Whoa, guess that's why they call it tipsy!"

Andy helped him to the nearest booth. "Get me a beer will you?" Bridge said.

"Sure."

"Another?" the bartender asked when he saw Andy coming.

"How long has he been here?"

"Least three hours. Since my shift started."

"You got any Odoul's?"

"Definitely." The bartender poured a nonalcoholic pint and handed the glass to Andy. "Rumor has it, his house was crushed by the windstorm."

"No shit?"

"No shit," the bartender said. "He isn't the only one. That storm has been good for business."

Andy delivered Bridge his pint and sat at the table.

"I don't drink much myself," Bridge said. His lip was still swollen from Danny's boot. "Find the stuff a bit imprecise." He put the pint to his lips and a stream of beer ran down his beard.

"Is Rita around?"

"Rita likes the sauce more than me, but it doesn't really jive with her gig." Bridge took another swallow, then sniffed the beer in the glass. He shouted to the bartender, "Just so you know, Bill, your shit has gone to shit!"

"Bridge, I heard about the house."

"I think of the sauce more as medicine," Bridge said. "It's got its time and place."

"Do you and Rita have a place to sleep?" he asked. "You're both welcome at my house."

Bridge just stared at his beer.

"At least nobody was in the house during the storm," Andy said. "Count that as a blessing."

Bridge rubbed his forehead with both palms.

"No one was in the house, right? Bridge?"

Bridge muttered, "I blame you for this."

"Me."

The bells on the door rattled, and Andy turned to see a clean-shaven man with blond hair swagger in. Behind him came two others, both wearing freshly ironed shirts and slacks. They spoke quickly and reminded him of the Starbucks executives he had guided a few years back—tidy and excessively caffeinated. Bridge turned and saw the newcomers.

"Real shortage of bars in this little town," the blond man shouted to the bartender.

"Churches too," the bartender said. "What can I get you?"

Bridge watched as the three men took a booth near the front.

Andy tapped his arm. "You have insurance, right?"

"Insurance." Bridge said.

"Yeah, won't they pay to rebuild?"

"The way I see it," Bridge said, "I'm screwed either way." He smelled the beer one last time, then pushed it down the table. The glass slammed into the wall and tipped over, spilling onto the seats.

The bartender turned. "Everything all right over there?"

"Sorry, Bill," Bridge said. "Think you got mold in your tap."

The newcomers laughed from their booth in the back corner. One of them was in the middle of a story. Bridge was squinting their way—he seemed to think their laugh had been at his expense.

The bartender tossed over a towel, and Andy used it to sop up the beer. "You could use that money and build anywhere you want, right?"

Bridge watched the newcomers.

"Bridge?"

The big man turned and discovered Andy cleaning up his mess. "Give me that," he said. "I don't need your help." He took the towel and laid it over the beer pooling on the table.

"You don't need anything. It's the same with all of you. Think you got everything you need. Don't need any help from anybody."

"They left a wall of naked trunks and expected them to stay up. Fucking dumbasses. Hasn't a one of them ever lived with Doug fir?" Then to the whole bar: "It don't take half a brain!"

"Hear that, brother!" a crimson-faced man shouted from his barstool.

The newcomers laughed again, and Bridge pursed his lips. "I can't even look at the place," he said. "The windows exploded over the lawn."

The newcomers clanked their beer glasses. These assholes obviously hadn't been here for the storm.

Bridge looked up to a rifle hanging on the wall beside the table.

"Hey, Bridge," Andy said. "How about we get out of here and grab some food?"

Bridge continued to study the gun. And one of the newcomers said, " . . . that shit heap looked better with a tree in it!"

"Or I could give you a ride somewhere," Andy said. "Let's get out of here, either way."

"You see that? That was my great-granddad's gun. A Winchester Model 94. He willed it to the bar."

A thin veil of rust covered the barrel.

Bridge turned to Andy, tears welling in his eyes. "I've lived here a long time," he said. "But I barely recognize the place anymore. Just wandering around lost like everybody else." He laughed, and the cut on his lip split open—a bead of blood oozed free.

Andy handed him a napkin.

Bridge held it to the cut. "What do you do when the place you belong ain't there anymore?"

Andy shrugged. "Hit the road, I guess."

Bridge chuckled, the blood soaking through the napkin. "And go where? There aren't any places left."

Bridge stood up, and Andy followed. Together, they walked to the bar, Andy holding Bridge's shoulder to keep him balanced.

"The bill?" the bartender asked.

The newcomers were watching Bridge. He still held the bloody napkin to his lip.

"Sorry about the mess, Bill." Bridge pulled a fifty from his pocket. "I'm paying for my friend here. And send a round to those fellas. You keep the rest."

Bill glanced at the newcomers. "Anything I should tell them?"

"Tell them," Bridge said, "to at least stop acting like they own the place."

Bridge and Rita had a room at the Ipsyniho River Lodge, a motel on the downstream side of town. Andy helped Bridge to their door and knocked. Rita answered. She went straight for Bridge's lip.

She caught a whiff and turned to Andy. "Where did you find him?"

"The Woodsmen."

While Andy waited at the door, she helped Bridge inside, laid him on the bed, and put a bottle of water within arm's reach. Lying there, he looked like a Bigfoot in a man's costume. "Can you turn the TV on?" he asked.

"Seriously?" she said. He nodded, and she removed a blanket that had been hiding the black box and laid the remote on his belly. Then she joined Andy outside, closing the door behind her. "I haven't seen him watch television since the Ducks were in the Rose Bowl."

"I heard about the house."

She glanced into the distance. "We're waiting to hear from the insurance people. I guess they're a bit swamped right now." She laughed, but there wasn't a trace of happiness in her face. "Got to be on time with your payments but they don't have to be on time with their help."

"If you need a place to stay," he said.

"That's sweet," she said. "But Charlie and Todd have been nice enough to lend this room as long as we need. Have you seen her?"

Shoshana. "No. I figured it would be best to stay away for the time being."

Rita nodded. "Seems wise."

Their eyes flashed across each other, and Andy looked to his feet. She blamed him too.

"I've been up there off and on all day," she said. "Given enough time, they'll heal."

"You think he'll get over this?"

"No. But you're a brother to him."

Some brother. He tried to concentrate on the pavement, on the sheen of water over the blacktop, the sky looking up at him. Maybe these molecules of water once rode the rapids of the Ipsyniho.

"Give him some time."

A bench sat beside the door, and she sat down, leaving space for him. He sat too, and together they surveyed the parking lot.

"Can I ask? Is she still . . . Is Shoshana still . . ."

"That's their business, Andy. There are rules about this stuff."

"Of course."

Rita was laughing.

"What's so funny?" he said. "I could use a joke."

"Nothing is funny. I don't know why I'm laughing." She shook her head, still laughing. "I guess we'll all be starting over."

"Starting over seems impossible right now."

"Yeah, it does. But it's all we got left."

CHAPTER 14

Jasmine didn't call until late the next morning, and the phone proved a profound intrusion on his perfectly thoughtless hangover. "If we go soon," Andy muttered, "we can still catch breakfast at Nearly Normal's."

She arrived with her hair wet from a recent shower, and her luggage was in the backseat.

He didn't ask until they were on the way there, the electric car gliding like an osprey. "Any word on the pregnancy?"

"She's still pregnant, though I don't know if that's the best thing, given, you know."

"She still wants to be pregnant, right?"

"Yeah, but she's not seeing things straight right now, know what I mean?"

Out the window, he watched the tear-shaped Christmas trees smear into a wall of green.

"You said you needed to talk to me about something?" Jasmine asked without taking her eyes from the road.

"It was nothing."

At Nearly Normal's, their server—a thin woman with blue hair and a tattoo crawling up her neck—placed a French press filled with thick coffee on the table. Andy ordered the powerhouse breakfast, Jasmine the vegan omelet.

"This place is wacky," Jasmine said, pouring a cup of coffee.

"Utter Ipsyniho," Andy said, watching a man with waist-length dreadlocks deliver a platter of buckwheat pancakes. "Organic, vegetarian cuisine served by free-range, antibiotic-free hippies."

"Yum yum." Jasmine pointed at the newspaper on the far side of their table, probably left by an earlier patron. "Have you heard about this?"

The headline read: Carnival's Executive Committee Investigated.

"There might be criminal negligence charges," Jasmine said.

Trey walked past the table, Chloe riding his back, her little arms wrapped around his neck. He nodded but kept going. Nikki was a step behind, and she shared a little wave with Jasmine.

They left the restaurant and crossed the parking lot to the Volvo. "Do you know his story?" Jasmine asked.

"What did you hear?"

"According to Shoshana, he lost his realty license or something. That's why they came up here. Got caught helping shady deals go through. Did a little time even. It left them pretty much destitute. Bridge and Rita have kept them afloat all summer."

Trey reentered the restaurant. He was carrying a small paper bag. Purple ink marks stained the sides. "Whatever you think about me, Andy, I only want to do good for this valley."

"Neat."

"What did I ever do you to anyway?"

Andy sipped his coffee. The truth was nothing.

"You know, you and me aren't that different. Maybe that's my sin, I remind you of yourself." He handed the bag over. "Chloe and Nikki picked a pile of these before the storm. Thought you might like one last taste."

Inside sat a pound or so of big, ripe river blackberries. "Thanks."

Trey turned to go, but before he did, he smiled. "Native or not, it hardly matters, right?"

After they'd eaten, Jasmine said, "Carter came up to the house this morning. Asked to speak with Shosh alone."

"What about?"

"She told me later. He said he didn't believe the story she'd told the Eugene cops, that it was an accident. He asked her if she needed help. Protection. He asked if she was afraid of Danny."

"What did she say?"

"She said no."

"What is it?"

"I don't know. I worry about her, you know?" Jasmine pushed her coffee away. "I tried to convince her to leave him. We were alone, and I told her to fly back to New York, that we'd find a place together, that she could make a fresh start. I told her that Carter didn't trust Danny and neither should she."

"What did she say?"

Jasmine forked at her food. "I shouldn't have said anything. Not yet. It is too soon."

"Danny would sooner die than hurt her."

Jasmine scoffed.

"Danny isn't like that, not normally. Think about what happened. His best friend slept with his wife."

"Andy," Jasmine said. "Trust me when I say this." Her eyes hung in a way he had not yet seen, weakened and shy. And he realized, for the first time, he was seeing the real Jasmine. "I know the violent type."

"He wouldn't hurt her on purpose. You've got him all wrong."

She shook her head. "Violent people are violent people. Some just learn to conceal it a bit better than others."

"People change."

"Not people like that." Jasmine was staring at her coffee. "My father, the only thing that changed him was death."

"Excuse me." It was the server. "Is there anything else I can get you? A gluten-free vegan cookie, maybe?"

"What's the point?"

The server fingered one of her dreads. "What?"

"Nothing."

Once they were alone again, Jasmine leaned over and whispered, "Where do these people come from?"

An hour later, Jasmine and Andy stood in his driveway, a breeze rustling the hazelnuts.

He smiled, unsure of what to say.

She stepped into him, pressing her cheek against his. "You're a good hugger," she said. "Things always work out for good huggers."

"You think?"

"Definitely. One has to believe something." She kissed him.

"Think there are any jobs in New York for a lousy fishing guide?"

She stepped away. "Well, I mean, we don't have blackberries in New York."

"Right."

"You could come out," she said. "I'm sure you could find something. My apartment is too small for two. You couldn't stay there, but I could help you find your own place. The city can be hard, though. You should know that."

"I couldn't handle all that cement anyway," he said.

"If you come," she was laughing now, "for christsake don't wear an 'I heart NY' shirt."

"Don't worry."

A minute later, as he watched the electric car drive through the orchard, a vacant emptiness settled on him—he might as well have been alone on the South Pole.

CHAPTER 15

Winter arrived that week, laying its heavy quilt over the valley. For days the ridges were lost to the clouds, and rain filled the ruts in the driveway. The river didn't respond at first, the water slowly saturating the soil. But then the water had no other place to go, and the river began its rise.

Pinned inside by the rain, Andy worked filling his fly boxes. As he tied, he thought of all the places he could go. Russia's Kamchatka Peninsula, or maybe Mongolia's interior; people said it was like the American West a hundred years ago. But these places would take some coordinating—he'd have to find an outfitter to fund his travel, for instance.

The equatorial environment had treated him well; maybe he should go someplace warm. There was always Islamorada. Wherever he went, he would stay, make a home, do things right.

After a few days, his fly boxes were stuffed with finished patterns. So he grabbed a novel, McGuane's *Ninety-Two in the Shade,* and curled up by the big window, a cup of coffee in hand. The rain slid off the roof and chattered against the deck. The squirrels ate their nuts while sitting in the lee of the woodshed.

He couldn't read.

He grabbed his fishing log and a pen and tried to write about the river, about the rains and the water levels. But the entry quickly careened off course. By the bottom of the first page, it was obvious he was writing to someone. A few pages later, he tore out what he had and started a proper letter. He wrote until his hand cramped.

That afternoon the electronic voice of the NOAA weather radio predicted floods. The Ipsyniho would leave its banks.

He drove toward town and found the community preparing for the overflow. Sandbags walled the fronts of stores. The Co-op was installing a ladder over their wall. People filled coolers with food, water, and wine. Andy found Bridge buying microwavable burritos. He looked as if he hadn't showered in days.

"I'm going crazy without a kitchen," Bridge said.

"You're welcome to mine anytime, Bridge. You know that. What are you doing tonight? Why don't you and Rita come over and we'll do a pizza or something."

"We can't," Bridge said. "Not tonight. *Sex and the City* is on."

The water broke the banks the next morning. Andy watched the brown currents from his porch, the water only a hundred yards away and creeping closer every hour.

Mr. Kepinger stepped around the side of the house. "Howdy," he said, without looking away from the river.

"Howdy," Andy said. He hadn't paid his rent, and he only had a hundred and sixty dollars to his name. "I'm sorry about the rent," Andy said. "I didn't mean for this to happen."

"We'll worry about that later, son." Kepinger squinted into the distance. "Let's get those bags up before we've got the Mekong Delta lapping at our door."

They worked until dark, filling sandbags and stacking them around the base of the house. The sweat mixed with the rain, and it felt good to be doing something.

"Last winter, I had to do this alone," Kepinger said between breaths.

That night, Andy ate dinner at the Kepingers' house, meatloaf with canned corn and green beans. And after dinner, as the waters rose, Mrs. Kepinger taught Andy to play pinochle. "You should come play with the wives down at the Senior Center," she said as she won another hand.

After dark, he had to wade the Ipsyniho to make it back to the house, a straight row of hazelnuts his guide in the blackness. He found the answering machine's red light blinking.

"Andy, it's your father. I just saw on the Weather Channel that it's going to flood out there. You should stock up on food and get some sandbags just in case. They say it's going to be a big one." There was a pause in the message. "Maybe if you get some time, you could give a call. Just let us know you're okay."

The next day, Andy spent hours watching the current slowly pass by, the debris washing with it. The only thing more enchanting than a river was a flood. In the main channel, the river roared downstream, the rapids and pools buried under a steady wash. Out on the edge of the flood, where Andy's house sat, the current was slower, tamer. But if given enough time, even a slow current would eventually undercut sandbags.

He had seen the Ipsyniho flood twice in his ten seasons there, both smaller overflows that receded within a day or two. But this flood was different. It scaled the banks, spread over the valley, and lingered—the heavy clouds continuing to come inland as the river struggled to wash the rain back out. In the distance, he watched tall trees topple, their roots undercut by the endless waters. On day three, he saw a drift boat where River Road should have been, it's sole occupant oaring steadily toward town. Through binoculars, he saw the guy had brown hair.

He spent the lonely time working on the letter to Danny. It wasn't long, but the finished draft mirrored his remorse, his sympathy. He wasn't asking for forgiveness or for redemption; he simply wanted him to know.

On day four, the clouds finally passed, and he watched an impossible sunset from his porch, the sky painting the flood waters red. Sometime around noon the next day, the river finally receded from the house.

He cleared a lane through the sandbags and drove up the muddy driveway and onto River Road. Most of the fields were still flooded, expansive brown lakes. In town, clearcut mud lined all the streets, a fine silty paste contoured by the currents that had delivered it. Children grabbed handfuls, packed them like snowballs, and heaved them at each other. In front of the Co-op, an abandoned raft sat high and dry—its bowline tied to the sandbags.

Inside the store, a man said, "This one stayed longer, but it wasn't as big as last year's."

After buying food, he walked over to the post office, and without pause, dropped the letter in the mail.

That evening, he put on his waders and took a walk across the flood plain. The water still plowed through the shoreside blackberries. A few hundred yards upstream, he noticed a mysterious rumbling under the currents. The rumbling kept a rhythm, almost like the samba at the Carnival. Finally, he realized the sound's source: boulders rolling downstream, pushed by the fast currents. And he found himself wondering if the Ipsyniho's steelhead noticed their river changing, or if they were too distracted by the business of surviving.

A week or so after the flood, Mr. Kepinger showed up at Andy's door. "I don't have the money," Andy said immediately. "Just say the word and I'll pack my shit." He had decided on Islamorada, if only because Ethan could get him plugged into immediate work.

"Nonsense, son." Kepinger flicked his toothpick into the yard. "I want to hire you, part-time, in exchange for the rent. These arms," he examined his shrunken limbs, the skin loose over the muscles, "well, I'm slowing down a bit these days."

"I'm planning on leaving soon," Andy admitted.

"What's 'soon'?"

"Once I get enough money to pay you back and buy a plane ticket." He had no idea how long it would take to raise the money, or how he would go about doing it.

"Until you got the funds," Kepinger said, "you'll work for me."

And so Andy started working around the orchard, pruning mostly, and burning the cut limbs. He also repaired the carport that had come free in the storm, and built a new woodshed beside the Kepingers' house. Mrs. Kepinger delivered dinner to his door each night. "I'm already making it. Ain't nothing to make one more serving." He left the clean plates on their porch each morning.

At night, he drank tea and reread his favorite novels, listening to the squawking geese migrating above the clouds. He found the slow evenings refreshing. He had avoided winter's respite the year before, and each dark night seemed to add an ounce to his drained reservoir. Every day, he felt more himself. Every day, he felt less alone.

Then one rainy morning he drove to Nearly Normal's for some breakfast. He had managed to scrimp by for nearly a month on a hundred and sixty dollars and the Whole Foods gift card his father had sent. It was time to treat himself to a coffee and a hipster enchilada. While reading the paper, Rita appeared in the chair across the table. Behind her stood a young woman, a mamma-to-be, the bulge barely perceivable under her shirt. Rita looked forlorn. "Poor Danny," she whispered.

"What do you mean?" Andy asked. "Is he hurt?"

"Shoshana left him," Rita said. "I thought you knew."

She explained that Shoshana had taken an apartment in Eugene. No one knew much about it, even though Trey had been checking on Danny every day. "It wasn't his idea, and he's having a hard time accepting it. He keeps telling himself that it's temporary, that she's coming back. But," Rita shook her head, "it doesn't sound temporary to us."

"When? When did she leave?"

"It's been a while. I'm surprised you haven't heard."

For days after that, he tried to go up to the yurt, to check on Danny, to take him food or something. But the thought of coming face to face kept him working hard around the orchard.

Finally, on a foggy day, he saw Shoshana in the Co-op. She stood behind a cart, examining a jar of pasta sauce. She had changed, cut her hair, and even through a thick sweater, the bulge was noticeable. For a moment, neither of them knew what to say.

He could tell she hadn't been sleeping much.

"You're still here," she said.

"Of course."

"I thought you'd skip town first chance."

"How are you?" he asked.

"Good. I can sleep on my side now." She looked at a jar on the rack. "By now, I'm sure you've heard."

"You've got a place in Eugene."

"No. I was going to, almost signed the lease, but at the last minute changed my mind. I've been sleeping in my studio, three blocks from here. Scooter and Sara, my neighbors, let me use their kitchen and shower. Real sweethearts."

"What changed your mind?"

She traced a finger over the jar's label. "Danny, I guess. And this little one. We'll never work, I get that now, but he loves this baby, and I'll be damned if I rob my child of its father."

A man said, "Excuse me," and they stepped out of his way.

Shoshana bit her lip. "Can I ask you something? At Carnival, you told me you called that day for a different reason, and I've been wondering. You never said what that reason was. If it's old news now and you don't want to talk about it, that's fine. But—"

"No," he said. "I called because, well, one day I saw a little girl, you know, with her dad. She was maybe six or seven, and she looked like you. A spitting image. She shook me up. I started thinking about things. Regretting things. I started wishing we hadn't gone, you know, to the clinic."

"The clinic?"

"Maybe we wouldn't have made it as a couple, but still. We had an opportunity and we just cast it away."

"You question that decision?" she asked.

"It was a long time ago. But still. Sometimes, when I'm thinking about things, I worry we rushed to the decision, that's all. And I wonder what things would be like."

"It was the right decision, Andy. We weren't ready. We weren't fit. Who knows if it would have made it to term anyway. I was only eight weeks along."

"I know. But I worry sometimes that I pushed us into it, that we rushed into it on account of me. If I hadn't said what I did, maybe we would have considered ourselves ready. Maybe we'd have a child now. Sure—"

"What do you mean, because of you?"

"The night you asked me to leave, a few days after we found out, I said maybe a baby isn't the best idea, and the next time I saw you, you'd made the appointment."

"I don't remember this," Shoshana said.

"Seriously?"

"If it's worth anything, I do remember thinking that I was going to the clinic whether you agreed with me or not," she said. "This is why you asked me to the dam?"

"Yeah."

"We made the right decision. Trust me. We were kids." She was rubbing her belly. "How's your father, Andy? Talk to him much?"

He pointed at her belly. "Is there anything I can do to help? Maybe you need some fish or something? I hear it's good for brain development."

"Go see him," she said. "That's what I need. He's seeing a therapist, an anger specialist, but Danny needs to see you."

"Okay. I'll do it."

She glanced toward the checkout line. "I should go. Scooter and Sara are making dinner."

He watched her push her cart down the aisle.

As she rounded the corner, she glanced back. "By the way, have you seen the new issue of *Rolling Stone*? Page eighty-something. Check it out, if you haven't already."

Near the front registers, he found the magazine. There it was: a man in a pink cowboy hat held a banjo over his head like a victorious soldier atop a captured hill. Andy was in the foreground, off balance and out of focus. He flipped back a page and found the title, "Northwest of Normal: Oregon's Cascadia Carnival Delivers a Bizarre Dose."

Shoshana's voice pulled up his gaze. She was chatting with the woman checking groceries, something about a new gallery opening in town. She was smiling.

CHAPTER 16

Finally, the rains let up and the river dropped into normal winter shape. The brown flows settled to green again, and the continuous flood current broke into distinct rapids and pools and tailouts.

Andy had called Ethan a few days before and asked about coming out. "Of course," Ethan said. "You're welcome to the couch at Lizzy's house." Lizzy was his new lady, as it turned out.

"What happened to the tarpon guide?"

"Ah," Ethan said, "she acted like I was her sport. 'Do this, do that.' And she kept taking my flies. No, I'm done dating guides."

Andy asked about what kind of work he could expect.

"There's always work on my buddy's head boat. Shitty work with cheap-ass clients, but it'll pay your bills until you can get a loan and buy a proper flat's skiff. You've got to have a skiff to make any real money. When are you coming?"

Andy told him that he needed to raise airfare first.

"As soon as you get it, let me know. I'll smooth it out with Lizzy."

Andy had been trying to visit Danny for days now, ever since seeing Shoshana in the Co-op. Twice he had climbed into the truck and driven upstream—once he made it as far as Danny's driveway. But each time he had convinced himself to wait, that it would be best to try again in a day or two, give things a little more time to settle.

But enough was enough. The only thing worse than confronting Danny was the constant fear of confronting Danny. And the river would be fishable soon.

Before he could stop himself, he dialed the yurt. Luckily the answering machine picked up. Danny's voice said: "It's me. Leave a message."

"Hey, I don't know if you're interested or not, but I'm thinking of fishing tomorrow. Should be at least a few winters around. I'll be at Millican fifteen minutes before light. Maybe I'll see you there."

Andy's own answering machine contained a message—the red light was blinking. The call must have come when he was outside. He clicked the play button and heard his father's voice, the fourth time this month. "Andrew, please pick up. I'm not too proud to beg." Pause. "How long are we going to keep doing this? I know we've had our—" Andy punched the delete button.

From the dresser, he grabbed his wallet and started toward the truck.

His father's voice. It had become more desperate—there was an edge of panic to it. Maybe something was wrong, medically or something. He was getting to that age.

To hell with him. He had made this bed. They barely knew each other anyway. They were only relatives on paper.

Andy stepped out onto the porch, the truck only a short cast away.

Fuck this. He shouldn't have to feel guilty about not calling. He should be able to live his own life, free from any of that old bullshit. What had that man done to deserve forgiveness?

And yet, Andy found himself just standing on the porch. He wasn't moving, wasn't climbing into the truck and driving into town. He could and he should; he had every right to. But he was just standing there with the keys in his hands.

The man didn't deserve forgiveness, but he was his father, and he just wanted a second chance. This *father* wanted a second chance.

He stepped back inside and held the phone. Besides, it would be easier to forgive him than to go on hearing these sad messages every week.

"Dad?"

"Andrew? Is that you?"

"I got the grocery card and I just wanted to give you a buzz and say thank you, or whatever."

"Is everything all right?"

"Everything's fine. I just wanted to call, to say thanks."

There was a pause. "I've been calling."

"I know. And I'm calling you now."

"We've been worried about you, with the weather out there and everything. First New Orleans, then Oregon."

"I've been thinking about leaving. A friend can plug me into the guiding scene in the Keys."

"The Keys are nice," his father said. "It's an easy flight from up here. When are you going?"

"I'm not real sure. I need to take care of some things first. Is everything okay? I mean, you've been calling a lot."

"Everything is fine," his father said a little too urgently. "It's just it's been so long since I've seen you, that's all. Four years this March. And we're . . . we're not going to be around forever, you know."

"Are you okay?"

"Do you think you'll still be in Oregon in June?"

"What's going on?"

"William and I are planning a trip. He's desperate to fish out there with his big brother. He idolizes you, you know. To him, you're this famous fishing guide with his picture in a magazine. William really wants to see you."

Then in a quieter voice, he continued. "I know how you must feel, son, how I made you feel. I wasn't what you needed, what you deserved. I see that now. My life's great mistake. Please, please let me make this right."

Andy focused on the fly tying bench, on a purple feather near the vise.

"You don't need to forgive me." His father's voice was shaking. "I'm not asking to be forgiven."

Tears welled up in Andy's eyes—he hadn't planned on this. He laughed. "It's okay."

"No, it's not."

Andy dropped into his guiding voice. "Water under the bridge. Seriously . . . the fishing should be good in June."

"It's not water under the bridge. I want to know you. I want to see you as you are. Please. Will you be there in June?"

"I don't know, Dad. We'll see."

Gordon's truck was parked outside the fly shop.

The store had been rearranged. The rods hung on a different wall, and the flies sat in new wooden bins. The picture board was gone.

"I just need some tippet," Andy said.

Gordon's hair was neater than ever. "Over there."

"Danny been working much?"

"Not at all," Gordon said. "He quit about a month ago."

"Have you seen him?"

"Nope. I've been running this place pretty much on my own." Gordon liked collecting the profit but hated doing the work. And he wasn't very good at it. "I've got a punk kid from the high school covering the afternoons. Thinks he's Brad Pitt. Doesn't know shit about the river."

Andy found a roll of twelve-pound mono and carried it to the counter. He needed to build short and heavy leaders for winter's weighted flies.

Gordon rung it up.

He had fifty-five dollars left to his name. He had studied those bills repeatedly. "What do I owe you?"

"Three fifty."

Andy handed over a five. "You know, I could help out around here, if you're looking for somebody."

Gordon scoffed, and turned to the sound of the door opening.

A man and woman stepped into the shop, their eyes already scanning the rods along the wall. Both looked to be in their late fifties; the matching khaki pants suggested young retirees. "Hoping to look at some two-handed rods," the woman said.

Gordon pointed at the wall. "Have at it. Let me know if you have any questions."

Andy leaned close and whispered, "I know I burned you earlier, but it won't happen again. Gordon, give me a chance. You can't let a high school kid run this place. If the shop doesn't offer expertise, what does it offer? People will just order their shit online."

Gordon handed Andy a dollar fifty. "Thanks for the cunning business advice." The phone rang, and Gordon put it to his ear. "Ipsyniho Fly Shop."

The man was shaking a rod, feeling its flex. "What about this one," he said to the woman.

Andy wandered their way. "What kind of fishing you looking to do?"

The woman answered. "I'm looking for a new winter rod. Something for around here."

Andy grabbed a thirteen-foot-four-inch Burkheimer off the rack—the store's most expensive rod. "Give this one a shake."

The woman sighted down the rod, then twitched it in her hands. She obviously knew fly rods.

"You've probably noticed that most Ipsyniho runs don't offer much casting room," Andy said. "I don't know about you, but I fish the river in winter with a Skagit line. The short head keeps the D-loop close while still sending a heavy fly as far as you need."

The woman eyed the rod's price and cringed.

Andy took a second rod from the wall, a mass-produced knockoff for half the price. "Most two-handers don't load well with short strokes, but these two do."

"They feel the same to me," the woman said as she examined the knockoff.

Gordon hung up the phone, and Andy felt his eyes. "The Burkheimer," he continued, "is made locally. The designer keeps a camp near Steamboat Creek when the fish are running. He built this rod to dovetail perfectly with the Ipsyniho. It's the distillation of years of local experience." Andy laid a finger on the knockoff in the woman's hands. "This one was made in a factory in China."

"Will I notice a difference?" the woman asked.

Andy nodded. "Definitely, although both will throw the line just fine. You'll find the Burkie to load and unload more consistently. You'll cast smoother loops with less effort."

The woman reexamined the knockoff.

"But," Andy raised a finger for emphasis, "the Burkie's real advantage is the company behind it. These are local people making a living doing what they love, not factory workers slaving away so upper management can get new yachts. And they make the rods ethically, recycling and reusing everything possible, keeping waste to a minimum. These people care as much about the health of the ecosystem as they do the bottom line. The price might look high, but some would argue that's what a fly rod should cost."

Gordon appeared beside Andy and introduced himself to the customers. He guided their attention to another rod on the wall, one that split the price difference between the Burkheimer and the knockoff. But it was obviously a rod better suited to summer fishing, and the woman took one look and discounted the suggestion. "No, I like this one," she said, holding the Burkheimer.

A moment later, as Gordon rung up the rod, he said, "Stop by sometime this week. We'll talk."

He saw her walking across the parking lot, but by the time he switched the truck off and jumped out, she had already disappeared into the Co-op.

He found Tallulah in aisle one, near the fruit bins. She wore knee-high rubber boots and a purple rain slicker, and seemed to be testing the scent of various oranges. "This one," she said, handing the fruit to a woman nearby. "It would go perfect with ice cream."

The woman smelled the orange. She had the same reddish blond hair and freckled face. And she wore rubber boots too, hers green with yellow stars. "Sharp," she said. "And spicy. I like it. But try this one." She handed Tallulah a bigger orange from a different bin.

Tallulah took one glance and said, "Oh, Mom, if we're just going to do navals, we have to get ice cream."

"You and your ice cream."

"It's my comfort food," Tallulah said, brushing hair out of her face.

The woman squeezed a big Valencia. "Aren't you a little young for all that?"

"Phish Food would really help take the edge off." A moment later, Tallulah spotted Andy. "Hey, you're that guy."

"How's Sam?"

"He flew south for the winter."

"Excuse me," Tallulah's mother said. She wasn't smiling. "How is it you know my daughter?"

Tallulah answered, "We met on the ship."

"The ship?"

"The one at Carnival. I told you about it. You never remember anything."

"A ship at Carnival?" She was asking Andy.

"A drift boat really." He introduced himself. "I had parked it along the shore, or under the shore actually. Tallulah took a liking to it."

She studied him with a doubting look, one born of motherly concern: she was clearly trying to decipher if he was a creep or not.

"I'm a fishing guide here in town. Live over on the Kepinger spread, just upstream of town. You know the place?"

"I know the place. Kepingers, the hazelnut people." Her concerned expression remained. "You live there alone?"

"For now. So you're from around here?"

Her face and hands still wore last summer's tan. She clearly spent a lot of time outside. "Lulu and I moved up a couple years back."

"We live on a farm," Tallulah said. "You should meet our goat. His name is Billy Ray Cyrus." Tallulah pulled on her mother's sleeve. "He likes blackberries, but he eats them too fast."

He shrugged. "They're good."

"Have you ever had Olallieberries?" Tallulah asked. "That's what we grow."

He shook his head. He knew Olallie was a Chinook term—there was a rapid on the McKenzie with that name.

"They have a more soulful flavor than blackberries," the woman said. "A cross between the loganberry and the youngberry, if you know what those are."

"I do," he said. "The loganberry is part blackberry, part raspberry, right? And I've heard of the youngberry, but never had one. Is it connected to the dewberry or something?"

"Exactly." And then she smiled: an especially warm beam that was so effortless, so casual that it had to be her natural disposition. So this is where Tallulah got her charm. "Most people don't know this stuff," she said.

"How come I haven't heard of the Olallieberry?"

"It's always been grown in northern California, in the same climate as Chardonnay, actually. The demand down there is huge. The few produced are bought up fast. But Lulu and I are learning the vines are more productive here, and the finished berries are bigger and more plump."

"And they taste better," Tallulah added.

"The Ipsyniho is berry heaven."

She offered her hand. "I'm Rebecca, but everyone calls me Ceecee."

"Except me," Tallulah said.

"So tell me, Andy," Ceecee was holding an orange to her nose, but her eyes remained on him. "What were you doing with a drift boat at Carnival?"

CHAPTER 17

The next morning, he arrived at Millican Boat Ramp to find the parking lot empty. Maybe Danny wasn't ready. Maybe he would never be ready.

Dawn's glow had yet to warm the clouds, and drizzle settled on the windshield. The air was humid and still—ideal fishing weather. Without Danny, though, it wouldn't be the same.

But then, the low rumble of a diesel and the clank-clank of a drift boat against its trailer. The truck rounded the last corner, and without using its blinker, pulled into the parking lot.

He could do this. He had to at least try.

Danny rolled down the window. "You got coffee?" His face was thinner and whiter and dark bags hung under his eyes.

"I wasn't sure you'd come," Andy said, his mouth ash-dry.

"First day the river has been fishable in months. Of course I'm coming." He was staying in the truck. "So you got coffee or not?"

"I brought a thermos."

Danny nodded toward the back of the truck. "Throw your shit in."

Andy set his dry bag in back and locked the rods in place, then carried his thermos around to the passenger door and climbed in.

Danny wore his customary fishing gear, the waders and sweater, the lucky baseball cap. But even through the bulk, he looked different, thinner—older. He was hunching over the steering wheel.

"You got a mug?" Andy asked.

Danny fished around at his feet and found a paper coffee cup. He handed it across, and Andy removed the lid and filled it.

"Listen," Andy said.

"Should be incredible fishing. Last year, I took clients the first day the water dropped. Weather just like this. Same barometer too." Danny gassed the truck and they swept onto River Road. "'Gangbusters' was an understatement."

"I want to say—"

"Not now." Danny was watching the road. "Let's just fish awhile."

They launched the boat below the dam, the darkness fuzzy with first light. Danny oared to the top of the run. "Time to see what the flood left us."

"I'll follow you through," Andy said. He wanted to watch Danny cast, watch him work the water. He wanted to see his old friend as he remembered him.

Danny grabbed one of the rods, anchored a hand on the gunwale, and stepped over the side. He waded into the current, already stripping line from the reel, and a moment later, fired his first cast—the fly struck him in the center of the back and was pinned to his coat. "Shit. Little out of practice."

"Normal for the first day out."

Danny couldn't reach the fly.

Andy leapt over the side and waded out. "I got it."

"I can get it myself." Danny twisted and turned, still trying. Short of taking off his coat, he would never reach the hook.

"There." Andy unhooked the fly.

Danny snake-rolled the line, loaded a D-loop, and fired a new cast—this time the fly disappeared toward the far bank.

They fished the first run, then the second. The river had changed again, the beaches shifted, the banks undercut, the troughs filled. And by the time they reached the Honey Hole, neither of them had hooked a steelhead.

Not that Andy really cared. He had taken to cutting his hooks at the bend, leaving just enough curve to feel the strike but not injure the fish.

He left his rod in the boat and stood in the current. He recognized no features of the run—none of the submerged boulders or slack pockets looked familiar. They had changed even from last year. "Normally, we'd have at least a grab by now."

Danny reeled up his line, pinned the fly in the handle's cork, and laid the rod along the gunwale. "There's no such thing as normal anymore."

Andy poured them each a fresh cup of coffee, and they stood in the current blowing at the steam and watching the water. Dense drizzle obscured the far bank.

"Did you get my letter?"

"Shit man, I can't even remember the last fish I caught." Danny laughed.

"We've got to talk sometime."

Danny finished his coffee. "Are you getting in or not?" He was steadying the boat so Andy could climb over the gunwale.

Andy didn't move. "I'm not asking to be forgiven."

Ridges formed in Danny's jaw and the vein appeared on his forehead. He was only one big step away.

"We've got to talk about it."

"You want to talk about it?" Danny roared. "You want to talk about it? What can you possibly say to make this better?"

"Nothing maybe, but we can't pretend it didn't happen."

"We don't have any other choice. I can't even look at you."

"Maybe this is the end, I get that, but still, we have to talk about it. Things can't be left like this, for either of our sakes."

"It didn't just happen. You don't get it. It happens every day, all day." Then, as if suddenly too exhausted to stand, he sank onto the boulder behind him. "There's nothing else."

Andy waded closer, an arm's reach away.

"All you had to do," Danny was shaking now, "was tell the fucking truth. Both of you. It would have been bad, but it would have been better than this."

"I know."

"She couldn't breathe. The whole drive down, every corner. Oh god, I hurt her so bad."

"I own this."

"It just went in. I didn't know she was there. I didn't. You have to believe me. Do you believe me?"

"I believe you."

"No one believes me. They whisper about it when they think I'm not looking."

"It was an accident. People know that. Shoshana knows that."

"I thought it was you. I felt it go in, I felt it . . . I felt it scrape bone, and I thought it was you."

"I wish it had been."

"And I was glad. Just for a blink. But Andy, I was glad." He was shaking his head. "You should stay away. I'm dangerous."

"Come on."

"You don't know the truth. You don't know."

"I know you."

"Maybe you don't."

"Of course I do."

"I'm . . . I'm the reason . . . " Danny was crying now.

"You're the reason?"

"I hurt everyone I love."

"Shoshana is on the mend, and like you said, you didn't mean to. This can be right again."

"I'm the reason he crashed. I'm the reason he went off the road."

"Who?" But then he knew who. Joel, his brother.

"You never wondered? You never wondered what happened? I passed him on the inside, that's what happened. I forced him wide. We were playing around, racing. But I'm the reason."

"I didn't know."

"No one knows. Only her. Please," Danny buried his face into Andy. "Please, don't tell. My parents, please. They can't find out."

They didn't fish much the rest of the day. They just drifted, together, surveying the river's new contours. Most runs had changed, and they discussed which areas would be most likely to hold fish.

"Look at that shelf. That wasn't exposed before."

The steelhead were looking for a specific type of lie in which to hold. It had to be a transition spot between fast water and slow where the unique aquatic topography provided the shelter they needed.

"Do you think I'm a violent person?" Danny was looking at the water.

"No, I don't. No more than the rest of us."

They drifted awhile in silence. "I think it will take us ten trips to get a feel for this place," Danny said.

"What do you have tomorrow?"

"I'm guiding tomorrow," Danny said. "You should drift, though."

"I'll be stuck to the bank."

"Stuck to the bank?"

Andy explained that he had lost his boat.

"You can't guide without a boat."

They drifted through a rapid and another pool, then Danny worked the oars to slow the boat. He stood on his seat for a better look at the substrate of the tailout. "I want to be better than I am," he said.

"Maybe that's what matters most."

Then they passed Steamboat, the little creek churning at full winter volume. The ladder of stones that normally separated the creek from the river was submerged, replaced by swirling and lifting currents.

"Has Willis sold?"

"To Cherry Creek." Danny pushed by the creek, the currents lifting the boat, then dropping it back. "You didn't know? It's been front-page news for two days now."

Cherry Creek would surely log the entire property, dumping silt and herbicides over the spawning grounds. Steamboat's steelhead wouldn't survive such maltreatment. The creek would become like all the others in the watershed. "This can't happen."

"We're not going to let it," Danny said. "The town is fired up. Enough is enough. Bridge is organizing a community meeting."

The river carried them downstream, and Andy watched the green currents of Steamboat disappear around the corner.

He couldn't abandon this place. "We have to keep trying."

After they had lifted the boat onto the trailer and stored the gear back in their respective trucks, Danny insisted Andy follow him back up to the yurt. "There's something I need to show you." With evening settling over the valley, Andy followed Danny up River Road.

At the house, Danny parked and raised his finger to say, hold on.

The yurt had changed. Debris from the windstorm remained piled on the deck. The gate to Shoshana's garden was open, and a well-worn elk trail lead inside. But the sign still hung in place. *Arousal From Below.*

Danny reappeared with something in his hand. "It's a shithole around here, isn't it?"

"It's been a tough winter."

"I'm going to clean the place day after tomorrow. I'm determined." Danny held up a key. "Pull around."

It was well worn, and Andy instantly recognized it. "I can't," he said. "No way."

"I don't need two. Pull around and I'll hitch you up."

"I can't take it."

"Come on," Danny said. "It's just sitting there. Might as well put it to use. Pull around."

He relented and followed Danny's hand signals until the hitch aligned. Danny used the key to open the padlock on the trailer, and a couple metallic clanks later, the boat was secured behind him.

"Step on the brakes," Danny called. The trailer's brake lights illuminated his thin frame. He walked up to the window. "She isn't pretty but she'll work."

"Danny, thank you."

"It's nothing," he said, handing over the key.

They stood there for a minute, the rain tapping the windshield.

"Let me know if you need help cleaning this place," Andy said.

"Maybe I'll give you a call tomorrow when I get off the river."

"I'll be around."

"Good." Danny slapped the side and backed away from the truck. "I'm going to be putting together a kid's room pretty soon. Let me know if you got any ideas."

"You're going to make a great dad, you know that?"

Danny shrugged. "I know a few things not to do, at least." He took off his hat and wiped his brow. "Go on," he said. "I'll give you a call tomorrow."

They waved. Andy eased down the driveway and Danny watched him go. A minute later, he was pulling onto River Road.

A gap in the western clouds opened, allowing the sunset to cast its warm beams over the Ipsyniho's green ridges. Backlit raindrops fell to the valley. He searched upstream and down for a rainbow, but didn't see one.

He brought the truck to full speed, heading due west. The drift boat was rattling behind, and the wet road home mirrored the red horizon.